REBEL

GHOST MOUNTAIN WOLF SHIFTERS BOOK 3

AUDREY FAYE

1

KENNEDY

"They're kissing. Again." Reilly throws himself down beside me with pleading eyes, like maybe I have the power to make it stop.

I grab his sidekick instead. Robbie likes to join in when Hayden and Lissa get all lovey-dovey, and I figure they don't always need five-year-old company. Besides, snuggling Robbie's soft white fur is one of my favorite things.

I roll my eyes at Reilly while I do it, though. I don't think he actually cares about the kissing, but he's figured out that teasing our alphas makes the pack feel good—and it makes Lissa's cheeks turn all pretty and pink. Or maybe that's just because of Hayden.

I look over at the two of them. They've stopped kissing, but the connection between them hasn't eased any.

I think they do this so that we can feel what lives

between them. Not the private stuff, although Ghost said she saw them crossing the perimeter last night with leaves in their hair and goopy smiles on their faces. This is different. Hayden will stop what he's doing sometimes and rest his cheek on top of Lissa's head, or she'll walk by and touch her hand to his heart, and every time they do it, our pack gets better.

Lissa doesn't want us calling them our alpha pair, but we're not blind wolves. And even if we were, we'd know. The two of them together are a gravitational well that holds everything in our pack in the right place.

I grin. I learned about gravitational wells from one of the books Reilly made me read. It was pretty good, even though it made my wolf twitchy to sit still that long.

I nudge the bear leaning against my shoulder. "A pack is kind of like a solar system."

He blinks and looks up at me, his eyes lighting with interest. "Yeah?"

I nod my chin at our kissyface alphas. "Lissa and Hayden are the star at the center, right? And the rest of us are planets and asteroids and stuff. We kind of have our own space and our own thing, but we shape our orbits around them."

He smiles at me in that way Reilly has that totally melts your heart. "You read the book."

I wrap my arm around his head. "Of course I did, doofus. It didn't even entirely suck."

He snickers from where I've mashed his face into my ribs.

Robbie licks Reilly. Then he licks my chin. Twice. I must taste better.

I glance up at the sky, getting a read on the sun. Growing boys need to eat, and so do teenagers. It must be at least an hour after breakfast. Shelley usually lets us raid the kitchen by then. "Want to go steal some cookies?"

"I heard that." Myrna grins at me and winks at the boys. "I wouldn't mind one if you're going raiding."

Shelley gets sad if we don't try to steal her cookies at least once a day, and it's a good day to be a raider. Mellie and Rio helped make the last batch and they're almost as big as my head.

"We'll go." Cori jumps to her feet, pulling Ravi up behind her. "We got caught yesterday, so we need to practice."

They only got caught because Jade wanted a glass of milk to go along with her cookie and she wanted it in the special pink glass from the very top shelf, which she had to get herself, and by the time they got all that sorted, Shelley was back to get the next batch out of the oven.

I crook my finger at the small girl trying to climb her daddy's leg. "Come here, cutie. We'll practice being pirates while they go get us cookies."

She looks torn, which makes Ravi's wolf puff up with happiness.

Cori shoots me a look of amused gratitude.

I grin innocently. I'm not an entirely clueless wolf.

Jade reaches her arms up, because daddies beat pirates, exactly as they should. He smiles at her, his eyes clear and happy. He's only run twice in the past three weeks, and he hasn't even made it as far as the inner perimeter before his buddies caught him.

Reilly is a really fast bear when he wants to be.

Lissa turns to Hayden and gives him a big, sloppy kiss, the kind that's supposed to make us laugh. "Want some milk to go with your cookies, sweetie?"

That's exactly the same tone and words she would use to ask Robbie, which makes her son sit up straight and the rest of us fall over laughing.

Hayden rolls his eyes. "You just want me to have to wash a million glasses again."

Lissa's grin is bright and sweet and full of mischief. "Yes."

Hayden nuzzles in, because he can't resist that look any better than the rest of us can. He might be our alpha, but Lissa did something really special to the gravitational well the first day she kissed him. Or maybe the day she beat him in the water fight. My wolf still isn't sure.

Reilly groans loudly, his hands over his eyes. "Tell me when it's safe to look."

Rio chuckles and drops to the ground beside us. "In about ten years, kiddo."

Reilly peeks between his fingers. "You waited until you were twenty to kiss someone?"

Rio manages to keep a straight face. The rest of us don't come anywhere close. I have no idea why I'm laughing, though. I kissed Ghost once, but that was just weird.

Rio grins at me and barrel-rolls over top of Reilly, squishing his bear to keep him happy, and neatly managing not to squish Robbie when he joins in on the fun. I stay where I am. Anyone who tries to barrel-roll over me will learn all about the new moves Ebony is teaching me.

Rio comes to a stop by my leg, two wriggling boys captured in his arms. "Do we have any duct tape?"

I snort. "You think that would hold a bear?"

He sighs. "Good point."

Reilly dissolves into giggles, which is always the easiest way to win any fight with him. Robbie apparently doesn't know what duct tape is or doesn't care. He just curls his furry white self up on Rio's belly and settles in. One pup who can nap absolutely anywhere.

I eye Rio in case he wasn't planning to lie around for the next hour. I have nowhere to be.

He moves Robbie gently to my lap. "I have to go help Shelley catch the cookie raiders."

That's probably code for something pups don't need to know about, but maybe not. Rio takes cookies very seriously.

Reilly makes space for him to leave and cuddles in against my side. I wrap an arm around shoulders that are going to get big soon and huff a contented sigh. His bear never used to do this. The stupidheads in charge of the pack teased him too much. I glance over at Lissa and Hayden, who are cuddling just like we are. And watching us.

Hayden hides a grin and kisses the top of Lissa's head.

I make a face, just like I'm supposed to, but that's my

human teenager talking. My wolf gets stupidly happy when they're like this. It makes the pack stronger.

Strong enough to maybe have room for a baby alpha.

I try to push that thought away. Too many people in this pack see everything. But inside, I can't hide from the truth. My wolf is getting stronger. A lot stronger, and I don't know why, but I hope she stops soon. I want to stay, but if she gets any more bossy, that might be impossible. Hayden's a really cool guy, but there's no way his wolf will deal with someone more dominant than he is in his pack.

That's not how wolves work.

I snuggle Robbie and try not to think about what it would be like not to be here. I could maybe go to Whistler Pack, because Adrianna Scott is the strongest wolf ever, but I don't want to go. I want to stay right here with my friends, and pups who love me, and grown-ups who let me be a kid and a kickass dominant and seem to like me just fine no matter what.

The parts they know about, anyhow.

HAYDEN

Kel's right. He always is, damn him. He thinks there's something going on inside Kennedy's head, and this close I can darn near smell it. She's thinking way too hard for a teenager.

I lean into Lissa. Which doesn't require much—we're

already about as close as two shifters still in their clothes can get. "Any idea what's going on with Kennedy?"

She tilts her head, studying our two baby alphas and the bear cub they've cuddled up with. "No. Well, maybe. What are you noticing?"

My green-eyed wolf, still full of mysteries. "She's more quiet than usual. Introspective. Those are usually warning signs with a teenage dominant. Could just be the usual growing-up stuff, but Kel doesn't think so."

Lissa sighs. "I sent her on an errand a few weeks back, but I don't think that would be making her thoughtful. I can check in with her, though."

That would be the right answer for almost every wolf in this pack, but I know something about being a baby alpha. "You asked my mom to talk to her, right? I'll give her a nudge."

Lissa rubs her cheek against mine, speaking to my wolf. "Are you sure she's got the time?"

My mother never has time. She makes it for what matters. "She likes Kennedy. A lot."

Lissa chuckles quietly. "Is there anyone she doesn't like?"

Nobody who can speak without their knees knocking together. Adrianna Scott is the consummate leader—personable, charismatic, inviting. Until she isn't, and the few people who've been on the receiving end of those moments still turn white when she walks into a room. "Sometimes baby alphas can internalize too much. Mom will dig it out of her."

"If there is something going on, Kennedy might not

want to rock her pack's boat. Just like a certain alpha I know."

I sigh. "I'm getting better." My wolf is getting used to the idea that letting his pack see what he wants and needs isn't going to break them. "Braden brought me his last piece of bacon this morning and I ate it. That's progress."

Her laugh soothes every raw place inside me. "He'd already eaten his body weight in bacon."

I grin into her hair. "He's a growing boy."

She shakes her head. "Want me to message Adrianna?"

They would both enjoy that, but my green-eyed wolf was looking longingly at the forest this morning, so I don't want to add to her computer time. "I'll do it. I need to feel like a useful alpha at least once a day, remember?"

She snickers. "You washed dishes."

If wolves had gravestones, that would be going on mine. Which is far too morbid a thought for a sunny summer morning. Especially one that started with a new crispness in the air. Fall is coming, which means I should call my sister, too. We need a den, preferably before it starts snowing on our heads. The kitchen might be fine for cookie raids and baking, but nobody wants to sleep in there.

I squeeze Lissa's arms. "You good?"

She smiles. "Yes. I have spreadsheets to play with."

That sounds like some kind of horrible punishment, but she never seems to think so. I roll to my feet. I'm feeling a bit twitchy today, and I don't think it's because the air was crisp this morning. I'll take a loop around the perimeter, catch up with my betas and Kelsey, who's up a tree with Ghost. Which means my betas are likely roaming in very small circles, trying not to look too much like they're keeping an eye on her. Watching Kelsey spread her wings is amazing, but if anything happened to her, half my pack would never forgive themselves.

Rio strolls over the small hill that separates the kitchen from the bend in the river. He's got Layla and Miriam flanking him and their two pups riding on his shoulders.

I catch his eye. Kennedy's more than capable of holding down the teeth-and-claws job at the den, but if it's thinking time she needs, I can leave the big, black wolf of death in charge instead.

He says something to Miriam that has her spluttering, but I don't miss his extra layer of alertness. I'm free to roam.

I kiss Lissa again, because I can and because it's literally happiness candy for my pack. She tastes like the apple-blossom tea she had with her pancakes. "Anything you want from the woods?" There aren't a lot of berries left, but I found where the hazelnuts live, and she likes them almost as much as I do.

My wolf isn't convinced a handful of nuts are as good for wooing as tasty rabbit snacks, but I'm working on him.

She smiles and lays her hand over my heart. "No. Enjoy."

It takes actual physical effort to back away from her. Which is a pretty sure sign our wolves are trying to tell us something, but that isn't a choice they get to make, and Lissa isn't the only one who wants to walk slowly.

It's not because I'm scared of where we're headed.

It's because every step is so damn good.

I blow her a kiss, which amuses Layla and Miriam almost as much as it disgusts Reilly. I look over at the kid who's gotten really good at bear dramatics, and then back at the only mated pair in sight. "If you two did more kissing, maybe he wouldn't be like this."

Miriam splutters again and ducks her head, but Layla laughs. Then she shoots me a look that absolutely freaking delights my wolf, because it's full of mischief and not a hint of reticence. She scoots around Rio, takes Miriam's face in her hands, and plants a kiss on her that would be really educational for Reilly if he were looking.

Cori and Ravi come over the hill, bearing cookies and grinning ear to ear, just in time to catch the grand finale.

Kennedy hoots at them. "Mated-pair kissing contest. It's pretty stiff competition, but I think you two can take them."

Ravi can't figure out if he's horrified or elated.

Cori's made of sterner stuff. She shoves the cookie tray into Rio's hands and advances on her mate with a look in her eyes that sets Jade to banging on Ravi's head, sure something exciting is about to happen.

Cori pauses, studies his face, and drops a whisper-soft kiss on his cheek. Then she reaches up for her daughter. "Want to give your daddy a kiss, cutie?"

Kennedy giggles behind me, thoroughly pleased with herself.

Whatever our teenage baby alpha has on her mind, it hasn't hurt her pack instincts any. My wolf turns and rolls his eyes at her. Troublemaker.

She looks at Lissa and back at me, raising a challenging eyebrow.

I shoot her the sternest alpha glare I can come up with on short notice.

That only makes her giggle harder.

Robbie's white head lifts out of her lap, wondering what ruckus is interrupting his nap. Reilly's hands come off his eyes. "What did I miss?"

Kennedy pats his head. "All the good stuff, dude." Said in exactly the right tone to pull him inside the joke with her.

He groans. "Did you take pictures at least?"

Lissa snickers quietly at her laptop screen. I grin down at her. Maybe the next time Kennedy offers up that same dare, I won't have to turn it down. In the meantime, I have alpha work to do.

My wolf soaks in the feeling of warm sun on his shoulders as I walk away, even though it can't hold a candle to the warmth in his belly. His pack has mated pairs and feisty teenagers and silly bears and adorable pups and a green-eyed wolf who kisses him sometimes.

Life is really fucking good.

2

KENNEDY

I walk out into the forest a little ways, keeping an eye on the internet signal on the sat phone. I got a message from Hayden's mom this morning. She's video-calling me and I'm supposed to be someplace private.

My brains have been kind of scrambled ever since I got the message, but Reilly brought me the sat phone at the right time, and Hayden made a joke about turning down the volume in case Adrianna yells, and Lissa gave me the kind of hug she gives Robbie and my wolf let her. Which is all good because it's a really bad idea to talk to Adrianna Scott with scrambled brains.

I find a tree where the sentries won't be able to hear and swing myself up on the lowest branch. It's not the easiest tree to climb, and I have to monkey around some. I might be fierce, but I'm also kind of short.

I get myself up to some decent forking branches and

wedge myself in against the trunk. I can see the ground, and anyone trying to sneak up on me, which isn't something my wolf will let me stop worrying about even if I'm inside the perimeter and as safe as a pup. I set the sat phone on my knees and wait.

The video-chat app rings at exactly the appointed time and Adrianna pops onto the screen, laughing. She shakes her head as she runs her hands over her mussed-up hair, plucking out leaves and twigs. "Hello, dear. Let me get sorted for just a minute."

I grin. She looks like Reilly after he's rolled around with the pups. "If something important came up, we can do this later."

Her eyes go quietly stern. "You're important. I sent the juveniles to find someone their own age to bother."

I bet she's not bothered at all. When she visited us, she had to go swimming in the river three times to wash off all the maple syrup and berry handprints and dirt the pups got on her. "Juveniles are menaces."

She laughs and picks another twig out of her hair. "How is Reilly?"

"He's good. His bear really likes how happy the den feels."

"That's good for everyone."

I nod. "Yeah." I don't really want to talk about how it makes me feel. It gets too close to things I don't want to say out loud.

Adrianna studies me.

I keep my face still. Phone screens are really small and maybe she can't see too much. Which is probably stupidcakes, but I don't want to talk about why I'm worried. I don't want her to be reassuring and I don't want her to be nice.

My wolf won't believe either of those.

She smiles. "Do you have questions for me this morning, or shall I ask some of you?"

They both sound dangerous, which makes me feel more solid. I know how to do dangerous. "Can I ask about baby alphas? Your pack has some, right?"

"Several, yes."

I try to find words for what my wolf wants to know. "You say they find their place in the pack, but how do they do that? And what is their place, exactly?"

"Not all of them manage." She's back to watching me carefully. "Some, like my son, have a deep need for their own pack, and eventually, with or without my blessing, they leave to find it."

I frown at the odd note in her voice. "You don't like it when they leave?"

She sighs. "I don't like it when they leave before I think they're ready. Which is admitted arrogance on my part. The hardest time is the teenage years. Our wolves feel like adults, ready to make their own place in the world, and for a baby alpha, the most straightforward way to do that is a pack of their own."

I make a face. "No teenager should be in charge of a pack."

She inclines her head. "Yes and no. A pack of their own, not really. It's too much responsibility too young. But you asked how the baby alphas fit in here, and one of the ways that seems to work best is for them to have a baby pack."

My wolf lights up.

Adrianna chuckles.

I make a face. I guess she can see just fine on a phone screen. "My wolf is also a menace."

She grins wryly. "That won't ever change. Mine is still a furry demon some days."

I want, badly, to ask more about that, but it veers too close to what I don't want to talk about. "How do the baby packs work?"

Her face morphs into teacher mode, but this is a class I'm really interested in. "All shifter groups need to pick a pack structure, a way to organize themselves. Our animals don't do well otherwise. But some of us thrive in certain structures and wither in others. Wolves generally need a hierarchy, and we tend to attract other shifters who find comfort in that same kind of organization."

I nod. She's written about this part. "But Whistler has almost as many cats and ravens and bears and stuff as wolves, right?"

She smiles, pleased. "You've read some of my writing."

All of it I could find. "You say things that make sense to my wolf."

Her eyes soften. "Thank you. That's a really lovely compliment."

I wriggle in my tree, uncomfortable. She sounds like she means it, and that's just weird. Everyone knows she's the best in the world at making sense to wolves.

Her lips quirk. "Even grown-up alphas like to hear that what they do makes a difference, my dear."

I make a face. "Sorry. It's just that you're really normal sometimes. It's weird."

Her laughter peals through the speakers on the sat phone.

My wolf wags her tail hard enough I nearly fall out of the tree. I settle her down. There's nobody down below to catch me if I take a tumble.

She wrinkles her nose. Wolves aren't supposed to be in trees.

I sigh and keep my chatty wolf's thoughts to myself. Adrianna is saying some really important things and my human needs to hear them, even if my animal can't manage to pay attention. I work backward to the last thing she said. "So Whistler has shifters who mostly like a wolf kind of hierarchy, even if they're not all wolves."

She nods. "Yes. We're structured primarily as a wolf pack, and that works very well, but it doesn't stop us from including good ideas from some of the other ways shifters organize themselves. Cats tend to have a lot of micro packs within the larger pack—smaller units within the whole, like families or mated pairs or tightly knit groups of friends. They happen informally at some level in every pack. You're already part of more than one, I suspect."

My wolf starts happily listing them. The sentries. Bailey's crew. Whatever I am to the pups. I wrinkle my nose, thinking. "A lot, but some are because our pack is still kind of messed up."

"That's an astute observation." She wraps a sweater

around her shoulders, one that matches the pink in Kelsey's blanket. "Not all smaller units are healthy ones, and not all of them are permanent. Some help the pack get to a new place and then they disband."

I wrap my free arm around my knees, vaguely uncomfortable again. "Most of mine are like that."

Adrianna's face softens. "Do you have family in your pack, sweetie? Or elsewhere?"

My heart twinges, but it's old aches. Ones that don't get to make me cry anymore. "I was a foundling. My mom left me on the edge of pack territory when I was about eight months old."

Sad understanding hits her eyes. "When you first shifted."

I wriggle away from her sadness. "Probably. That's what Myrna says. She's the one who found me, chewing on the basket I'd been left in." That's a good part of my story. Every time she tells it, I can hear the truth in her voice. She loved me right from the first moment she saw me.

Adrianna laughs. "Hayden mostly chewed on shoes, but when Jules was a pup, she chewed everything. Shampoo bottles were her favorite."

My wolf winces. "Those must taste awful."

Adrianna's eyes twinkle. "You'd think, wouldn't you?"

This is so not what I expected to be talking about. "Is Jules a baby alpha too?"

"No, thank goodness. Two of us in one family are plenty. She learned how to hold her own, though. She's very good at managing the bears and other cantankerous clients she deals with in her work, and she credits her brother with helping her develop those skills."

I'm probably not supposed to laugh at my alpha, but I do anyhow. And I think about how Hayden probably learned a lot of things in his little family pack, too. "His wolf doesn't mind if Ebony beats him up."

Her eyes twinkle. "I hear Ebony isn't the only one who can do that."

My cheeks turn hot. "Just one time. Mostly he's better than I am." That's not exactly true. He's bigger, and that gives him some advantages I haven't all the way figured out how to match yet. But I will.

My wolf shies away from my human thoughts. Good alpha. Strong alpha.

I want to cuddle her up like I do with Robbie. She just wants to be loyal teeth and claws. It's not her fault she's getting stronger.

The sat phone is quiet, Adrianna watching me steadily.

I cringe. I'm letting my guard down way too much. "So, your family pack helped Jules learn to stand up to alphas, and Hayden learned to not be at the top of the hierarchy sometimes."

Adrianna smiles. "When he was still alive, that was James. Submissives are often at the top of the chain in a family. In friend groups, too."

I blink, astonished, but she's totally right. Bailey would do anything for Lissa, and my wolf lets Ghost boss her around all the time. "I never thought of it like that."

Adrianna's head tilts curiously. "Most dominants aren't all that happy to consider being at the bottom of a hierarchy."

I swallow. That's getting way too close to the secret words I don't want to say. "It's kind of cool, actually." Ghost is going to make big faces when I tell her, but I hope she gets one of her special smiles, too. "I'm not always a baby alpha, then. Just sometimes."

She studies me a moment longer. "Small groups are a chance to have different kinds of roles—to find ones that meet the needs of your wolf and your human, both. Doing sentry duty for your betas helps feed a desire to be helpful teeth and claws, or taking care of the pups can help a dominant remember what it is to feel soft and happy and safe."

My throat closes.

She smiles gently. "That's not a weakness, sweetie. I cuddle a lot of pups."

My breathing sounds like the wind over by Lonely Peak. "Because you don't want to be alpha all the time?"

"I'm always alpha." She exhales slowly. "But I want to be an alpha who holds on to her own softness, always, and never forgets why she needs to be hard."

I barely catch my whimper before it escapes.

I'm pretty sure she hears it anyhow. "I see both in you, Kennedy. A generous, fierce strength, and a heart that hasn't forgotten how to be young and playful and gentle."

I can't speak. At all.

Adrianna chuckles. "Forgive me, my dear. Don't let

me decide who you're meant to be. I see a lot of my younger self in you, and I think I was speaking as much to her as I was to you."

My throat tries, but I'm not getting any closer to being able to talk.

She picks up a mug of tea almost as big as her head and takes a sip. "So. Small groups. All packs have them. Done well, small groups enhance the strength of the pack. They're how we learn and develop skills and meet needs that might be harder to address in the larger pack. Some happen naturally, and some benefit from a little encouragement."

I know one that she encouraged. It's one of our pack's favorite campfire stories. "Kel still complains about the one you made for him."

Adrianna laughs. "That one wasn't my doing."

I blink.

"I made it formal. But the forming of the three of them was Hayden's choice. His wolf knew what he needed to be happy, and he went out and found it."

My heart stutters.

Adrianna's smile is full of wry, gentle humor, even on a tiny phone screen. "Already finding yours, are you?"

I gulp. "I try not to. I try to just be a helper and useful teeth and claws, but sometimes my wolf thinks she knows things, and she's hard to ignore."

"Good. That's the last thing you should be doing."

I'm so confused. We're trying to be one pack, not a bunch of small ones. The small ones make Hayden's wolf sad. Or at least that's what I thought, but I'm realizing I wasn't seeing all of them. There are micro packs right at the den. The mamas. Rio and all the pups who really like candy. The people with a certain kind of scar on their hearts that my wolf doesn't understand, but she can feel. They belong to Kelsey.

None of those baby packs are hurting. They're helping. "A small pack can be a good thing."

Adrianna sets her chin on her hands and smiles. "Yes. They can be divisive and weaken the whole, or they can be a fierce source of energy to help a pack grow and heal and be better."

My human is so dazed, but my wolf is blazing like the hot summer sun. She wants this.

Something in Adrianna's eyes blazes right back. "Your wolf knows things. That's a gift. Use it. Don't deny your pack that part of who you are."

I manage a wild nod that isn't really yes or no and would die before it disappointed Adrianna Scott.

She takes another sip from her huge mug. "If you already have a baby pack, who's in it?"

I blink, but as soon as she asks it, I know the answer. "Reilly." I pause a beat, because the next part feels weird. "I want to say Robbie, too."

Adrianna shakes her head. "Listen to your wolf, sweetie. Baby packs don't work by human rules."

I wrinkle my nose, because both my human and my wolf are sad about that. "Then not Robbie, not in the same way. I love him a lot, but he's Hayden's."

Adrianna's eyebrows go up.

Oops. I'm not supposed to say that stuff out loud.

"Can you pretend you didn't hear that? They don't think they're mated yet."

Adrianna's laugh is like Kelsey's when Rio tickles her, full of joy and sunshine. "Is that the story they're going with?"

I make a wry face. "Yes."

She shakes her head. "But your wolves know. Which is why Robbie feels like Hayden's. He could be yours as well, but baby packs aren't about how much you love. They're about connecting for a purpose. You can meet Robbie's needs as his packmate. What can you offer Reilly in a baby pack that's special?"

My human is clueless. My wolf knows instantly. "Friends at his back."

Adrianna nods a little. "That's the dominant's answer. Dig for the rest."

I squint at the screen, nonplussed. Then my human sees another piece. "People who really know him and who pay attention. Sometimes he gets too quiet and he could get lost in the big pack, even when everyone loves him. He might not get heard, and he's a really smart bear."

"Yes. Exactly that." The approval in her eyes somersaults my wolf. "That's precisely what a baby alpha can do with her power. You make pack more focused and meaningful for Reilly's bear, and you make sure he gets to fully contribute."

That sounds so fancy. "I mostly just wrestle with his bear and read the books he gives me."

Adrianna smiles. "What does Hayden do most days?"

My wolf goes entirely still. "Alpha things."

Her lips quirk. "I bet they look a lot like wrestling with Reilly's bear."

They do. So much. I want to protest, to argue that isn't what alphas do, but I'm looking at one who still has twigs in her hair.

She smiles again. "Is Reilly the only one? Your baby pack doesn't need to be big. Hayden's wasn't."

I gulp. Rio and Kel would both die for Hayden, and they help him be amazing every single day. Which feels so very out of reach, until I think about the look I sometimes see in Reilly's eyes, and the way it makes me feel—and that he's not the only one who makes me feel that way. "Ghost. And Hoot." And maybe Kenny, but he'd be really mad about that, and so might a lot of other people.

Adrianna flashes me a grin. "Reilly's going to end up running with a pack of teenage girls, is he?"

I grin back. "That's not so bad. We're pretty awesome."

She laughs. "Indeed." She studies me for a minute, her eyes twinkling. "You started this conversation asking how baby alphas find their place, and it appears you've already done a lot of the work to find yours."

That sounds so much more organized than I feel. "Maybe by accident."

"Part of being an alpha is instinct, and part is thoughtful intention. So that's some homework for you. Contemplate your baby pack and how you might thoughtfully build on what your wolf is already doing."

My wolf preens.

I manage not to roll my eyes. Her head is going to be so big after this conversation. "So I should think about how I can help each of them be stronger, and how we can help make our big pack stronger."

"Exactly that." She smiles gently. "Remembering, of course, that strength comes in a lot of flavors."

I nod furiously. "I'm not a jerk, I promise."

She chuckles at me over the top of her mug. "You aren't. But you've forgotten one part. Don't forget to let them help you be stronger."

My heart tumbles.

I don't say anything—but I think it.

Stronger is the last thing I want to be.

GHOST

I try not to cry. It doesn't really work, though. My nose is all snotty by the time I'm back up my tree, and I have to swipe at my eyes with my sleeve, because I'm supposed to be keeping a lookout.

But I can't stop thinking about what Kennedy said.

And what Adrianna Scott said back.

I didn't mean to eavesdrop. I just wanted to see if K wanted any of my chocolate. She gives most of hers to the pups, so I always keep a couple of my squares for her.

I swipe my sleeve over my eyes again.

Baby pack. We're baby pack and that's just like family and it's okay and I didn't even know my wolf was scared about that until just now. She wants, so very badly, to be part of the big Ghost Mountain Pack. But she doesn't want to lose her sisters.

Or Reilly.

The ones who make her strong.

I blow my nose. I need to finish my shift and then I need to find Hoot and Reilly, because we have a job to do and Adrianna Scott thinks we can do it. That's the biggest, most important thing anyone has ever said about me and she didn't even know I was listening.

But she's right.

We need to help Kennedy be strong. Which is a big job, because she's really scared and I'm not sure why. But that's okay, because I know something that maybe even Adrianna doesn't know. All of us in Kennedy's pack—we know what it feels like to be really scared.

Kennedy is the one who taught us to be brave anyhow.

3

KENNEDY

My wolf settles on the grass, her belly finally full. A small brown ball of fur immediately pounces on me and growls. I try not to laugh. Mellie's been practicing her dominance moves this week and she gets really cranky if we don't take her seriously. I pin her on top of my belly and let her hear the rumble in my throat. A gentle warning not to bite off way more than she can chew.

Her eyes widen.

I ruffle her fur. She needs more playmates, poor kid. Some dominants who aren't quite as big and scary as I am. Until then, I need to let her growl at me, because Braden just ignores her and nobody will let her boss Kelsey and Jade around. Even tiny dominants don't get to have bad manners in this pack.

Reilly joins us and holds out some apple slices.

I lay one on my belly and Mellie backs away from it, growling. This time I laugh. "Wolves don't eat apple, do they, cutie?"

My wolf heartily agrees. I like apples though, so I pick it up and eat it.

Mellie licks my chin, which probably tastes like maple syrup, because Braden fed me my pancakes this morning and he has really terrible aim. I flip her over and scrub my fingers on her belly, which makes her tongue loll in a silent wolf laugh.

Reilly grins. "She chased a squirrel this morning. She was really mad when she couldn't follow it up a tree."

Dominant wolves are sometimes not too bright. "Did you shake it out for her?"

Reilly wrinkles his nose. "No. That would be cheating. And mean to the squirrel."

I wrap my arm around his head. His bear likes wrestling. "Some friend you are."

He snuggles in instead of busting loose, so apparently his bear is feeling mellow. "Kel says you're supposed to come find him when you're done your lunch and not covered in pups."

That doesn't sound terribly urgent, but it would be really easy to stay covered in pups all day. They like me, and when they crawl all over me and lick my chin, it's hard to be worried that I'm a big, bad wolf.

However, I am loyal teeth and claws, and this pack doesn't have nearly enough of those for me to sit around all afternoon. I hand Mellie to Reilly. "I think Shelley was hoping for some help in the garden." It's a small garden and it got planted late, but we had fresh lettuce for dinner last night and it made Shelley and Eliza and Kelsey so happy that even Rio ate some.

Reilly grins at his small charge. "No digging up the potatoes this time, silly. And no barking at the zucchini."

I snicker. Zucchini are pretty scary. Sometimes one will show up that's three feet long and nobody even saw it the day before.

Mellie makes a pouty face, but in this pack we don't leave any job to the submissives, even when the dominants really suck at it. She'll learn. I helped make salad last night, even though my wolf thinks eating leaves is a silly idea and it would be much better to feed the lettuce to the rabbits so they can grow into tasty bunny snacks.

I roll my eyes at my pouty animal. Hayden's wolf is already terrorizing the bunnies. I can be a shifter who eats lettuce and maybe even likes it.

Reilly holds out his hand to pull me up. I let him help, and think about what Adrianna said. Instead of just punching his shoulder like I usually would, I bump up against his bear and try to find my words. "You're really good at helping Mellie see why quiet things are interesting."

He ducks his head, but not before I see the surprised pleasure in his eyes.

Hayden's mom is a really smart wolf. I give Reilly's bear one last bump. "Don't let the zucchini eat you."

Reilly nods solemnly. Then his bear giggles as Mellie butts his chin with her head.

I leave him to deal with bossy toddler antics and head

for the woods. I swing by the kitchen on my way out and grab a canteen and some snacks for the sentries—the kind that aren't green and leafy. And I think, because I want to be a baby alpha who builds up my pack instead of messing it up, and there are still a whole lot of really big things wrong around here.

By the time I get out to Ghost's tree, I've eaten half a strip of jerky and figured out the big holes in my first three ideas. My wolf is good at stealing bandanas and not so good at being thoughtful. I sigh. This being-a-responsible-baby-alpha stuff is hard.

"If you're thinking that hard, it's probably a bad idea."

I glare at Kel, who totally needs to stop sneaking up on people.

Ghost snickers quietly up in her tree, which means she saw him coming.

I growl at both of them, just because. Then I lean against the tree and eye Kel. "You have stuff for me to do?"

He helps himself to some of my jerky. "If you've got a few hours."

"So long as it doesn't involve zucchini."

He snorts. "Mellie cut a new tooth last night, and she did it on Ebony's tail. If I can get you to do her run today, I might be able to convince both of them to take a nap."

Ghost laughs.

I grin. Our pack mostly sucks at napping. "I can do the run. You want me to check on the dominants and swing by Bailey, right?" That fits in strangely well with what I was sort of planning to do anyhow. Almost like Kel can read minds. Which might be true.

He nods. "Pay particular attention to anything you hear out at Kenny's camp. Word is they maybe have a house in town."

That's new. "All of them?"

He shrugs. "Not sure. Ebony caught the tail end of a conversation."

I grin at him. "So I get to go eavesdrop?"

He raises a wry eyebrow. "Don't you always?"

I try to look innocent and well behaved. "I don't usually have permission."

He shakes his head, but I can tell he thinks I'm funny. "Don't torment them, but get close enough to listen if you can. If they're leaving, we have some decisions to make."

His words suddenly make it all the way through to my brain, and they hurt my wolf. "It will suck if they go." Especially for Eliza, because one of them is her stupid-head son. And for Myrna and Shelley, because they remember most of those assholes when they were babies.

"It might for a while." He meets my gaze steadily. His wolf isn't even a teeny, tiny bit scared of mine. "But remember, it hasn't really been that long since they got kicked out of the den, and heading into town isn't leaving the pack. We have to keep our eyes on the long game."

He's got a point. Leaving the pack means doing the lone-wolf thing or heading to Vancouver, not holing up in a house in town so close to pack territory they can probably still smell it.

"A move like that might also create opportunity to

reel in a couple of those jackasses, so keep your eyes and ears open. Their humans are all talking smack, but their wolves might not be so convinced."

I look up, because Ghost has some seriously good eyes and ears, and maybe, just like Reilly, she could use some help from a loud baby alpha to make sure she gets heard. "I could talk to Ghost and the other sentries before I go out. See what they've noticed."

His eyes glint with something that might be approval. "Intel is always good. Keep your betas in the loop."

I nod solemnly, just like Ghost is probably doing up in her tree. I don't feel so tangled anymore. I have homework to do and a job to do for my pack, and Adrianna says the best alphas are the ones who listen hardest.

Today, I'm going to practice.

RIO

I take a good look at the two teenagers sitting on a rock, so deep in conversation they've completely lost track of their surroundings. Which is entirely acceptable for a submissive who's off sentry duty and inside the inner perimeter, and bordering on astounding for one of our fiercest sets of teeth and claws.

I'm not surprised. My wolf was pulled out here by a very particular vibe. One I've only felt one other time in my life—about three seconds before a ten-year-old wolf calmly decided an arrogant sentinel and a cranky Special Forces veteran were his pack. "Adrianna got to her."

Kel snorts. "You think?"

I do, and it's about damn time. "Somebody needed to give her a push."

His lips quirk. "My official position is that this pack doesn't need a teenage baby alpha running amok."

"That's not what she's doing."

He eyes me skeptically.

I grin. "Remember when Hayden realized we were his pack? That was running amok. This looks almost responsible." More importantly, she's not trying to do it alone. Ghost is doing most of the talking. Kennedy is listening with her entire being, which is a skill most fourteen-year-old baby alphas don't even have on their radar. "How much of that did you coach?"

"None of it." Kel studies the two on the rock, listening in his own way. "Ghost has said more in the last hour than I've seen her say in a month."

That's interesting. And hopeful. Signs of more than one wolf trying to step into who she might one day be. Baby alphas tend to catalyze that kind of rising. "Ghost is a smart choice for her baby pack. She'll help hold Kennedy's compass steady."

Kel smiles faintly. "That's Reilly's job. Ghost's is going to be different, I think."

I blink. I completely missed that. Which is why packs have all-seeing betas. "Damn. Any others?"

He shoots me a look. "You tell me."

Sentinels can see things even betas can't. "Some of Bailey's crew, maybe." It's hard to tell. I haven't been able to get close enough to the shadow pack to get a good read. Not without seriously pissing off their leader, and my wolf has been oddly reticent to do that.

Kel nods, like he had that figured out before I did. Which is probably true. "I'm sending her out to do Ebony's run. That will let her sniff at most of the shifters within easy reach of the den."

Paws on the earth is always good advice, especially for baby alphas who are thinking really loudly and need to hear what their wolf has to say.

He sticks his hands in his pockets. "Are you going to step in? She'll need a mentor. One closer than Whistler."

The big, black wolf of death already figured that out. "Yes."

Kel smirks. "Excellent. Then you can tell Hayden she's headed off to yank on dominant tails."

I sigh. "She needs to be thinking and listening to her wolf, not obeying the letter of whatever law you laid down while she neatly sidesteps its intent."

He snorts. "She can do that and mess with an asshat or two."

If she can't, she hasn't been paying enough attention in class. I glance over at the guy who's been teaching them. "Keeping her steady while she figures this out is going to take all hands on deck."

He nods quietly. "I know."

I bend over and pick up a tattered hoodie that smells like Ghost. We might not have as many hands in this pack as we did when Hayden fought his way to peace with who and what he is—but we have really good ones. My wolf respects the small and mighty hands of this pack very much.

He's just not sure Kennedy will let them be enough.

4

KENNEDY

I trot along the crest of the ridgeline and finally spot what my wolf smelled ages ago. Hoot, sitting on a rocky outcropping. One I can't get to, at least not without wings or a long run, because there's a big crevice separating her ridge and mine.

She maybe wants it to stay that way. She's so quiet. So still.

The wind lifts up her hair, blowing it into her eyes, and she swipes at it. She's sitting with her knees tucked up against her chest, watching the long, sloping hillside below. The one that has a view all the way back to the den. A place she was happy, once.

My wolf whines quietly. She loves Hoot. Sad Hoot is bad.

I scratch behind my wolf's ears. We need to listen

today, even if that means watching sad Hoot instead of romping over and asking her to play.

My wolf puts her head on her tail and pouts. She thinks that's a really dumb idea.

I don't like it either, but I listened to Ghost earlier and I learned some things I didn't know, because even though I was asking her about Evan and Damien and Kenny and Colin, she said some words in between those that felt really important. Ghost wants something and I don't know exactly what it is, but I could hear it trying to work its way free.

Which was a hard surprise, because I thought I was a pretty good friend, but now I think I'm maybe one who talks a lot and assumes she knows things and doesn't listen nearly enough. I know how to be teeth and claws. Listening is hard, especially when you want to hear the deep-down stuff that people mostly don't say.

My wolf droops. She wants to be strong for her pack.

I sigh. I need to let her droop. There are other ways to be strong, and maybe if I learn some of those, I won't be so dangerous. I lift my head a little, trying to listen better. Hoot's not saying any words at all, but her body is, and her face, and if her wolf was howling, she'd be singing a song of so much sadness and yearning.

I might not understand what Ghost wants yet, but I know what Hoot is wishing for. Some of it can't ever happen, because evil teeth and claws broke her family and it can't ever be put back together again. But she wants one thing that maybe can happen.

She wants to be at the den.

My wolf whimpers. She wants laughing Hoot. Playful Hoot. She could chase Hoot back to the den. Hoot likes chases.

I wish it were that simple. The den would love her. She's funny and her wolf is feisty and she never forgets anything about anyone and she even likes to eat lettuce. But she won't leave Bailey, not ever. Bailey needs her and she needs Bailey and the ghosts in the woods so badly need them both.

I want to put my paws over my eyes and whimper like a pup, but I don't. I need to listen, and I need to think. My wolf picked Hoot for her baby pack and there must be a reason. I just need to figure out what it is.

GHOST

My wolf is sick and tired of sitting in trees.

I try to soothe whatever's chewing on her tail. We do this every day. It's important work and it keeps the pups safe. She's just being silly.

Except she's not being silly. She's listening to the wind, only this time it isn't the kind that blows through the trees and teases my nose with promises of bonfires and crisp leaves and cloudy mornings. It's a special wind, one that's coming from Kennedy's heart and delivering a message straight to my wolf's ears.

I have to help my friend be strong. I need to run at her side.

I can't do that if I'm sitting in a tree.

I scan the ground and listen for the sentry calls, the ones that say nothing has changed and all is well and the den is safe. Usually it makes me happy to hear them and proud to be useful. Today I want to hoot back an alarm, even though nothing is wrong except for confusing whispers in the wind.

The ferns to my left rustle faintly, which means Kel wants me to know he's coming. That's normal. He does circles of the inner perimeter a lot. Ebony says his wolf finds it soothing. I wonder if he has days when that doesn't work and his wolf just wants to scratch at every part of him. I wait until he's almost below me before I drop out of the tree, landing like a cat just like Dorie showed me.

Kel doesn't look surprised. He never does, even when I know he didn't hear me coming. "Do you need a break?"

I don't know how to answer that. I just look at him, all the thoughts in my head suddenly stuck.

He nods a little. "Walk with me?"

That's normal, too. He often asks one of us to do a loop with him when he wants to ask questions or bump shoulders with our wolves for a while. We all like it. He's quiet and he doesn't smile much, but he's got this goodness inside him, all the way down deep. Even Adelina's wolf likes him, and she doesn't like anyone.

I glance over at him, trying to figure out what to say.

He walks silently beside me, waiting. He always does that with submissives. He bosses Kennedy and Ebony and even Hayden around sometimes, but with the rest of us, he just waits. It makes my wolf feel special. Like maybe being restless is important instead of just silly.

I watch his feet. You can learn so much about someone from the way they set their paws on the earth. Kel walks with respect, and sadness, and a determination that won't stop until he dies.

I blink. My wolf feels a bit like that today. I dig for words—the ones that feel determined. "How do I help Kennedy?"

Kel steps over a small pile of leaves blown up against some twisted tree roots. "She's a baby alpha. Do you know what that means?"

I swallow. I know what Kennedy thinks it means, but I don't want to say that. I don't want her to be right. "That she'll have her own pack one day."

"Maybe." He looks over at me. "Some baby alphas stay in a bigger pack."

Kennedy's voice sounded funny when she talked about that part. "They make a small pack, right? One that's helpful. So they can maybe stay."

A frown moves across Kel's face. "Yes."

My wolf likes that so much. Kennedy is amazing, but most of her jobs have been to use her teeth and claws. This one is about using her heart. "She's going to be really good at that."

He smiles a little. "So are you."

I squint into a sudden beam of sunlight, more unsettled by his words than the glinting brightness. They match the whispers in the wind. "I'm supposed to help her."

He nods. "It goes both ways. She has responsibilities to you and you have responsibilities to her."

I look down at my feet. "I can feel them."

He huffs out a breath. "All betas can."

I crash to a stop, staring at him.

He chuckles quietly. "I take it the two of you hadn't figured that part out yet."

My words scramble over each other. He can't be right. "We're a baby pack of three, or maybe four. We don't need a beta."

"Your pack might not. She does."

The restless thoughts in my head all suddenly freeze. "Is Kennedy going to be okay?"

His eyes are solemn. "Nobody can answer that."

My wolf plants her paws. I've never felt her so determined. So fierce. "How do I help her be okay?"

He looks at me, and he's so, so serious. "You trust your wolf, you trust your pack, and you damn well ask for help if you need it."

I stuff my hands in my pockets, look down at the ground where my feet need to stay, and remember the words in the wind. "Okay. I'm asking."

I feel his surprise.

I don't let it stop me. "I need to stop sitting in a tree."

KENNEDY

I move cautiously through the scrubby brush and spindly trees. The ferns around Kenny's camp are drying out in the late summer, and they get crunchy and loud if you're not a careful wolf.

I keep my ears open. Trevor and Baird were easy to find, but they were just moaning about beer. I need better information than that. Ghost thinks Damien and Evan and Kenny might all come back to the den. My wolf is really skeptical, especially about the last two, but Ghost says Evan is mostly a jerk on the outside and something else on the inside, and she thinks Kenny might come to the den if someone else needed him there.

Which is interesting and smart and sneaky and I want to listen hard and see if she's right. I bet she is. Quiet wolves learn a lot more than loud ones.

I catch a fresh scent trail and swing left. It's not Kenny. He's usually in his fur, which means I have to be more careful, because wolf noses aren't stupid. This isn't wolf scent, though. It's Evan, and he's alone. Which is weird. Usually he's riding Damien's ass or hanging out with Baird and Colin and being a lazy doofus.

Ghost thinks that's cover—that he's a wolf in a cage and we just have to figure out how to let him out.

Even if she's right, I'm not so sure letting him out is a good idea. Evan didn't used to be such a jerkface, but he always thought I was just a stupid little girl. Even before. Not all the dumb shit these guys believe came in the door with Samuel and Eamon. But he was friends with Layla and Miriam back when the rest of the pack used to give them grief, so maybe he's not all the way a jerkface, either.

I don't remember that part so much, but Ghost does.

She's quiet, but she really watches.

Evan isn't being quiet. My wolf tucks in behind a clump of downwind rocks. He's stomping in circles, kicking trees and muttering, and he's kind of stinky. I stick my head around a rock to see if he's talking on his phone, but all that does is get me a bigger whiff of stinky Evan.

My wolf wrinkles her nose. He reeks worse than Robbie's feet, and those get really smelly. He looks bad, too. Cranky, and like he's been pulling at his hair. And no phone. He's definitely talking to himself.

Bailey does that sometimes. It's never a good sign.

I look around to see if there's a way to sneak closer without getting caught, but all I can see are skinny trees and dry ferns, and Ghost might be able to use those as cover, but I can't. I could jump on Evan and beat him up and make him talk, but Kel said I wasn't supposed to torment anyone, and using my teeth and claws just because someone is raggedy and talking to himself probably counts.

My wolf isn't so sure. She thinks maybe a fight would help him feel better.

I sigh. She forgets. Evan isn't very nice, even when he feels better.

He swings another kick at a tree, still muttering. His boot bounces right back off, which just makes him mad, so he punches the tree instead.

I shake my head as he yells really nasty insults about the tree's mother. Those I can hear just fine. And what he yells after, too.

Three words that mean Ghost is right.

KENNY

Damn fool girl.

Sneaking up on dominant wolves and not paying any bloody attention to who's behind her. I consider kicking a rock so she'll figure out just how vulnerable a position she's put herself in, but I don't feel like getting chewed on today, and there's an even chance Evan would join the brawl just to try to deal with some of the twisting in his gut.

I have no doubt Kennedy could take us both, but she'd go home with enough bruises that teeth and claws would come looking for us, and they wouldn't be in a good mood.

Which wouldn't help anything. I'm already planning to slink off into the woods. I don't need any more wounds to lick. I've failed about as completely as a guy still breathing can fail. They're all leaving, just as soon as Colin and Baird get the keys to their new place. Six guys off to discover that the world doesn't give a fuck about who they are, and I couldn't convince even one of them that pack is worth eating crow for.

I guess they have plenty of reasons not to listen to me.

My wolf watches Kennedy as she spies on Evan, both of them so full of intensity I can hardly stand it, even from here. Jason used to be like that when he wasn't being a starry-eyed dreamer like his mother.

The part of me that used to have a heart twinges with phantom pain. Jason tried to see the best in everyone, even Samuel. They used it against him, used it to kill a sweet fourteen-year-old kid, and I wasn't there to keep him safe because they played me like a fucking violin and then threw my son's dead body on the strings.

Throbbing starts behind my eyes.

I sigh. Another hour and it will be a hammer. That's just enough time to find one of Hayden's lieutenants and tell them to keep little girls at home where they belong. Before she gets hurt—or has to hurt someone else.

It's not a friendly warning. My wolf stopped taking the high road so long ago he can't even remember what it looks like.

I'm doing it so that I can slink off into the woods in peace.

KENNEDY

I stop on the bank of the small stream, enjoying the cool dirt under my feet. This is one of my favorite places in our whole territory. The only way in is to climb a wet, slippery rock face, so I'm always alone. I bend down and scoop up some of the water, slurping it out of my hands. My throat sighs happily. It was a hot climb.

I toss another couple of handfuls on my face and then I wade in deeper, over toward the small waterfall. It's the baby cousin of the one that tumbles down the rock face I just climbed up, but it's so pretty. It's tall and not very wide, and it glistens in the sun, and there's a space on the rocks behind it where my wolf likes to curl up on a hot day.

Today I want something different, though. I back up under the falls, letting the cold water beat down on my shoulders. I tip my head back and let it rain down on my scalp, too. My muscles aren't sore, but my brain is. Listening is hard work, especially when you hear things that you don't know how to fix.

Ghost wants something, but I don't know what it is.

Hoot wants to come home, but I don't know how to get her there.

Evan wants out. Which is a really hard, unhappy cage to open, even if he is a jerk.

And Kenny wants to disappear.

I scowl, which just gets water in my eyes. Evan isn't in my baby pack, but Kenny definitely is, even if that doesn't make any sense. My wolf didn't bother to explain. She just knows. He was an idiot and tried to sneak up on me, and I could feel him tugging on that same place inside me where Reilly and Ghost and Hoot live. My wolf still wanted to bite him, though. For the sneaking part. And for wanting to disappear. We have enough ghost wolves in our woods already.

I let the baby waterfall beat on me as I think about my baby pack. Maybe they can help me fix some things. Reilly's bear could sit on Kenny. He's getting really good at that. And Ghost might have some ideas about Hoot. For the rest, I need to be smart and quiet and sneaky and scary.

I'm really good at the last one. The rest are harder.

I sigh and tip forward into the small pool, careful not to get too close to the edge of the big waterfall. That's probably a metaphor or something, but I just want to be a teenager and not have so many hard things to think about.

My wolf doesn't want that, though. Today was confusing and frustrating and hard and sweaty—and she loved every second.

5

HAYDEN

She's dusty, tired, and more at peace than she's been for days. And clearly she wasn't expecting a welcoming committee.

I hide a grin as Kennedy stares at the motley crew she's chosen for her baby pack. Some of them don't know that yet, but she does. My wolf has felt the elastic bands she's been stretching around them all day. Even he didn't expect all of them to be at the den when she showed up, though.

I eye Rio, who's standing beside me looking bemused. "Should we be letting her claim a cranky dominant three times her age who could actually give her wolf some grief?"

He snorts. "Could we have stopped you?"

Yes. Kel could have ground me into dust when I was ten. "She should be smarter than her alpha."

"Okay." He nods affably. "That's a good angle. She might listen if you approach it that way."

Not a chance in hell. I watch as Kenny stomps over to Kennedy, irritation mostly masking the grief in his eyes. I don't bother hiding my wolf's grin as Ghost steps in between them, her arms crossed in a truly excellent imitation of Kel.

"Huh." Rio huffs out a surprised chuckle. "I didn't see that coming."

I eye my cranky, psychic beta, who's carefully standing close enough to intervene and far enough away so Ghost doesn't know that. "He did." It's entirely possible Kel kicked it into motion. He knows just how much backup a baby alpha can need. And Ghost isn't all of it. I glance at the trees on the other side of the river, where Hoot is standing in the shadows. Feeling the bond, even if she doesn't understand why.

A baby pack doing what the best of them have always done.

I turn my attention back to the standoff between a wiry, beaten-down wolf who's far too close to giving up and a teenager who usually chooses to be invisible. Kennedy has stepped forward, close enough to have Ghost's back, but she's not interfering. She's staring, puzzled, as her wolf tries to sort out the dynamics she can smell.

Kenny shifts his gaze to the baby alpha who's trying to claim him. "You let me sneak up on you today. You're going to get yourself hurt. Stay away from my camp."

My wolf readies his claws, but Kennedy meets his gaze calmly. "I knew you were there."

He snorts.

"You were at four o'clock behind me, you scared the crap out of a mouse that was hiding under the rock you were skulking behind, and your wolf kept wanting to lick your front left paw, but you wouldn't let him."

His jaw doesn't actually drop, but it's a close thing.

I wait for her real kick to his gut to land. There are only two reasons a wolf leaves their back turned on another dominant. He won't want to believe either of them.

Rio mutters something under his breath.

I smirk. "I don't think she needs sentinel help. She's got this."

"Maybe." He doesn't take his eyes off the standoff. "Smartass attitude eventually got through to Kel, but I don't know if it's enough to bring Kenny back to life."

My wolf sobers. He's good at reading broken wolves, and he knows we had the easier job. Kel's sense of his own worth was badly battered. Kenny's is dust. His loyalty to pack isn't, however. Which Kennedy has clearly already added in to her math.

It's a gutsy play. My wolf is so fucking pleased she's making it. And already working on how he can have her back.

I snort. He's going to have to get in line.

The forces in the watching pack shift and Reilly walks through with a plate of Myrna's grilled ribs in his hands. Hoot is right behind him, holding the stainless steel containers we use to send dinner out to the sentries. Reilly offers Kenny a cautious smile. "Would you like some dinner? The ribs are really good."

Kenny looks like he just got punched again. "Nah, thanks kid. I need to head out. I just want Kennedy here to stay safe."

Hoot smirks. "She would hate that."

Reilly snickers and then looks mildly alarmed.

Ghost shakes her head at both of them, long-suffering beta to idiot baby packmates.

I lean against Rio. "How did I not know she's a mini-Kel?" She hasn't got his poker face, but she's handling a tricky situation like a pro. Reilly isn't at all sure he wants to be in a baby pack with a wolf who was mean to him, Hoot's wolf is stirred up enough to really be pushing on her human, and Kennedy is still coming to terms with what she's started. Ghost is already quietly walking the walk.

Rio just smiles. Watching wolves step up is his favorite entertainment ever.

These ones aren't done. Hoot takes the plate from Reilly and stuffs it into Kenny's hands. "Sit. You want hot sauce with those or Myrna's magic green sauce?"

He doesn't manage to answer, probably because Kennedy and Ghost bracket him and neatly herd him toward the nearest log. Reilly scampers off in pursuit of more plates. He might not be sure about Kenny, but he's more than willing to trust his friends. He gets as far as Shelley, who's hotfooting it toward him with a tray. She walks back over with him, sets the tray in willing bear-cub arms, and starts doling out food.

Kenny gets a second plate and two helpings of magic green sauce. Ghost gets a huge salad, which makes her smile, and Kennedy gets a sizable plate of ribs topped by a single lettuce leaf, which makes her laugh. Last off is a big stack of the special honey-spice ribs Myrna makes for bears who like to set their mouths on fire.

Shelley tucks the empty tray under her arm with brisk efficiency and turns to go, but I don't miss the victory in her eyes. Or Kennedy's thoughtful study of Shelley's back. A wise baby alpha, recognizing her allies.

My wolf preens. Smart pack. Sneaky pack.

Ghost bumps against Kennedy's shoulder and says something that makes both of them laugh and Kenny snort. Hoot follows up, and whatever she says nearly spills Reilly's plate of ribs and turns Kennedy as pink as Kelsey's knitted blanket.

I chuckle quietly. One baby alpha about to discover what I did at ten years old—baby packs are about as biddable as hurricanes. "Do you think Kenny knows he's about to get his ass moved back to the den?"

Rio smirks. "Nope." He sobers. "It needs to happen. His wolf is gutted about the other guys leaving."

They haven't left—they're just throwing an elongated temper tantrum. But the man who still considers himself their beta probably isn't seeing it that way. "So we're going to take him in?"

"Was that ever in doubt?"

Not unless someone has an objection. Judging by what Shelley just engineered, the most important voices in this pack have already spoken. "Are you going to help him get here?" It's not a long walk to the den from his camp, but there's no way he going to make it without serious assistance.

Rio shakes his head quietly. "No."

I frown. I don't leave baby packs with jobs they can't handle. I study the four young shifters clustered around a befuddled man who's slowly beginning to eat his ribs. I don't know enough about Hoot or Ghost, and Reilly has good reasons to be cautious. But I know baby-alpha instincts, and Kennedy's are stellar. "Can they actually pull this off?"

"No." Rio smiles. "But they'll get help when they need it. And this is already helping Kennedy."

It is. Her wolf is visibly steadying, and even more visibly plotting. She's also entirely missing the far quieter calculus of a juvenile bear and a couple of our best sentries—and the growing dismay of a man who hasn't entirely lost his beta instincts.

Three wolves and a bear, realizing that they're needed.

She's got herself a baby pack. Now we'll see what she does with it—and far more importantly, what they do with her.

KENNEDY

I didn't know.

I hug my wolf tightly and apologize every way I know how, because all that time I was trying to make her behave, I didn't listen. She needs this, just like Ghost needs to be alone in windy places and Reilly's bear needs us to bump into him a lot. She needs a pack that's hers, and she needs her big pack, too.

I didn't know that was a choice, but it obviously is, because everyone is wrapped around us, plates and pups in their laps while they have easy conversations and listen to Ravi's guitar, just like we do most nights. Nobody thinks I'm breaking anything, except for maybe Kenny, and he doesn't get to vote. I keep looking over at Hayden, but he just smiles at me and says more silly things to Lissa to make her laugh, like it's no big deal at all that I claimed some of his wolves.

Sort of, anyhow. I didn't take them away. They're still his, too. My wolf doesn't really understand how that works, but she likes how it feels.

I won't tell her it's a cat idea.

I take another big bite of spicy ribs. My wolf doesn't understand why I want so much sauce on tasty meat, but she's willing to go along. She saw the lettuce leaf. I shake my head at Ghost, who's eating a whole bowl of them and looking totally happy about it. I have no idea how she convinced her wolf to become a vegetarian.

Reilly's eating salad too. He says grizzly bears are adaptable and they eat lots of things. I think he just wants Ghost to feel like she belongs. He's kind of awesome like that.

Kenny isn't eating very much. That's okay. He's here, and I didn't expect that. He can yell at me every day if he keeps coming to the den to do it. I can't believe Ghost squared off with him, though. And Hoot practically shoved that plate into his belly. I know they boss me around sometimes, but they used to go invisible when any of the jerk dominants were nearby, even Kenny.

My wolf snorts. Kenny is so at the bottom of this baby pack's hierarchy. Which his wolf should hate, but he's nibbling on a rib and kind of listening to whatever Reilly's talking about, and Reilly's eyes aren't so cautious anymore. I need to watch that. Bears who got picked on shouldn't forgive too easily, even if I'm pretty sure I know why Kenny did it.

I look up as a shadow blocks the light from the setting sun. Kel sits down beside me, a plate of ribs in his hands and six rolls sitting on top. He tosses one to each of us, in the exact order my wolf thinks we've sorted our hierarchy.

Tricky beta.

Kenny makes a strange face as he catches the last one, like he wants to be mad or grumpy or pissed off, but he can't quite get there. He takes a big bite out of his roll instead.

Kel nods at Ghost. "Have you sorted out a new sentry rotation yet?"

Ghost shakes her head and hugs her bowl of salad to her chest.

Kel leans back against a log like he can calm her down just by being chill. "Should we do that now?"

Ghost gulps and looks at me. "I don't want to be a sentry up in a tree anymore. Kel says we can use more wolves on the ground, instead."

I chew really slowly, trying to figure out why gravity is suddenly trying to pull me into the sky. "You love sentry duty."

She looks down at her lettuce. "It's time for me to do something different."

I want to talk, a lot, but I remember that I'm supposed to mostly listen. Which might take a while. Ghost isn't usually very chatty and she's already used an awful lot of words today. So I start with what she's already said. It's fine if she doesn't want to sit in a tree. I can take on more shifts. I look at Kel and shrug. "I'm good with that."

He takes a bite of his ribs and doesn't say anything.

My wolf straightens. I'm missing something. Something that he doesn't think I should be patient about. I glance carefully at Ghost. "What do you want to do instead?"

She shrugs. "Stuff."

Hoot glares at me, just in case I don't get the message. Stop pushing. Don't be a jerk.

Right. I sigh and pick up the last of my ribs and try thinking hard, instead. I'm almost finished stripping the yummy meat when I figure out the part I missed.

I grin down at my fingers. I've been paying lots of attention to Lissa and my tricky betas. Sometimes one answer can solve two problems. I take a bite of my roll and chew slowly, because my wolf likes to be a troublemaker sometimes. Then I glance casually at Kel. "It's going to be harder to cover the perimeter like that."

He has a really good poker face. "Yup."

I sit on my wolf, because she's going to hate this next idea. "I heard that most of the dumbasses are moving into town. Maybe we don't need a perimeter guard anymore."

Hoot sits up straight, her eyes flashing. Kenny sits up straighter.

Kel eyes me like I tried to steal his hot sauce, but his hand flashes a quiet signal where no one else can see it. *Keep going.*

I lean back and break my roll in two. "There aren't really any threats to worry about anymore." I stuff warm, tasty bread into my mouth to stifle my wolf's growl. It's warm and chewy and it tastes like butter.

"Are you nuts?" Kenny's eyes are mostly wolf. "There are pups at the den and not nearly enough teeth and claws to protect them if some asshole comes strolling in because you couldn't be bothered to set a perimeter guard."

He's not talking to me. He's talking to Kel, underestimating me because I'm still a little girl in his eyes. A dumb one who thinks dens don't need guarding. I'm going to have to do something about that, but not yet. This matters more. I swallow my roll and shrug at Kenny. "Fine. You take a shift, then."

He eyes me suspiciously.

This would be easier if he wasn't a smart wolf. I smirk to distract him. "You might have to improve your woodcraft first, though."

Dominance punches out of Kenny's wolf, aimed straight at my nose.

Crap, I guess that doesn't get to wait. I let my wolf beam bossy juice at him for a nanosecond. Just long enough for his eyes to pop. "Turn it off right now. That's not allowed in the den."

I look over at Hoot and Ghost, who haven't budged. Brave wolves. "Are you two okay?"

Ghost stabs her salad and glares at Kenny. "You don't get to win arguments that way. Not anymore. Especially when you're wrong. Your woodcraft is better than the other jerks, but it's not good enough." She pauses a beat and fires his own words back at him like bullets. "We have pups here at the den."

I grin at Hoot. Even Bailey knows to tread carefully when Ghost gets mad. It doesn't happen very often, but when it does, it's a really bad idea to mess with her. I eye the fork in her hand. She probably can't do too much damage with that, and if she does, Kenny totally deserves it.

"I agree that he could use some lessons." Kel nods his chin at Ghost. "Are you volunteering to work with him?"

I glare at him. That's a bad idea. She won't stay mad very long, and her wolf is too submissive to bite Kenny if he's a jerk.

Kel just raises an eyebrow.

Crap. I'm missing something again. My wolf tries to think fast. Ghost has awesome woodcraft and she could make Kenny a lot better, but not if he doesn't respect her. Then I realize that lessons can take a lot of shapes. "He can patrol with me. Ghost and Hoot and Reilly can try sneaking across the perimeter."

Reilly looks thrilled.

I hide a grin. His bear is sweet and smart and patient and really bad at sneaking. But he's working hard at it, and it will be a good test. If Kenny can't track a sweet, dorky bear, no way does he get a solo shift on perimeter duty.

Then I catch the glint in Ghost's eyes.

Maybe Reilly won't be so easy to track after all.

Kel sets down a well-gnawed rib and nods at Kenny. "You can partner with me or Kennedy until one of us decides you're good enough to patrol alone."

I nearly choke on my roll. There are some things Kel never lets anyone else do, and deciding who is good enough to protect the pups is one of them.

Hoot bangs her hand on my back until I can breathe again. "I'll ask Bailey if I can stay for a few nights."

Kenny's head shoots up. "Bailey is still here?"

My wolf goes to instant red alert. She's not nearly as fast as Kel, though. He doesn't even move and he's a lethal threat aimed straight at Kenny's throat.

Kenny just closes his eyes. "I mean no harm. She was kind to my son. That's all."

Hoot's breath catches. One raspy inhale. Two. Then, her eyes blazing with pain and memory and grief, she does the very last thing I expect her to do. She scoots in and wraps her arms around Kenny's neck. He sits, frozen, as she tips her forehead into his shoulder and murmurs words drenched in sadness. I only hear the last three. "I miss Jason."

My wolf howls for all the others she misses, too.

One of Kenny's hands floats up, a bewildered, lost leaf.

Ghost whimpers.

I wrap my arm around her. Reilly is already leaning in from the other side. There are so many things we can't fix—but we can help with this. Together, we lean in to Kenny's floating hand and help it land where it needs to go.

He sits, a quiet, frozen man with his hand on Hoot's back, his eyes staring at something nobody can see. We press into him anyhow. We all remember Jason. He was a big, silly, laughing, dopey kid.

The day he died, Bailey almost broke.

I hold on tight to the man who did.

6

KENNEDY

I squint at the rising sun. I have no idea why my wolf dragged me out of bed this early. Hardly anyone is stirring except for Shelley. She's sitting with a big mug of tea, watching the mist rise off the river.

I see motion on the far bank and stick my head a little farther out of my sleeping bag. It's Kel's dapple-gray wolf, blending in with the forest until he shifts and reaches for a pile of clothes at the foot of a tree. He pulls on a pair of shorts and a hoodie and scans the den as he wades through the stream.

My wolf snorts. Silly beta. There are no big, bad guys trying to steal Shelley's tea, and they'd probably regret it if they did. She can be kind of grumpy in the morning.

Kel skirts the pile of sleeping mamas and pups and stray sentries. It's really cool to see Hoot and Ghost there.

I stretch and make a face. I'm never up before the pups.

"They're gone." Kel speaks quietly as soon as he's close. "The guys at Kenny's camp left for town late last night. Took their things."

I frown. "Kenny, too?"

He shakes his head. "He's sleeping out there alone."

"Not if I have anything to say about it."

I blink and turn to look at Shelley.

She sets down her tea and stands up, brushing dirt off her jeans. Then she shoots a brisk glance at the two of us. "Well, are you coming to help or not?"

Kel clears his throat. "Help with what, exactly?"

My wolf grins. She loves it when the submissives get bossy. She also thinks it's really funny when Kel plays dumb. We all know what needs to happen. There's no way Kenny gets to sleep out there all alone. Not now that we know how sad he is inside.

"He needs to sleep here where we can keep an eye on him." Shelley is taking no nonsense from anyone this morning.

I wiggle out of my sleeping bag. "We tried last night." Hoot was bossy and Reilly tried to sit on him, but he just walked away. I tracked him for a while, but I left once he wandered back to his camp. The other guys were still there, though. I never would have left him alone.

Shelley snorts. "All his excuses for staying out there just moved into town."

He has more excuses than that, but I don't think she's going to listen to any of them.

Kel's lips quirk. "Would you like teeth and claws for company, or Myrna's frying pan?"

Shelley grunts, but she totally thinks he's funny. "Frying pans can't carry tents and whatever he's got for gear. The two of you will do."

I bet he doesn't have anything. He took a big pile of stuff out into the woods last night and left it near Bailey's turf. I don't say that, though. My wolf is too happy that Shelley's all feisty and grumpy and bossy. I fold up my sleeping bag and pull on the fleece I was using as a pillow. It isn't nearly as good as fur, but it's bright green and my wolf likes it.

Shelley nods at me like I did something smarter than just getting dressed, and leads us off in the direction of Kenny's camp. I glance over at Kel and keep my voice low so I don't wake up the pups. "Want me to go steal us some cookies?"

His lips quirk.

Shelley rolls her eyes. "No cookies for breakfast."

"I'm a growing wolf." I try a pouty face. Hoot is really good at them.

"You're a menace," says Shelley wryly.

I grin. That, too.

Kel reaches into the pocket of his flannel shirt and tosses me a squished granola bar. "Here. So you don't die in the next ten minutes."

I like granola bars, but I still make a face. I'm a teenager. I have a rep to maintain. "It's covered in pocket fuzz. And it looks like you sat on it."

He swipes it out of my hand. "Fine. I'll eat it."

I consider trying to reclaim it, but my wolf is still waking up and I'd probably just end up on my back on the dirt. "I hear old men need their strength."

Shelley chuckles.

My wolf grins. She likes amusing her elders.

Especially ones who are going to help fix her pack.

ADRIANNA

"Mom." My son glares at me through the phone screen. "It's the crack of dawn."

I smile. "Do you have something better to be doing, sweetheart?"

Lissa snickers and sticks her head into view. "He doesn't. We're on patrol. He's just cranky because he has to go over the pack budget with me later."

I imagine he plans on nodding and smiling and agreeing with whatever she wants. Which is a very smart plan. Jules sings the praises of the spreadsheets Lissa sends her for their den build, and my daughter has extremely high standards when it comes to herding columns of numbers.

Hayden wraps an arm around Lissa's head. "I'm not cranky."

He isn't, and they're adorable, which warms my wolf and wreaks havoc on my intentions to wait another couple of weeks before I visit again. However, that isn't why I called. "We've got a young raven with engineering leanings who's coming down to do an internship with HomeWild. Ebony arranged it. Jules is very pleased. She's also talking about setting up more of a presence in the north. With all her bear clients and her lead designer up there, it only makes sense."

My son eyes me dubiously, as he should. There is no doubt at all where Jules will locate that presence. "We're not ready for that."

I grin at Lissa. "He thinks I'm the boss of his sister. How quaint."

She laughs. Hayden just shakes his head, but I can see the pleasure he's trying to hide. Family ties have always been so very strong for him.

I settle back with my morning mug of strong, black tea. Which I shouldn't be drinking, because I was also on dawn patrol and I need to take a nap before I engage with any more of this day, but there are some rituals which don't bend to common sense. "It will be a while yet. But setting up internships and exchanges is an excellent way to build stronger connections between north and south. I'm very pleased with Ebony's work so far."

Hayden snorts. "So what you're telling me is that you can't boss my sister around, but you're doing a fine job of co-opting my beta?"

I hide a grin behind my mug, which won't fool him at all, and doesn't need to. He knows that Ebony needs a way to expiate her guilt, and an astonished young raven who could barely keep her feet on the ground this morning was a nice start. "Do you have any pack news?

My favorite bear hasn't sent me an update for days. We're growing restless down here."

Lissa laughs. "He's kind of busy at the moment."

That's interesting. I eye them both. "Doing what?"

My son gives me a look that would be scorching if I were any closer. "Kennedy's forming her baby pack. He's been recruited."

"Good for her. A baby pack will steady her wolf, and your pack as well, if you let it."

Hayden rolls his eyes. "You didn't raise a complete idiot."

Lissa kisses his ear. "No, she didn't."

He melts. There's no other word for it. I smile at the both of them and try not to look too much like I'm about to go browse knitting patterns for baby booties. "You look very happy together."

Hayden groans. "Mom."

I take a sip of my tea.

He shakes his head. "I only got here a few weeks ago. The world will not end if we take our time and give everyone a chance to adjust, including the two of us. And Robbie."

Robbie is a smart pup who will be more than happy to grow up wrapped in love. But Myrna's astute commentary in her last video chat with my mother appears to be correct. Hayden isn't just being patient. He's embraced the magic of running slowly. James would be proud. "You're just like your father. It took me the better part of a year to convince him we were mated."

Lissa perks up, those gorgeous green eyes of hers inquisitive and amused.

I smile at her. "He wanted me to be sure. Silly wolf."

She turns more than a little pink.

Hayden doesn't bother with words this time. He just growls.

Lissa taps his nose. "Be nice to your mom."

My wolf wants to howl her delight. *This*. This is exactly what she would have wished for him. A partner capable of challenging and balancing him in every way. It's a very fine reason to take their time. They won't love each other any less for moving slowly.

I hide a sigh. The matching grandmother-and-grandson t-shirts will need to remain in my closet for a while yet. Which will annoy my wolf. She decided Robbie was hers the moment he knocked her over and licked her nose. Her patience ran out ages ago.

Hayden rubs his cheek against Lissa's pink one. "All my wolves are picking on me. A guy could develop a complex."

Not him, but I'm more interested in the sudden look of concern in Lissa's eyes.

She reaches up and touches his face with gentle fingers. "She wasn't aiming at you."

Hayden rests his forehead against hers. Then he looks at me and sighs. "Kennedy claimed the pack's old beta for her baby pack."

My eyebrows go up of their own accord. "The one you kicked out of the den?"

"Yup." He smiles faintly. "Baby packs, causing complications since forever."

I sip my tea and hide another grin. He would know. The moment when he laid eyes on Kel and decided to claim him ranks as one of the most fiercely uncomfortable of my life. "How is she handling it?"

He sighs. "Cautiously, at least by her standards, but they had their first scuffle last night. He let his dominance loose, because while I think he respects her strength, he doesn't yet respect her leadership."

Lissa smiles. "To be fair, she was goading him."

Of course she was. "I presume she squashed him like a bug." Dominant jerks, even potentially redeemable ones, rarely understand anything else.

Hayden makes a wry face. "She responded in kind and nearly choked the whole pack."

The ability to emanate pheromonal command is one of the fiercest weapons of a dominant wolf—and one that is so rarely justified. Especially when there are innocent bystanders who are far too experienced with its abuse. "Are your submissives all right?"

Lissa looks almost insulted, which eases my worries considerably.

Hayden chuckles. "None of them are remotely scared of Kennedy's wolf."

That's more than lack of fear—it's profound trust. A willingness to stand under an elephant's raised foot. "That's to her credit."

He looks straight at me. "It is. It's the first time I've had a true read on her, though. She's a powerhouse."

My wolf sits up straight, finally smelling the actual issue. "Strong enough to challenge her alpha?"

Lissa's hand goes to Hayden's chest as she shakes her head sharply. "She wouldn't. Ever."

Hayden nods, his hand quietly covering hers. "I agree. But her wolf is going to figure out at some point that she might win if she did. And so will mine."

My heart aches, for my son and Kennedy both—but empathy isn't what he needs from me. I look straight into the eyes of the son I raised. The wolf I raised. The man I raised. "She might have a problem with that. You won't."

I see the flash of hesitation in his eyes. He isn't certain. He can't be. Until it happens and his wolf has to face it, he won't know. Which is smart and self-aware and brave and none of it will change the math of one dominant wolf facing another.

Math that has the potential to shred both of them.

I do what I can. I let him see the eyes of the wolf he still considers his alpha and every bit of confidence and faith she can put into a single look. And I send strength and gratitude to the small, fiercely tender hand covering his heart.

I have reason to know just how much that small hand might matter.

KENNEDY

That whole thing about letting sleeping wolves lie? They aren't kidding.

I put myself right where Kenny's half-awake, snarling wolf can see me, because if he wants a rumble, I'm more than happy to give him one. "You wake up in a worse mood than Kel. Also, your sleeping bag is total crap. What happened to your good one?"

He shoots me a dirty look as he rolls to his feet. "This one's fine."

I bet he left his good one in the woods for Bailey. I can't let him know that, though. Little girls aren't supposed to know that big, bad wolves are softies under their snarls. I look around at his pathetic excuse for a camp. "I see your minions finally left you."

Shelley snorts. She's gathering the few things left by the fire pit, which doesn't look like much more than a small frying pan and a fork. "Minions have better manners than those boys."

"That's disrespecting boys," I say quietly. "They're men. They should act like men."

She blinks.

Kel raises an eyebrow. "Calling them minions is more respectful?"

Darn betas. "No. But at least I didn't call them something that actually exists in this pack."

His lips quirk. "Good point."

Shelley reaches for a stray spoon, but I see thoughtfulness in her eyes. The kind that maybe makes it okay that I spouted off at my elders. My wolf likes that.

Kenny stuffs his sleeping bag and a couple of shirts

into a duffle bag that looks older than I am. "I'm not coming to the den. I'll show up for my patrol shifts."

Shelley takes the bag right out of his hands. "You're pack. When you work to protect the pack, you get fed. I'm not lugging your food all the way out here, so you can damn well camp somewhere inside the inner perimeter."

Kenny scowls at her. "I'm not eating your food."

She looks right at him. "Bets?"

I so need to work on my poker face. I sneak a look at Kel. It somehow seems wrong to let a submissive fight this battle, even though it's really fun to watch.

Kel tosses the small bag with kitchen gear in it, which rattles as it hits the middle of Kenny's chest and bounces off. "Anything else you need to pack up?"

Kenny ignores the gear at his feet. "You have rules. Dominants need to stay outside the perimeter unless a submissive vouches for them." He shoots Shelley a dirty look. "Not you."

She opens her mouth, ready to launch the verbal equivalent of Myrna's frying pan at his head.

Kel holds up a quiet hand. "Not her. Me."

My wolf sits down hard. She so did not see this coming.

Neither did Kenny. He stares like Kel just sprouted snakes with little beady eyes out the top of his head.

"We need more teeth and claws. You don't entirely suck. You'll do." There's no kindness in Kel's words, which is exactly right. Kindness would kill Kenny. "This pack doesn't create second-class citizens, so Shelley is correct. You'll sleep where we can smell you, and eat when everyone else eats, and take your turn at picking up after the pups and folding laundry and digging holes for Rio."

Kenny isn't blinking or breathing or possibly even alive.

Kel's eyes glitter with something entirely scary. "And if you fuck up, you'll answer to me."

My wolf wants to growl, because if Kenny fucks up, she's totally dealing with him. But even she can tell that's not the most important thing that needs to be worked out right now. Kenny needs to come back to the den where Hoot can hug him and grieve with him and Reilly can drown him in bear sweetness and Ghost can quietly believe he's redeemable.

Then I can kick his ass.

So I don't growl. I just step forward and look at Kenny and hold up my littlest finger and make my first baby alpha promise out loud. "We won't let you be an asshole. Pinky swear."

His laugh sounds awful and rusty and cranky and broken.

But it's also really beautiful.

7

KENNEDY

This day is completely out of control and we aren't even done breakfast.

I shake my head at Ghost. She woke up as soon as we got back with Kenny, probably because he was trying to argue with Shelley about where he was going to sleep. Which Ghost solved without saying a single word. She just marched over and took his sleeping bag and plunked it down under a pretty willow on the far side of the river. Then Eliza gave him a pillow from her special stash and Kelsey put a handful of flowers in a mug by the tree and Myrna started asking him about what colors he wanted for his knitted blanket.

The blanket might be done by dinner. The submissives of this pack do not mess around.

I sigh. I hate knitting, because it involves sitting still and being polite with pointy things, but Hoot is sitting over by Ghost and looking all eager and a little shy, and Reilly has been getting knitting lessons from Rio and Kel for weeks and he's getting really good, and this is probably the kind of little-pack-inside-the-big-pack bonding activity that a baby alpha shouldn't sulk about.

I wander over to the big tablecloth that Eliza and Shelley spread out for us to sit on. There's a huge pile of yarn in the middle. Kelsey is busy piling skeins of her favorite colors into Kenny's lap. Which is really brave, because I don't think he was ever one of the assholes who ordered her to shift on demand, but he didn't stop it, even when Samuel and Eamon weren't around. Picking his battles, maybe, but my wolf thinks Kelsey is a battle everyone should fight no matter what.

Which is why they didn't let me stay at the den. I wasn't pragmatic enough. That's what I heard Bailey and Ebony say one night when they didn't think I was awake.

I watch Kenny, because I don't really know what pragmatic means, but his wolf is as broken as my favorite mug when I accidentally dropped it off a waterfall, and he's really close to Kelsey. He's just sitting quietly, though. Maybe because Myrna has her daddy's frying pan right beside her.

Even teeth and claws respect that kind of threat.

My wolf takes a good, long look and decides Kenny doesn't smell like jerk. Not yet, anyhow. I don't think he knows how to knit, so this could get interesting. None of the guys in our old pack did, but there's no way that's going to fly today. Everybody knits, even those of us who are hopeless.

Kelsey picks up a skein of pretty purple yarn.

Kenny winces.

She holds it up to her cheek and smiles at him sweetly.

He exhales like she stabbed him and nods at the pile in his lap.

Myrna cackles. "I'm knitting that one."

He shoots her a dirty look, but there's no weight behind it. I don't think he has any weight left. His wolf feels like he would float away if Kelsey blew on him hard.

Ravi casts Kenny a sympathetic look and sits down on a stump near the tablecloth, his guitar in his hands. He knitted a cute striped hat for Jade that she wears all the time, even when she's swimming in the river, so he probably gets a pass. Our wolves like music, and his is all soft and happy and hopeful lately.

Maybe because Cori knitted him a hat that matches Jade's.

I check in on the rest of my baby pack. Reilly is already knitting and talking to Kel and helping Robbie with the ball of yarn he's winding, so he's good. He feels solid in that weird new place inside me. Ghost does, too.

Lissa sits down beside Hoot, who's on the very edge of the tablecloth, looking unsure of herself. She pulls two balls of blue yarn and a spare set of circular needles out of her bag. I don't know what she says, but it makes Hoot snicker and Hayden roll his eyes.

My wolf eases. She doesn't need to hold her baby pack steady by herself. She has help.

A ball of yarn thunks into my chest. I look around

and spy Ghost, looking awfully pleased with herself. She holds up a set of knitting needles, the straight kind that I know how to use without tying them into a knot.

I sigh. Those are her bossy eyes, so I'm clearly not escaping the knitting deal. I walk myself over and flop down beside her, trying not to sulk. I had a good run last night, so my wolf can stop being difficult for once and just enjoy being lazy. I pick up a skein of yarn that needs to be rolled into a ball.

Ghost takes it out of my hands. "That's Robbie's job."

I only growl a little. "Fine."

She snickers and holds out needles that already have a row of neatly cast-on stitches. "Here, work on this one. I'll get yours started."

I take it and snort. "You just want it to look like an actual square."

She looks pointedly at the needles in my hands. "No, I want you to look like a dominant who knits for her pack."

Jeebers. I lean into her, because my wolf needs to make sure she still smells like Ghost. "What's gotten into you? You're all feisty and stuff."

She just smiles and does something fancy with her needles that makes a ruffled edge on the square she's starting.

Yikes.

HAYDEN

I stare down at the pointy sticks in my hands, not at all sure how I got roped into this. I tried to take perimeter duty, but Rio just snorted and headed into the woods, and it's hard to argue that the big, black wolf of death needs help. The most likely danger in these woods is currently sitting three feet away from me with a pile of yarn in his lap, looking poleaxed.

Which means I have no excuse not to be knitting. My designated instructor deserves fair warning, though. "Ronan tried to teach me for years. He swears I'm a lost cause." I look over at the big crochet hook Kelsey is wielding like a boss. "Maybe I'd do better with one of those."

Myrna snorts. "Those are for the pups."

She might change her mind if she crashes against my utter inability to comprehend the difference between knit and purl for long enough. But even my wolf doesn't truly mind. There are good examples to be set even in sucking at things, and maybe I can be enough of a distraction that nobody pays too much attention to the quiet lesson Shelley has started giving Kenny.

I make a sad face at Kelsey. "I don't think anyone wants a blanket square with this many holes in it."

Myrna chuckles and tugs on the yarn I'm supposed to be keeping taut. "Any wolf in your pack would take one of your squares, holes and all."

I want to tell them to have higher standards, but I can't, because the very first square Kelsey ever made is hot pink and only vaguely square and in a central place of honor in the blanket that will be mine when it's done, and my wolf gets all gooey every time he sees it. I sigh and squint at my knitting needles again. "Why don't they put hooks on the ends of these? Then maybe I wouldn't lose so many stitches."

Kenny glances up from his painstaking efforts to knit a stitch, looking an awful lot like he agrees with me.

Which makes my wolf bite at my ribs. I need to set a better example.

Ebony's lips quirk. She didn't miss Kenny's look or my wolf's reaction. "You know you can't get out of this by being terrible, right?"

I glare at the maniacally neat rows of sedate navy stitches hanging from her needles. "We all have things we're good at. This isn't one of mine."

Reilly looks up from a square of bright orange. "Maybe you need to knit left-handed, like me. I could show you."

I'm pretty sure switching which hand does what isn't going to make this better. "I think I'm just doomed, Riles." But I'll be doomed with a good attitude and patient persistence, even if it kills me.

Kel shoots me an amused look over the complicated diamond texture in lime green he's somehow managing to knit despite Mellie's help. "You're good at washing dishes. We'll probably keep you."

My wolf grins as half a dozen balls of yarn bounce off Kel's head. They won't make any difference to his smartass ways, but I like that my pack stands up for me. And I like the utter astonishment in Kenny's eyes. I pick up a stray ball that didn't quite make it to Kel and give it an assist.

He bats it away with his needles.

Mellie growls at me from his lap.

He grins. "Exactly. Stop messing with our knitting, Alpha."

Mellie pulls one of his needles out of all its stitches and waves it around gleefully. The competent knitters of Ghost Mountain Pack all smile at her like she's cute and not a demon pup of yarn destruction. The rest of us wince and get a tighter grip on our needles.

Kel starts picking up stitches without even looking. "Hey, kiddo. Did you have a good swim?"

Braden drops into his lap beside Mellie, fresh from his dip in the river to wash off his breakfast. I hope we have functional showers before winter sets in, or he's going to be one seriously sticky pup. Mellie hands her buddy a lime-green ball of yarn to hold. It's the one attached to Kel's square, which isn't going to make his job any easier.

Not that I think his focus is on his knitting. There's no one in this pack who understands despair and self-loathing better than Kelvin Nogues. Or their most effective antidotes. Pups. Simple tasks. Steady, everyday bonds of pack. All quietly wrapping around a man who is steadfastly ignoring us—and his wolf, who isn't.

I twist my fingers into the hieroglyphics necessary to attempt a purl stitch and growl as my needles stage a rebellion and dump half my row into the abyss. Kennedy curses under her breath, and I look up to find her glaring at a yarn situation that closely resembles mine. She shoots me a grin and points her chin at Robbie, who's turning yarn remnants into a fearsome snarl. I snort. A trifecta of baby alphas who can't knit worth crap. Our pack probably thinks that's funny.

Kenny damn well needs to see dominants walking the walk, however, so I scowl down at my needles and manage a couple more stitches without anything going drastically wrong. Then my wolf issues a Lissa proximity alert. I set down my needles, because I'm a man who knows my limits, and pat the empty space beside me.

She sits and snuggles against me for a moment, smelling like dish soap and mint tea. Then she leans forward and pets Myrna's knitting. "That's so pretty."

My wolf sulks. He's pretty, too.

"Glad you think so." Myrna picks up a ball of the same purple that's on her needles. "Make me a flower for the middle?"

Most of my pack can knit a decent square. Lissa knits the kind of things that come with patterns and graphs and pages full of mysterious notations, and have lots of holes in them on purpose.

Lissa examines the needles in my hands and chokes off a laugh. "Maybe I'll help Hayden first."

Kelsey giggles.

I wrinkle my nose at her. "Thanks a lot, cutie."

She beams at me, her smile full of her special brand of sunshine. I'm glad to see it. I quizzed Lissa pretty hard last night. Kelsey and Reilly both have plenty of reason to be wary where Kenny's concerned. He wasn't the worst of the asshole dominants, not by a long shot, but he's earned some of the guilt in his eyes. And some of the wariness in a bear cub's when he thinks no one is looking.

Lissa moves in closer and rests her chin on my shoulder, soothing my wolf. She knows exactly what's on my mind. She keeps her voice casual as she reaches for my sad, bedraggled stitches. "You've mostly got it right."

I snort. She's astute and sexy and her wolf can run like the wind, but she's a terrible liar. I hold up my train wreck of a square. "I get to cast off soon, right?"

She snickers and picks up one of Myrna's skeins of purple yarn, starting the process of winding it into a tight ball that will snarl far less easily when it meets up with pup antics. "Maybe we're looking at this the wrong way. You're really good at making holes. I can show you a simple flower design."

I shoot her a look of not entirely feigned horror.

The giggles that squirt out of her turn my wolf to canine mush.

KENNEDY

Lissa is my hero. First, because she can knit like a boss, and second, because she has this way of reaching right into Hayden's wolf and out through him to the rest of the pack. My whole baby pack felt it. Hoot and Ghost and Reilly got all happy and warm, and maybe I kind of did, too. Kenny didn't, but that's okay. He still felt it.

My wolf thinks that it's maybe like getting warm again when you've been really cold. There's a lot of shooting pain and tingling and itching before it starts to feel better. I flip my knitting around to go the other way and smother a groan when one of the needles slithers out. I always get the ones that are cursed.

Hoot scoots in beside me and holds out her nice, neat square. "Here, trade you."

I shake my head vehemently. "No way. Circular needles hate me."

She snickers. "They're inanimate chunks of wood and plastic."

I stab my needle into some loops of yarn that might or might not be my runaway stitches. "I bet they rise from the dead at night and become zombies who knit shifter fur into squares for their undead children to eat."

Dead silence.

I look up. My entire pack is staring at me.

Oops. "Sorry. Pups. Forgot."

Myrna snorts. "You're fired from telling bedtime stories."

I never get to do those. Mine all have fights in them and then the pups get too riled to sleep.

Reilly grins at me. "You could write a story about zombie knitting needles for the newspaper."

Evil bear. "It would be really scary and then no one would ever knit again. Think how sad Ronan and his rooms full of yarn would be."

Reilly's eyes fill with hero worship, just like they do

every time he thinks about the badass polar bear who's his biggest fan.

Hoot clears her throat. "Does he really ask you to catch him fish?"

Reilly beams at her. "Lots. Every time Ames flies north in her plane. He has to bribe her to stop here. She says our field is too rocky and it tries to put new dents in her plane."

Myrna grins. "She might say that, but she turned as pink as a raspberry when Kelsey played a song for her birthday the last time she was here."

Hoot sighs happily.

That special place inside me that holds my baby pack vibrates quietly. Hoot's not sitting on a ridge looking down at the den and she's not sad and she's not up a sentry tree looking out instead of in. She's right here, hearing our stories and asking Reilly questions and slowly inching her way in from the edge of the tablecloth.

My wolf wants to bite at all things that will try to pull her away again, but I need to be way smarter than that. Because she deserves this. So much.

She deserves a chance to be the guardian of happy things, too.

Hoot smiles shyly at Kelsey. "I heard you play yesterday. You're getting really good."

Kelsey makes a noise that sounds an awful lot like Hoot's happy sigh.

Ravi sets down his guitar and smiles. "She'll need a bigger guitar soon, I think."

Kelsey shakes her head firmly.

We all hide grins. I bet she'll still be playing that hot-pink baby guitar when she's as old as Myrna. She loves it that much.

Ravi's eyes twinkle. "A good musician knows when she's found her instrument."

Myrna chuckles. "Mine's a frying pan."

Reilly smiles. "Shelley's is flour and sugar and butter. And Lissa's is a bunch of numbers on a computer."

Smart, funny bear.

Layla laughs and tickles her son's belly. "Braden's is getting really sticky."

Baby alphas help the big pack see their little pack. "Ghost's is listening to the wind. Reilly's is seeing exactly the right way to be kind."

The pleasure on both their faces nearly stops my wolf's heart. Then it makes her mad. Mad enough to be reckless, and I can't stop the next words before she says them. "I'm not sure about Hoot's yet because she isn't here enough and I want her to be. And Kenny needs to stop thinking that his is being a bad guy."

His wolf curls in on itself. Hoot backs away, right to the edge of the tablecloth.

Crap. I didn't think. My wolf vibrates, desperate to fix what she just broke.

Hayden looks right at me, his eyes full of sympathy. Then he smiles at Hoot. "I'd like to see more of you, too. Especially if you know how to wash dishes."

She laughs, her ears turning pink. "Nope. I was raised in the woods, sorry."

Shelley elbows Kenny, hard enough that he almost

falls over. "He used to be pretty good with a dishrag, if he hasn't forgotten how."

Kenny doesn't say anything, but his wolf isn't all curled in and trying to disappear anymore.

I close my eyes, embarrassed and thankful for my pack.

Ghost's fingers slide quietly into mine. She's trying to offer comfort, but all it does is remind me that I don't know all of what she wants, either. I'm just a clumsy baby alpha stumbling around and crashing into things. Some of them have turned out okay, but that's not good enough.

Her fingers squeeze harder.

I sigh. Myrna says that thing about steps forward and steps backward, but it never made much sense until now.

I think it might be time for a consult.

8

RIO

She bides her time, which is interesting. Her wolf lurched hard when her baby packmates wobbled, something I only caught the tail end of as I switched off perimeter duty with Ebony. But that was two hours ago, and Kennedy is only coming to find me now, her wolf smelling of guilt and resolve.

I already talked to Kel. She didn't do a damn thing wrong, but she doesn't believe that. Which might or might not be today's problem to solve.

Kennedy picks up the spare shovel lying by the pile of gravel. Eliza and Danielle headed off a few minutes ago to refill the wheelbarrow, which is a hefty job given that my truck is parked a mile away. But the pack lugs groceries and pea gravel with equal lack of complaint, so no way is my wolf going to be the one to argue for a handier parking spot.

Air without gasoline fumes smells too much like freedom.

I spread what I've already shoveled onto the loosely marked path between the kitchen and the bend in the river. Steady traffic has worn the grass away, and if we don't shore that up some, we'll have muddy paw prints everywhere come fall and wetter weather.

Kennedy adds a scoop of the small, rounded gravel that won't irritate pup paws to a sparse spot and levels it out, carefully matching what I've already done.

I keep working. Dominants generally learn best when nobody makes any attempt to tell them what to do, and she's clearly no stranger to the business end of a shovel.

"Will this be enough?"

I glance at her, not sure if we're talking about pea gravel or baby-alpha desires to fix everything in the universe.

She makes a face. "I meant the path. I haven't figured out how to ask about the other stuff yet."

I smile. "You just did."

She sighs and sticks her shovel back in the gravel. She's smart enough to fill it with a reasonable load instead of the muscle-straining kind, which is a lesson it took me at least another decade to learn. "I screwed up."

I shrug. "Maybe. Welcome to being alive."

She snorts. "I screwed up because I don't know what I'm doing and I spoke without thinking and I'm not used to what I say mattering so much."

At least half of that is full of shit, but I focus on the part that isn't. "By claiming your baby pack intentionally, you've created a new level of connection. You'll feel and affect each other more strongly." I smile a little wryly. "That can take some getting used to."

She glances at me, curious. "What was it like when Hayden joined up with you and Kel?"

My lips quirk. "Annoying. I thought I was hot stuff. A sentinel, wild and free, roaming through his pack as he willed and everything he touched turning to gold. Then I got to spend several months having my ass repeatedly kicked by a ten-year-old and an old guy who hated my guts."

Her smile is young and oddly vulnerable. "Kel doesn't hate you."

I keep my smile equally gentle. Kenny isn't the only live volcano in her baby pack, but he's likely the most cryptic to her young heart. "It felt that way. When someone hates who they've become, that rings pretty loud, especially in a newly formed baby pack."

Her wince travels all the way to her toes. "I made it ring even louder by what I said to Kenny."

I let my wolf lean against hers. "First rule of a baby pack? You can't protect the others. None of you can. You'll all try and you'll all fail."

Her head shakes, her wolf utterly rejecting that nonsense.

The reckoning on that is coming, but it won't be me driving. "Trust your pack. Both of them. You had good instincts today. You spoke truth that needed to be said out loud, so that the larger pack can grapple with it."

Kennedy stabs the gravel with far more force than

necessary. "I could have said it in a way that didn't make Kenny and Hoot feel bad."

"Maybe." I pause just long enough for her to own the lack of certainty that needs to be the constant companion of every decent alpha. "Or you could have truly fucked up and not said anything at all."

She wrinkles her nose. "I didn't say anything you don't already know."

Her wolf did, but that doesn't matter right now. "True. So why did it matter that you said it?"

She growls at the gravel, which calmly ignores her. "I don't know."

I spread more gravel and wait.

She sighs. "Because now it's part of our pack story, just like Myrna's frying pan and Shelley's cookies and Reilly's sweetness."

She's got the same astonishing gift of insight as her alpha. I lay my shovel down, because there's no more gravel to move until Eliza and Danielle get back with the wheelbarrow. I toss Kennedy one of my canteens, which is full of Shelley's excellent lemonade. "Exactly. You know how when you're knitting and you drop stitches, you end up with a great big hole?"

She giggles as she unscrews the canteen lid. "Duh."

"Hoot and Kenny are two of the dropped stitches of this pack." I know how he got there. I'm still gathering the confused fragments of her story, but I know enough to know that the raw grief I've seen in her eyes is only the very tip of the iceberg. "You're collecting them back up."

Kennedy stares at me, her jaw slack, the canteen halfway to her mouth.

I grin. "Don't spill Shelley's lemonade, or she'll put me back on water rations."

Kennedy hastily jams the lid back on the canteen. Then she sits down, all confused, ungainly wolf.

I join her on the ground and fish out the cookies and apple slices Shelley also sent, just in case I couldn't walk a dozen steps to the kitchen if I got hungry. "It matters some, how gracefully you get them back on the needle. But what really matters is that they get there. Then the pack can knit them into the next row."

She takes a cookie, and her cheeks dimple. "I suck at knitting."

I reach out and break off half her cookie. "You did just fine today."

She breathes in and out, her wolf trying to decide if she wants to believe me.

I don't push it. This isn't my first baby-alpha rodeo—and some stitches are worth gathering really carefully.

LISSA

I pull up a tiny, innocent weed that will turn into a monster if we let it, and toss it into the small gardening bucket. It misses and gives Robbie a chance to jump on it and reduce it to weed shreds. Which probably means there will be more of its kind in a week or two, but at least he didn't attack the salad greens.

He licks my knee and runs off to the edge of the garden where he's been playing chase with Kelsey and Mellie. I smile as he gets in the way of one of Mellie's more enthusiastic tackles.

"He's doing a really good job." Ghost squats down beside me, watching the three pups. "He's helping Mellie figure out how to play so that it's fun for Kelsey, too."

That's a really lovely description for helping a dominant pup learn her manners. I shift my bucket so it's easier for both of us to reach. "He's had a lot of good examples lately."

She smiles. "He watches Kennedy a lot."

I make a face. It deeply annoys Hayden when I do what Ghost just did. Now I know why. "He watched you this morning when you helped Kelsey be a real part of welcoming Kenny to the den."

Ghost frowns down at a weed she just pulled. "She brought the flowers over. I just made sure he wasn't mean to her."

I touch her shoulder. "You did exactly what Robbie is doing with Mellie. You made sure the dominant wolf gave the submissive one space to be who she needed and wanted to be."

Ghost tries, unsuccessfully, to melt into the ground.

I smile. Salad greens aren't very good cover. "You reminded me quite a bit of Kel this morning. Silent and effective and a little bit scary. Having you down from the trees is going to be very good for our pack." Especially

Shelley. This little garden is about so much more than salad greens.

Ghost weeds half a row before she speaks again. "You're a lot more blunt than you used to be."

I laugh, which makes three pups stop their tumbling long enough to look over at us. "You're a lot feistier than you used to be."

She's silent for the rest of her row. "I think Kennedy needs me to be feisty."

There's so much in her voice. Need and fear and love and vibrant, quivering loyalty. I pull up a few more weeds and collect my thoughts. "We lived in fear for so long, and it made all of us smaller. We kept our hearts alive, but we hid away so many of the pieces of who we are." I reach out and touch my fingertips, feather-light, to the back of her hand. "Submissives give to our pack. It's how we're wired. But we also need to make sure that we get what we need."

She sits back on her heels and looks over at the pups, smiling. "This doesn't suck."

I laugh. "It doesn't, especially if you like lettuce."

She wrinkles her nose. "I can eat whatever."

I sigh. It's almost like Hayden set up this conversation so that I had to look in an uncomfortable mirror. "If you do that, you'll make Shelley and Kelsey sad and the pups will never eat anything green. Too many of the adults in this pack are terrible role models."

Ghost blinks.

I smile as a small red wolf trots over and bumps against her knees.

Ghost scratches behind her ears. "Want to make a really big salad for dinner, Kels? We can make the one with candied almonds and orange slices."

I hide a grin as Kelsey shifts into small girl and runs off to collect her sundress. "Need any help with candying the almonds?" Ghost can forage like a pro, but she's new to cooking anything more complicated than trail bread and oatmeal, especially on our finicky stove.

She shakes her head, quiet pride in her eyes. "I paid lots of attention when Shelley showed me the last time. I think I'm good."

I watch as she walks off toward the kitchen, hand in hand with Kelsey, two deeply submissive wolves with gorgeous hearts and impeccable instincts and an odd fondness for lettuce—who are stepping up just as fiercely as the baby alpha they both love.

I hope, so very much, that we're a pack that might finally be able to do right by all of them.

KEL

I'm not the right wolf for this, but I'm the one who's here.

Story of my life.

I sit down beside Shelley. She's picked a nice spot, one a little upriver from the den with a pebble garden that makes the stream burble and just enough overhead tree branches to soften and dapple the light.

The soldier in me knows it's the kind of light that's

good for camouflage. Shelley's not hiding, though. She's thinking, and feeling, and watching a wolf who needs to do more of both. She sighs quietly, running her fingers along a blade of grass. "It's hard for him, being back here. His son was Kennedy's age when he died."

I nod quietly. "You knew Jason?"

She smiles sadly. "Of course. He was pack."

That's all of an answer and none of one. I wait. I've heard the story of Kenny's son from four wolves, and they all told vastly different tales.

"He was more like Braden than Kennedy, really. A big kid who hadn't grown into his paws yet. He drove Kenny nuts some days, not thinking before he acted, but he could always make you laugh. Even after Samuel took over, Jason somehow kept that cheerful innocence about him."

She didn't.

"He was dominant enough that Samuel thought he might be worth something one day. Eamon harassed him some, because that man was pure evil and hated anything that made us laugh, but I wasn't really worried about Jason. None of us were."

The awful truth of war—they had plenty of others to try and save.

She wraps a blade of grass around a finger and lets it spring free again. "Kenny thought Eamon was the bigger threat, the one who would poison the pack the worst. So we focused on trying to drive a wedge between him and Samuel. They were cousins, but it didn't really seem like they liked each other most days."

Evil creates its own kind of loyalty. "You worked it from the inside. As Samuel's mate."

She doesn't say anything. She just watches water burble over pebbles, the weight of the world in her eyes.

I don't do her the disservice of trying to take it away from her. That kind of weight can only be unloaded by the person carrying it, and most of us never get all the way there. "Why did you mate with him?" That's another story with a lot of versions. She's a warrior in all of them.

"I thought he might get kinder. That it might help stabilize the pack." A sad shrug. "There were so many innocents, and I was foolish enough to believe in fairy tales. I thought maybe I could change him."

I've seen it work. I've also seen it eat people alive. Hope is the most corrosive acid ever invented. "That had to be hell."

She shrugs. "Some days I was able to make a difference. I lived for those days."

When I bled like that in service to others, they gave me a fucking Medal of Valor.

She sighs, her eyes still on Kenny. "The day Jason died wasn't one of those days. I failed him. We all did."

I know way too much about the guilt that comes from people dying on my watch. "Some say it was an accident."

She wraps the blade of grass tight enough to turn her knuckle white. "Maybe."

"You don't think so."

The grass snaps free. "No."

She needs Rio, but he's not the wolf who saw her sitting on a riverbank. "Kenny was planning a takedown of Eamon."

She nods. "Yes. He was still technically beta, but Eamon was pushing on that. Sidelining him. Making it harder for him to protect what he could. So Kenny planned to challenge him. The rest of us were ready to distract his other lieutenants until it was over."

Brave, stupid wolves. "What happened?"

Her eyes close. "Samuel got wind. Kenny never wanted to be alpha. He's a beta down to his bones, just like you are, but Samuel couldn't see that. Wouldn't. Nothing I said touched his fury."

I very carefully don't ask what his fury did in reply. Healing trauma is almost never about reliving the punches.

"I found Ebony and sent her to warn Kenny."

Honorable warriors never expect the knife in the dark. "Samuel didn't go after Kenny."

She shakes her head. "No. He acted like he didn't know anything. Ate dinner with his lieutenants, had some beers down by the river." She swallows. "A week later, Jason lost his footing on a ridgeline and fell off a mountain."

Something even wolves with oversized paws don't generally do by accident.

"We all knew." Shelley's voice is thick with tears, ones I know she won't shed where anyone can see. "Ebony found Jason's body. She looked for evidence, but there wasn't any. Nothing we could use. Nothing we could take to the police or the high court, and we were so busy trying to get the pups to safety."

My wolf very carefully reaches out and sets a hand on her back. "That's always what matters most. Always. Even when good dominants are breaking all around you."

Shelley's breath catches. "How do you know that?"

Because they're still broken. "I talked to Ebony. She told me that you chained her to a tree."

A sniff that somehow manages to be indignant. "She was going after Samuel. She would have died."

I shake my head. "You captured a trained soldier."

A small shrug. "I drugged her tea. A couple of the others helped. We didn't have a choice. Kenny was at the bottom of a mountain holding the remnants of his son and Kennedy was playing an awful game of chicken with Bailey to try to keep her from committing suicide on Samuel's claws. There were no other dominants left strong enough to keep Ebony from doing the same."

Always, in the depths of hell, it's the submissives who rise. Damn fucking heroes, every last one of them. "You kept the pups and your warriors alive."

Her eyes are back on Kenny. "I don't know if that one's going to make it."

I offer her the best hope I can. "He's still here."

9

KENNEDY

My wolf thinks this is a really smart idea.

My baby pack is going to think I'm crazy.

Maybe I am, but this will be way more fun than knitting. I look over at Kel, who just smiled faintly when I asked him a really big favor, and then followed me while I rounded everyone up and came over to where Kenny is sitting and quietly untangling some nasty old wire.

He definitely needs more fun in his life.

Kel doesn't say anything, so I guess it's my job to get this rolling. I look at my baby pack. "We're going to have a fighting lesson. I brought water and snacks, but if anyone needs to pee or put on easier clothes to fight in, you should go do that." I look pointedly at Kenny's jeans, but he ignores me and keeps playing with his wire.

Whatever. The rest of my pack is studying me kind of dubiously, but I don't care about that, either.

Reilly glances at Ghost and Hoot and clears his throat. “You’ve been teaching me a little, but I’m not very good yet. I don’t want my bear to hurt anyone.”

Kel ruffles his hair. “You can hurt Kennedy and Kenny all you want.”

I grin. I hope Kel lets Reilly throw Kenny over his shoulder like I’ve been teaching him. We need more truth and respect in this baby pack, and more stories out where the big pack can see them. My wolf is better at making that happen with fights than with knitting.

I hope so, anyhow. Kel is here for backup in case I’m wrong.

His eyes scan the five of us. “I think we’ll start off with everyone human.”

“I’m the smallest, then.” Reilly nods happily.

My wolf shakes her head. Silly bear, giving up his advantages so easily.

Kel studies our little group. “Sometimes you get to fight from your strengths. Sometimes that doesn’t work out and you have to fight from your weaknesses. My job is to make sure you have tools to use no matter what.”

That’s not exactly the lesson I asked for, but it’s maybe an even smarter one. It also sounds an awful lot like something Bailey would say. I look at Hoot under my eyelashes to make sure she’s okay, but she doesn’t look too upset. Just kind of thoughtful.

Kel follows my glance, and he looks kind of thoughtful, too. He nods his chin at Reilly and Hoot. “What do these two have in common that could be a weakness in a fight situation?”

I keep quiet, even though my wolf is grumpy. They're not weak.

Kenny snorts. "They're puny."

Kel catches Hoot by the scruff of the neck just before she launches. "That's not a weakness. That's an opponent foolishly underestimating their strength. Some of the best fighters I know are no bigger than these two."

Hoot blinks at him, which totally makes her look like an owl.

I shoot Kenny a dirty look and let Reilly see me do it. I really hope Kel lets him dump Kenny in the dirt. Kenny isn't a complete asshole, but he's still covered in a lot of asshole dust, and maybe the best way to deal with that is to rub him around in the dirt for a while.

Kel smiles faintly, like he can hear my wolf. "Reilly and Hoot also have a challenge in a fight setting that the rest of you don't have to worry about. What is it?"

Ghost tilts her head. "They both have humans who don't like to be aggressive. And animals that maybe don't agree."

I hide a grin. We've both had to sit on Hoot's scrappy wolf.

"Exactly." Kel nods at her approvingly. "You have a less-complicated pairing—your animal and your human tend to agree on the right course of action. These two have a different situation, which can cause problems in a fight, but it can also create opportunities." He looks straight at Reilly. "How?"

Reilly stares. He's still getting used to the idea that his bear isn't totally sweet like he is.

"We can be two different kinds of fighter," says Hoot softly. "We can calm things down, or we can be scrappy."

My grin flees. Hoot mostly doesn't get to be scrappy. Bailey needs her to be the other kind of fighter way too often. Maybe this lesson was a really bad idea.

Kel's wolf sits up straight, but the rest of him stays easy.

I hold my breath. He's a really smart beta. Maybe he can help me fix this.

He smiles faintly at Hoot. "You're exactly right. Today, you're going to use that to your advantage." He nods my way. "I want you to pair up with Kennedy. She's going to underestimate you because you're small and your human smells submissive, and you're going to let her think that. Right up until the moment you see an opening and get scrappy like your wolf and land a punch."

Hoot's eyes widen.

Kel grins at her. "You know how to throw a punch, right?"

She holds up a fist just like Bailey taught her.

"Good." He waves a hand in my direction. "Land one anywhere you like."

I'm a little surprised, but I roll to my feet and drop into a fighting stance. A purely defensive one. I'm way more dangerous than Reilly's bear, and if I accidentally hurt anyone, Kel will kill me really slowly and roast my bowels while he does it.

He looks at Ghost and Reilly as Hoot stands up uncertainly to face me. "Your job is to be annoying. Kennedy relies too much on her focus when she fights.

Distract her. Mess with her concentration. There are plenty of ways to help tip the outcome of a fight without using your fists. Work together and find them."

My wolf likes that. Reilly isn't a fighter, but he's good at strategy, and Ghost is really sneaky. Which Bailey would never use in a fight because she needs the submissives and pups to stay safe, always, but that took away part of their strength. I want them to have it back.

Even if I'm their target.

I settle a little deeper into my stance. My wolf picked this baby pack. She knows better than to underestimate them.

Reilly looks carefully over at Kenny. "What's his job?"

Good bear. Making sure a packmate is included, even if that packmate is being a stupid lughead.

"He has the simplest job, and the hardest one." Kel waits until Kenny looks up from his wire. "Watch and learn."

My wolf frowns. Something about that isn't quite right, but she doesn't have time to think about it, because Hoot walks right up and tries to throw a punch at my nose. That is so not what the instructions were, but I don't want a bloody nose, so I duck.

She grins and backs away. "Just making sure you were paying attention."

A pinecone bounces off the back of my head. Reilly giggles.

I sigh. At least it's not knitting.

KENNY

I'll give them this much—they're better than the dominants I was supposed to be training. Which isn't a high bar. I never wanted those guys to be any good.

Hoot might be tiny, but she's got a decent fighting stance and enough sense to make her movements unpredictable, which is the only way I can imagine her ever winning this fight. Ghost isn't making any noise at all as she moves around tossing pinecones. Reilly sounds like a bear as he retrieves one and throws it back, but that's just lack of attention. I've seen him out with Ebony, working on his woodcraft, and he's better than most of the dumbasses who just moved into town.

He's also just a kid, and right now he's focusing on his hands and forgetting about his feet. He pauses as Ghost makes a signal behind her back, all quiet and eager and so shiny it hurts my eyes. I have no idea how he got through the last six years with that much innocence still attached. I also have no idea why a man as capable and deadly as the one teaching this lesson isn't doing something about it.

Shiny is an irresistible beacon for evil.

My wolf winces as Ghost starts singing something horribly off key to go along with her pinecones. Unfortunately, it distracts Hoot at least as much as the baby alpha she's supposed to be trying to punch.

"Focus," says Kel quietly. "You have an invader

threatening your den and unknown allies trying to help you."

Hoot's eyes turn fierce. She starts circling Kennedy in a basic fighting stance again, a lot more serious this time.

For good reason. She lived through that invasion. The version without allies. I swallow down the bile rising in my throat. I thought I was one, for a while.

Kel shoots me a look.

Damn nosy beta. I swallow again and focus on the lesson.

Hoot has decent instincts, even in her human form. The circling is smart, or it would be smart if the girl in the middle wasn't as deadly as a snake. I saw Kennedy take down Baird, but this easy stance of hers is a lot more telling. Absolute, honed control. The kind that only comes with a whole lot of training and experience.

I knew there were wolves hiding in the woods. I had no idea they were hiding this.

I dip my chin in silent respect to the wolves who trained her—and to the ones who kept her alive.

Hoot tosses a decent right hook and Kennedy dodges just far enough for it to miss and not a hair more. She fires a grin at the smaller girl. "Close."

A pinecone hits right where the fist was aimed.

Reilly snickers and takes a step backward—right onto another pinecone. Which dumps him ass over teakettle into my damn lap. I manage to get the rusty wire out of the way before he impales himself on it. "Watch where you're going, kid." It comes out gruffer than I mean it to. I've watched a kid not much bigger than him lose his footing way too many times in my nightmares.

He scrambles up, his eyes full of alarm and hurt.

Dammit. I gentle my voice. Some. Shiny needs to come off. It gets people killed. "You always need to know what's behind you in a fight." I pick up the pinecone, tossing it up and catching it again. "Especially if you're the one who left the damn thing under your feet."

His fists clench.

Fuck. There are really big reasons I'm not the guy giving these lessons anymore.

"Reilly." Kel, with a stern set to his tone that makes the bear cub jump. "The fight's not over. Any minute now, Kennedy's going to invade the den because you and Ghost aren't doing your job and providing a distraction so that Hoot can land the punch that will take her out."

Reilly scrambles for a pinecone and fires it at Kennedy's head. He misses by a mile.

Damn kid. I sigh and toss him the one in my hand, exaggerating the motions, the flick at the end that will give it loft and speed. He watches intently and does a half-decent job of fielding it and lobbing it at Kennedy's head.

This one doesn't miss. It hits her square between the eyes as she whirls in response to a sentry call, death streaming from every line of her wolf.

And totally misses the punch that lands square in her gut.

KENNEDY

I toss myself on the ground by my packmates and glare at Kel, since he's the only safe person I can be mad at. I'm pretty mad at my wolf, too. I can't believe we fell for that.

Ghost holds out a water canteen, her eyes still pointed at the ground. "I'm really sorry. I shouldn't have done that."

Kel snorts. "You did exactly what I told you to do."

Ghost finally looks up, her eyes flashing fire. "I used an emergency signal to win a pretend fight. That's playing dirty and it hurt all of our animals and it wasn't for a good reason at all."

Kel's eyebrow slides up. "Would you like my opinion?"

Hoot snickers and elbows Ghost. "He probably thinks that's his mean look."

Reilly gulps, but he manages to grin at Hoot. "That *is* his mean look."

My wolf snorts. Good pack. Picking on the scary beta so Ghost feels better. Sadly, he's right. "I didn't think. I reacted, and that's on me. Anyone could sneak in here and use one of our calls as a trick, right? But my wolf was annoyed because of all the pinecones and the singing, which was really awful, by the way. I lost my grip on her for a second."

Which nearly caused a train wreck, and completely made Kel's point. "That's what I was supposed to be practicing, so now Kel's probably going to have you guys hoot when I'm sleeping and throw pinecones when I'm knitting and set off fireworks when I eat dinner to see if I end up with a fork stuck up my nose."

Reilly winces, even as he giggles. "I bet that would hurt."

Not nearly as much as watching Ghost turn white after Hoot punched me.

Kel raises an eyebrow in my direction. "I suggest you eat with a spoon for a while."

I make a face. This was supposed to be a fun lesson for my pack, not another chance for him to make me eat dirt. I guess I should have expected that—he makes Hayden eat dirt plenty. "I goofed. They were really annoying, though."

He pats Ghost's shoulder. "Obviously you need more practice dealing with sneaky beta tactics."

Huh. I roll my eyes like I'm supposed to, but my wolf doesn't miss how Ghost sits up really straight, or the slow rise of Kenny's eyebrows. I didn't know baby packs had betas, but of course they do. Kel is such a smart wolf, even when he's really annoying.

He eyes the five of us. "You all have things you need to work on. Kennedy's going to have a lot of distractions in her life for the foreseeable future. Hoot needs to learn how to throw a follow-up punch. Ghost has some work to do on trusting her instincts, even when they aren't comfortable ones. Reilly's going to practice hitting what he's aiming at, and Kenny needs to find a dictionary and look up the meaning of *watch and learn*."

All five of us scowl at him in unison. Mean beta.

10

EBONY

Uh, oh. I watch the guy striding my way and fire off a quick signal to the other one he's looking for. There's more fire in Kenny's eyes than I've seen in days, and that might be a really good thing.

Or not.

Kel arrives at the same time Kenny does and somehow manages to make it look like casual coincidence. He leans against a tree and nods at me. "Hayden's doing a perimeter run with Danielle and Eliza and Reilly, working out the new circuit."

We're prepping some submissive pairs to do patrol duty. Which gives my wolf nightmares, but she sees the quiet pride in their eyes and she knows damn well they aren't weak. We're still altering the perimeter, though. The new one doesn't have any nasty obstacles that might get in the way of reinforcements, even bears who might trip over their own claws. Reilly's been having a blast testing just how fast he can get from the den to each section of the perimeter. I shake my head at Kel. "That bear is damn speedy when he wants to be."

He snorts. "Wait until he figures out how to coordinate all of his limbs."

I bet. I never heard of any bears in Special Forces, but that doesn't mean they didn't exist. "Need any help?" It's an inane question. He'd tell me if he did. We're just killing time, ignoring the steam coming out of Kenny's ears until he decides to use actual words.

I'm actually pretty happy to see the steam. He was doing a disturbingly good imitation of a dishrag wolf when Shelley dragged him in here.

He finally crosses his arms and looks at both of us. "What are you planning to do about that girl?"

I expected the tone, but not the topic. I raise an eyebrow. "Want to be a little more specific? There are a lot of girls around here."

His grunt tells me where I can shove my sense of humor. "Kennedy. The one who can wipe the ground with all of us."

My wolf sobers. Kennedy's pinecone moment caught Kel's attention too, and it's the second time in as many days that Kenny's been close enough to get a measure of our baby alpha's dominance. Probably not an accurate one, but fucking huge doesn't have to be all that precise to be scary.

And he's clearly scared.

With good reason. The last alpha wolf he knew with

that kind of power was a demon-spawned psychopath. "She's a strong, loyal dominant. She's nothing but good for this pack."

"She's more than strong."

At least he's smart enough not to question her loyalty. "She might be able to take my wolf, but I have a few tricks up my sleeve yet." I nod my chin at the guy who's rapidly teaching Kennedy how to get around most of them. "So does he."

Kenny's face twists. "What are you going to do when she's stronger than your alpha?"

He's got guts. Way too much negative attitude, but guts. "He's your alpha, too."

A short, sharp nod. He's not here to challenge the hierarchy. He's trying to make sure we're awake.

I sigh. His manners are a lot rough around the edges, but underneath the crossed arms and scowl is a guy who still cares about his pack, and one who maybe gives a good-sized damn about Kennedy, too. It's a start. I shoot a quick glance at the submissive wolf who could likely take us both down to see if he has anything to add.

Kel shrugs. "She might be stronger than Hayden already."

I clearly missed the big pot of truth oatmeal this morning.

Kenny's scowl threatens to go nuclear.

My wolf growls. I spent six years tolerating that crap so he didn't blow my submissive cover. It ends now. "You're not beta anymore. Maybe think about that before you open your mouth again."

His grunt borders on rude, but it isn't really disagreeing. "She's dangerous."

I snort. "So am I. So are you."

He shoves his hands in his pockets and stands his ground, which pleases the fuck out of my wolf. "She's a different kind of dangerous."

She's a different kind of everything. "We're going to support her and support this pack. What are you going to do—slink off into the woods?" It's a low blow. We both swallowed our share of helpless the last six years, but I didn't have to eat breakfast with the guy dishing it out.

He winces. "I can't help her."

Kel hits him with a look that could melt steel. "The hell you can't."

Kenny's eyes widen.

Kel's not nearly done. "How many dominants do you see around here who come anywhere near her weight class?"

My wolf acknowledges his point. There are a couple in the woods, but she's loved them forever, and family is its own kind of dominance hierarchy.

"The worst thing you can do is be scared of her." Kel's scowl makes Kenny's look like a little kid practicing in the mirror. "If you believe in her wolf's ability to break this pack, you give that idea power. Don't fucking do that."

Kenny doesn't say anything. His face just hardens—in that way of mountains right before they crack.

Shit. He's not ready for anything that requires being hopeful yet. "You being here is steadying her. It gives that strength of hers some value. She's the only wolf in her baby pack who can kick your ass."

Kenny snorts. "Maybe."

Kel's lips quirk. "You might let on that you know that. Respect for submissives goes a long way in this pack."

Kenny sighs. "I was too hard on the kid yesterday."

Damn. I don't want to like him. Not until we've chewed off more of his jerk. "Reilly had six years of hard words from you. That doesn't fix overnight." I hold up a hand. "I know. You were trying to get him out of the line of fire, but he doesn't know that."

"He might," says Kel quietly. "He's been easier with having you around than I expected."

"Damn fool kid." There's no heat in Kenny's words, only regret.

He doesn't get to turn back into dishrag wolf. Not on my watch. "Work on it. He's a good kid. Help him learn. Teach him how to be a decent infielder, maybe. Our team could use a good one."

The pain that hits his eyes is a living, breathing thing. "I don't do baseball."

He did, once. "You do now."

The look he shoots me is full of venom.

Kel raises a wry eyebrow. "You know that Ebony can also wipe the ground with you, right?"

Kenny just shakes his head and stalks off the way he came, muttering under his breath.

I toss an arm over Kel's shoulders and grin. "That went pretty well, don't you think?"

He chuckles. "If you keep putting burrs under his saddle, he's going to take a swipe at you."

That might get interesting. "Ghost will protect me."

He eyes me. "She might."

I nod. Kenny might have only had eyes for Kennedy after the pinecone hit, but Kel noticed something else. Her dominance smacked hard against every shifter in her baby pack—and three of them weren't scared at all. They were all dealing with their own shit, but fear of the lethal weapon inside their leader wasn't even on the list.

One baby alpha, gathering the pack she needs.

KENNEDY

This is so weird. I dip a fry carefully into the little paper container of ketchup. I've been watching the other people in the diner to see how they do it, and they all have the little containers. Maybe we should get some for Braden. I nibble on the fry. It's salty and smells a little bit like chicken, which is definitely weird.

Hayden picks up one of his burgers and takes a big bite. He watches me as he chews.

My wolf wriggles. She likes burgers, but she's not used to this many humans, or this much quiet attention from her alpha. "Will you teach me how to drive?"

He steals one of my fries and grins. "Nope. You're not old enough, and I'm not tough enough to deal with Rio if you steer his truck into a tree."

I snort. "That's why there are roads. How old were you when you learned how to drive?"

His lips quirk. "I didn't learn in Rio's truck."

I roll my eyes. "Come on. It's full of pea gravel. It won't even be able to go that fast."

He manages not to snort root beer out his nose. Barely. "That isn't how the laws of physics work."

I groan. "I have to take physics in school this year. Reilly checked."

Hayden chuckles. "No letting a bear do your physics homework for you."

I make a face. "He can tutor me though, right?"

He smiles. "Absolutely." He steals another one of my fries. "You're good at making Reilly feel useful and needed."

I give him one of the looks I use on Myrna when she's being really annoying. "He *is* useful and needed."

Hayden takes another huge bite of his burger and nods.

I sigh. I've been trying to believe what Adrianna said, but my wolf isn't all the way convinced. Which means I need to stop being a stupidhead and ask. "He's part of my baby pack. You don't seem to be mad about that."

"I'm not." He steals one of my fries.

My wolf has no idea what that means. "What about the others?"

His grin is wry. "I'd tell you that claiming Kenny is a dumb idea, but you're basically following in my footsteps."

I take a tasty bite of my cheeseburger and think about

that some. "Was Kel as lost as Kenny when you first claimed him?"

"More in some ways. Less in others."

I swallow and take a swig of root beer, which doesn't taste right for how it smells, either. Diner food is really strange. "How do I help him?"

He sighs. "I want to tell you to leave that part to us. But that's probably not how it's actually going to work."

My wolf wrinkles her nose. Of course not. But that might get kind of complicated. "How will I know when my part is, so I don't take a part you're supposed to be doing?" I need a baby-alpha instruction manual or something.

He pours some of his fries out onto my plate. "It's not neat like that. There aren't any parts with my name stamped on them. Whistler has a lot of baby alphas and even more people who sometimes do alpha jobs because they happen to be the nearest wolf when something like that is needed."

I make a face. That sounds like a hot mess.

He laughs. "One thing I know is that it gets easier if there's good communication. So tell me some things you think I need to know about your baby pack. What are we getting wrong?"

I nearly choke on my burger. I stare at him, wide-eyed, as I manage to swallow down the onions and mustard that are suddenly burning my throat.

He calmly hands me my root beer. "You're a smart shifter with good instincts, and except for maybe Reilly, you know the wolves of your baby pack far better than I do. You also have an alpha who has big shoulders and no problem hearing that he's fucked up."

I'm still staring. I probably need to stop that soon. I also need to be careful. There are some stories about my baby pack that aren't mine to tell. Lissa says we need to wait until Bailey and Hoot and the others are ready to speak for themselves. I gulp. "Can I think about that for a while?"

He looks at me, his head tilted. "If you want."

Crap. I stab another fry into my ketchup. "Your mom thinks about things. She doesn't just say whatever pops into her head."

"Is that what you think?" He chuckles. "Sometimes that's true. She can be thoughtful and deliberate and weigh her answers. Other times she moves so fast she has an answer between one breath and the next."

My throat closes.

He studies me for a long time. Then he reaches out and wraps his hand around mine. "That's how your wolf works, doesn't she?"

I want to nod, to blink, to tell him the truth. Instead, I carefully extract my fingers and dip another fry into the little paper container.

HAYDEN

It's the damn ketchup. She keeps drowning her fries in it, just like my mom does. It's hard not to see the parallels.

Except Adrianna Scott never had to do this alone.

My heart bleeds for the wolf on the other side of the table who believes no one can walk with her on this, even as she gathers us around her. My mom had two parents who believed in her absolutely and a pack that didn't shake when she rumbled.

I can at least give Kennedy an alpha who doesn't.

I steal another one of her fries, which seems to amuse her wolf, and consider how best to do that. I know there are stories I haven't heard yet, and my green-eyed wolf has given me a decent map of where not to push, but I also need to do my job. Which maybe starts with helping Kennedy do hers. "Baby packs are tricky, especially at the beginning. What's the biggest challenge in yours right now?"

She makes a face. "Getting Kenny's wolf to stop being a stupidhead."

I eat more burger so I don't grin. "What do you think will help with that?"

She demolishes another handful of fries before she replies, but it's a thoughtful move, not a defensive one. "You give Ravi jobs to keep him at the den."

Kel does, but she's clearly been paying attention. "Yes. Most wolves need to feel like they're contributing to pack. That goes double for wolves who are struggling."

The debate waging inside her is far more obvious on her face than she knows. I wait patiently. She needs to trust her alpha to see her brain and her heart, not just her teeth and claws.

She growls at an innocent fry. Then she squares her

shoulders and looks me straight in the eyes. "I think perimeter patrol is the wrong job for Kenny."

My wolf cocks his head curiously, impressed by her vehemence—and her certainty. "He's a dominant. It's a natural fit."

She's shaking her head before I'm done speaking. "He did too much of that when he was trying to be a good beta and a bad beta at the same time."

Out of the mouths of smart baby alphas. "Good point."

Her wolf relaxes a little. "It doesn't let him see and feel what's happening at the den. He needs that. He needs jobs that will keep him in the middle of everything." She wrinkles her nose. "Like knitting."

I grin. "Better him than us."

She laughs, a bright teenager again, hanging out with her alpha and eating her body weight in fries.

Which she is, but I don't lose track of the really vital point she just made. The one that applies to a lot more wolves than just Kenny. We have way too many packmates living on the periphery. The last thing we need to be doing is handing out jobs that keep them there. "What jobs would you assign him?"

She shrugs, and I can see her wolf's impatient annoyance with an answer not found. "I don't know."

I dump the last of my fries on her plate and steal a few. "The right role for a wolf isn't always obvious. I bet you'll know it when you see it."

She tilts her head. "Did you? With Kel?"

Memory swoops in, fast and furious. "I did, yeah." I

smile. It was the first time I knew all the way down to my bones that I could actually make a difference for him—that I wasn't just an annoying kid bent on making him crazy. "He was the baby walker."

She stares at me, her mouth half-open.

I laugh. That was pretty much his reaction. "He walked the halls with the babies when their parents were trying to sleep. It was the perfect job for him. He couldn't sleep at night for months after he got back, and he needed to remember how soft pack can be. And how loud. We had one tiny girl who Kel swore broke his ears."

She winces in amused sympathy, but her wolf is studying me intently. "You picked that job for him? When you were ten?"

She misses nothing. "I did. That's how alpha instincts sometimes work. One day I was sitting in the dining room listening to one of the moms talking, and I just knew. I told her Kel could help. He grumped and scowled, but she didn't care. She just tracked him down the next time her son wouldn't sleep and handed him this sweaty, howling baby."

Kennedy listens silently, a wolf who can smell the incoming magic.

I will never forget it. "Kel's whole face changed. Until that moment, there was a part of him that was missing. He found it in a baby's cry."

Her whole heart sighs.

My wolf will be seriously cranky if she ever leaves his pack. He adores her, and he will damn well do everything he can think of to lay the groundwork for her to stay.

Starting with keeping her busier. "I'm thinking that Kenny isn't the only shifter in your baby pack who could maybe use more work to do. I bet you all had a lot more responsibilities out with Bailey."

Her eyes get very careful. I watch the struggle on her face—and then I watch the decision. "That's part of why Hoot can't come live at the den. She still has them."

I grab hold of my wolf and his righteous frustration before he does something stupid. "I didn't know that." I should have. The math is really obvious now that I'm staring right at it. "This is why baby packs are helpful. You see things. You can make sure I see them."

She reaches for the last fry and scrapes up the last of the ketchup from an impressive row of paper containers. "The whole pack needs more jobs. Most of us, anyhow."

I make a wry face. I had somehow convinced myself that an extended camping vacation was a good thing. A chance for everyone to relax and heal. "We'll have more when the den arrives and school starts."

The look in her eyes is really clear. We can't wait that long.

Damn. I should be paying her in something a lot fancier than burgers and fries. "I'll talk to the betas and Lissa."

She nods solemnly.

And here I thought I was going to be helping her. "In the meantime, listen to your wolf and your instincts. You're likely to figure out some of the right jobs for your baby pack before I do."

She looks at me, one eye skeptical and the other one proud.

Time to use one of my better alpha skills. I stand up and wrap an arm around her head. "Let's head back to the den. We have a mountain of pea gravel to unload if you can move after all those fries."

She giggles into my arm. "You ate most of them."

I snort and scoop up the root beer she didn't quite finish. "Pants on fire."

She elbows me and I let her go, which is probably a good idea. Human guys don't tend to wrestle with the female teenagers in their care. She snorts and snags the cup out of my hand. "I have no idea what you're talking about. And that's *my* root beer."

I push the door open and hold it while she walks through, a much more content wolf than when we walked in. One successful conversation with a baby alpha. A really humbling one.

Now we just have to deliver pea gravel without hitting a tree.

11

KENNEDY

Hoot elbows me hard enough that I nearly trip over my feet. "I can't believe he let you drive the truck."

It was way fun, and I only came close to a tree that one time. I grin at Hoot. She's already extracted a promise for future driving lessons from Rio. Which is one of the reasons the wolf following us is so cranky—she tried extracting them from him, first. I turn around, because if I'm supposed to find jobs for my baby pack, I need to know more about them. I don't remember very much about Kenny from before. I was too little and he was too annoyed by little girls. "Are you a good driver?"

He scowls at us both. "We're supposed to be working on tracking skills, not walking through the woods making so much noise a horde of deaf zombies could find you."

I snicker. "That's a pretty good line for an old guy."

That doesn't make him look more cheerful.

Hoot flashes him a grin. "We are tracking. Smart wolves can do more than one thing at once."

She's supposed to be trying to cross the perimeter along with Ghost and Reilly, but she decided to switch teams. I tried out one of Kel's scowls when she did that, but it just made her giggle. My wolf is okay with that. She thinks scowls are overrated. Hayden isn't a very bossy alpha and people still listen to him when it matters. And Hoot is working through just as much stuff as Kenny is, behind her smart-ass grins.

I don't really know how to help with any of that, but at least this way I get to walk beside them both.

I watch how Kenny's feet fall on the ground, because that's a big part of good woodcraft. He's not all that bad. "Those are sucky boots for this. They're clunky and loud."

He raises an eyebrow. "I know."

I frown, because that makes no sense.

He frowns right back. "They're the boots I've got."

Hoot makes a funny little sound. "You got them on purpose. Back when Samuel was in charge. So that you'd be easier to hear."

He eyes her like she might explode.

I keep watching Hoot, because she just might. Her family paid the biggest price of all when Samuel was in charge. But she doesn't blow up and her eyes don't get all hollow like they do when she's remembering the worst stuff. She just studies Kenny, like he fell off a shelf and she's not sure where to put him.

My wolf has thoughts on that. I bump against his shoulder. "You were only kind of an asshole. Admit it."

Hoot snickers.

Kenny ignores us both.

I tuck that away. His wolf is good at being calm, even around really annoying teenagers. The den doesn't have very many of those yet, but it might one day.

Hoot tests out an owl call, shakes her head, and tries again. She's practicing a new one. Some kind of owl Reilly found for her on the internet. He's such a sweet, geeky bear.

Kenny rolls his eyes.

He can be an aggravating wolf all he wants. It's not getting him out of tracking practice. "How many times have we crossed their trail?" Ghost hasn't been leaving much of one, but so far she's not cleaning up after Reilly.

Kenny smirks. "Three."

I look over at Hoot.

She grins. "Four. One of them was just Ghost."

I raise an eyebrow at Kenny. "You got lazy and missed one."

My wolf waits, alert, expecting him to snap at me. Instead, he nods at Hoot. "I only picked up Ghost's trail twice. You're good. So is she."

Hoot's eyes widen at the compliment. "Ghost is the best. Maybe even better than Kel."

He snorts. "She's not nearly as mean or as tricky as he is."

I eye him. "She can be plenty tricky. Let's circle back

to one of the places you missed." I bet it was when she went up the tree. Ghost is a really excellent monkey.

He looks at me like he might just leave instead. "It would be a lot smarter to do this furry."

Not while Hoot's with us. Her wolf is a scrapper, and she kind of wants to bite Kenny. Which might be bad for baby-pack morale, because Ghost and Reilly would be mad they missed it. "Good perimeter guards have to know what they're doing in both forms."

He opens his mouth and closes it again, a resigned look in his eyes.

I wince a little. Right answer, wrong tone. "It was a reasonable suggestion and I gave you a snotty response. Sorry."

Hoot looks a little surprised, but we can't help Kenny turn back into someone he can be proud of by being jerks ourselves. Bailey might be a tough wolf, but she made sure we all know how to apologize.

He nods quietly.

Good enough. I loop us back toward the last incursion I spied and keep my eyes open. Ghost is good enough to cross our path three more times while we backtrack, and Reilly is better than his first two trails made him look, so she's probably setting us up. I scan the trees, using my peripheral vision like Dorie taught me. Spying cats is really hard. Wolves are easier. They don't look quite so much like branches.

I see something pale that might be Reilly's legs, but it turns out to just be a trick of the light. Hoot is mostly watching the ground. Kenny isn't watching much of anything, or that's how it appears. My wolf doesn't think he's as checked-out as he looks. Which is interesting. Kind of like his boots, maybe.

A guy who's had a lot of practice looking different than he really is.

I don't want to feel sad about that, because he's also done a lot of things to hurt wolves I love, but I do anyhow. Ebony says he had the hardest job of all. I don't believe her—I think that was Shelley. Or maybe Rennie. Or a lot of other people with Hoot's last name.

My wolf growls. She doesn't want to think about that. We're out tracking and we have a job to do.

Kenny looks up sharply. Hoot spins to her left a split second later. I jerk to attention, but it doesn't take long to figure out what I missed. A bear crashing through the woods makes really distinctive noises.

Reilly runs into view with Ghost hot on his heels. They both shift, breathing hard. "Bobcat," says Ghost, taking the t-shirt Hoot hands her. She doesn't put it on, though. She looks at me, waiting for instructions.

I grab my wolf. We need to be smart, and Ghost isn't panicking. Quite. "Cat we know?"

Her head nods, a little wildly. "In, and then back out again. Maybe twice. I'm not sure about the second time. We were running pretty hard and I didn't stop to check. He didn't cross the inner perimeter, but he came close."

Kenny's steps forward, his face hard. "Show me."

I grab his arm. "Stand down. We know him."

He shakes me off. "That doesn't mean he's friendly."

If he won't respect me, he needs to at least respect the pack hierarchy. I shoot a look at Hoot. "Go get Kel."

"Already here," says a calm voice from behind us.

"Intruder." Kenny's voice is sharp. "Bobcat."

I growl. He so does not get to be in charge of this. "I know who the cat is. He's a friend."

Kel eyes me like I have really bad choices in friends.

Whatever. I roll my eyes, because Kel might not be in my baby pack, but keeping him from being serious all the time is totally one of my jobs. "He's not trespassing, exactly. Lissa sort of invited him."

That gets his wolf's attention. "Then he needs to knock on the door like a polite visitor and let us get a good look at him."

I make a face. He has reasons for not doing that, and even if he didn't, he's a cat. Annoying wolves is one of his favorite games. "He doesn't know you. He's trying to figure out if he can trust you enough to knock." Which means that all the stuff I said when I delivered Lissa's pebble wasn't good enough, even though I talked for a whole day.

"Maybe." Kel's watching me like I might grow horns any minute, but he's also listening, and that makes my wolf proud.

I try to be worthy. "I'll take Ghost and go find him."

Kel and Kenny don't even take enough time to breathe. "No."

I ignore Kenny. He's not the boss of me. Kel kind of is, so I meet his gaze straight on. "Why not?"

His eyes are full of that weird silence right before

lightning strikes. "Because chasing down dumbass bobcats isn't your job."

I keep my wolf's snarl inside my head. He's not disrespecting her, even though she thinks he is. Of all the adults in the pack, he sometimes has the biggest thing about trying to keep me safe. When he's not teaching me to be a better badass.

I look around for Hayden, because I know this is a job my baby pack can do, but he's nowhere to be found. I take a deep breath. "We can do this. Ghost is a really good tracker, and he's just one bobcat. I don't know why he's being a dumbass, but we shouldn't be ones back."

Kel's eyes narrow. "He crossed into our territory with questionable permission, which is a potentially hostile act. Until we know it isn't, we don't put our submissives in harm's way."

I cross my arms and glare at him. "Nobody sneaks up on Ghost."

She steps in beside me. She's breathing kind of funny, but she straightens her shoulders.

My wolf very smartly backs up half a step and tucks in behind the shifter who can win this fight.

Kel's snort is half-laugh, half-growl. "You two are a hell of a tag team."

I grin at him. "I'm just the muscle. She's the brains."

Ghost makes a strangled-squeak sound that my wolf thinks is really funny.

Kel sighs and shoots her a very pointed look. "Can you keep Kennedy out of trouble?"

She nods solemnly. "Yes."

My wolf wrinkles her nose. That probably means we can't go chew on a bobcat.

Kel shakes his head, but that's not our answer. The quick nod at the end is.

Ghost turns to me, her eyes wide. Which helps my wolf get her act together. Baby alphas who volunteer their packmates for big jobs need to help them deliver.

I grin at her. "Let's go find a bobcat."

She swallows.

I try not to worry that I pushed too hard. She's a really amazing tracker. "Come on. It will probably take longer because you have to keep me with you and I make lots of noise."

Kel gives me a look that says I better stick to her like glue. "Dominant wolves rely too much on their teeth and claws to get them out of everything. They don't put in the time to learn how to be silent on their feet."

Ghost's eyes narrow. "Kennedy got your bandana. She's really good."

I roll my eyes at him where Ghost can't see. Troublesome beta.

He shrugs. "Bobcats are a lot harder than bandanas."

Ghost straightens again. "We'll find him."

I eye Kel as I toe off my sneakers, because Reilly's bear is disappointed and Kenny is irritated and worried, and maybe I should try to do something about that stuff before I go.

His lips quirk. "I'll take these two back to the den. The bobcat doesn't cross the outer perimeter without at least two sets of teeth and claws riding his ass, so you signal Hoot when you've got him close."

Hoot is already up a tree somewhere. I can hear the owl calls.

"Are you seriously sending two girls out to find a potential threat?" Kenny's voice is low, but his incredulous question punches through the air anyhow.

My wolf snaps to attention.

"No." Kel eyes him. He's weirdly relaxed, but his hand signals say that if I so much as twitch, I'll be shoveling pea gravel for the next century. "I'm sending the pack's best tracker and a dominant who has excellent control when faced with guys who make poor choices."

Ghost stops breathing. My wolf wants to give Kel a really big hug for saying such nice things, but that would mess with his whole tough-beta routine.

He tips his chin at the woods. "Go. If you lose him, no heroics. Send up a flare. Bobcats are sneaky as hell."

I flash him a grin. "We know."

His eyes narrow.

Crap. He maybe doesn't know about Dorie yet. I pull my hoodie over my head and toss it at Reilly. I'll take my t-shirt and shorts with me so we can have a chat with a bobcat when we find him. I turn to Ghost, who needs to breathe really soon.

It's time to go chase a kitty.

RIO

Ebony circles behind Kenny and Reilly and starts herding them back to the den. I walk over to Kel's shoulder and watch two young wolves disappear into the woods.

He glances over at me. "You weren't wrong about those two."

Neither was he. "Lissa counts the cat alpha as a friend. Ebony says he's well respected by the local packs." None of which replaces having eyes on him, especially if your name is Kelvin Nogues. But it might help his wolf rest a little easier until two teenagers get back.

"Yeah."

Damn overprotective wolf. And also one who really likes to mess with cats. "How hard was it not to go with them?"

His lips twitch. "Hard enough."

I lean against his shoulder and sigh. "Maturity sucks."

He laughs, and some of the tension in his wolf eases. He chooses to put himself in harm's way first, always, and it's not an instinct that's remotely amenable to reason, even when his brain and his heart and his beta gut all know this was the better choice.

I add a sentinel paw on the scale. Ghost and Kennedy can handle one bobcat, and the den is going to need Kel. "This is going to be an interesting exercise for the pack."

His eyebrows slide up. "How so?"

"When do you figure is the last time they had a visitor?"

He winces. The answer to that was painfully clear when Adrianna came—and this is a visitor who knew them as they once were. Which is a picture I still don't have fully in focus, but I know it's a damn sight different than a fire pit by the river and a pile of sleeping bags. I'm also pretty sure the lack of fancy accommodations isn't going to be what the cat alpha notices first.

He nods slowly, his beta brain already working all the angles.

I offer up my wolf's two cents. "Lissa set this in motion. She has a better read than anyone on what the submissives of this pack can handle."

His eyes drift in the direction Ebony and her charges went.

That's a different problem. "Is Kenny going to be an issue?"

"For Kennedy, no. She already knows she needs to deal with him."

It took Hayden a lot longer to realize he had to get a cranky ex-soldier in line. Probably because the other guy in his baby pack was being a jerk. "Is he going to handle the guilt that's going to land when the cat shows up?"

Kel sighs. "I don't know. He wasn't anywhere close to the worst of the assholes, but he's the one who's here to face the music."

Which says something about Kenny's wolf that he's nowhere near ready to acknowledge. "His baby pack will help catch him. They're a lot smarter than we were."

Kel snorts. "We had our heads up our asses for years."

I grin wryly. "Pretty much. Anything you need me to do besides chomp on a cat if he shows up unexpectedly?"

His eyes are back on the woods. "That's my job."

It's the job of the guy we both call our alpha, but none of us are going to have a chance to chase a kitty for a while. We need to give a baby alpha and her very worthy packmate time to deliver him first. "Hayden says he had a good chat with Kennedy."

A wry eyebrow. "Did he say anything more than that?"

"That she eats a lot of ketchup on her fries."

Kel huffs out a laugh. "Of course she does."

I'm quiet a moment, getting a measure of his wolf. "You don't seem all that concerned about her."

"Is Hayden?"

"A little." It took a lot of sentinel digging to sniff it out, though. "He's keeping it well tamped down."

A small nod. "He would."

That's as much as I have to say. I don't blow oxygen on fires I don't want lit. "Are we worried about a bobcat who has no sense of self-preservation?"

Kel snorts. "He's a cat."

Still. "He could have called first. Or walked in the front door."

"He'll have heard," says Kel quietly. "Would you knock under those circumstances?"

Not a chance. "Nope. I'd send Kelvin Nogues to sniff around. So I figure it's kind of interesting that this guy came to check things out himself. He's either an arrogant asshat or a cat who's got some cards to lay on the table."

He smiles faintly. "Yup."

Still expecting me to figure shit out myself. "Given that Lissa likes him, I lean toward the latter."

A small twitch of his shoulder. "Maybe."

Annoying wolf. Unfortunately for him, I've had his number for a really long time. "Think he's going to let Ghost find him?"

Finally, a real smile. "She's not going to give him a choice."

12

LISSA

I glance over at Ebony. "You sure this is where we're supposed to meet him?"

We've been sent out to this very specific tree to be the greeting committee for our incoming visitor. Hayden is on pup-guarding duty back at the den on the off chance we've accidentally let a feline psychopath get this close, which I'm letting him get away with because a cat is yanking his chain and his wolf has a right to be annoyed.

Ebony snorts. "He's a cat. Of course I'm not sure. He might have gone for a run through our territory just to be difficult."

A different day and a different cat, she might be right—but not this one. She has no way of knowing that, though. She doesn't actually know the Lonely Peak cats. She wasn't here for very long before Samuel took over, and we didn't exactly have a lot of visits with local packs after that. "He's not a jerk. He's truly not."

She rolls her eyes. "Chill. My wolf knows how to play nice with cats, and I've had a couple of chats with this one while I was making contacts for my northern-liaison job."

I forget she has that, most days. Until I see her salary land in the pack bank account and try to convince her to take some. So far, I'm not winning that fight. "I should have let you invite him."

She shrugs. "He knows you. He doesn't know me, and from what you say, he's got reasons for being careful. He seems like a decent guy, though."

He is, but he sometimes makes a lot of effort not to come across that way. "How do we do this?" It's a big question. The outcome of this visit matters so very much. We've been in isolation for six long years.

Ebony snorts. "We wait for Kennedy and Ghost to drag his sorry ass here. Then we walk in with him and make sure he doesn't do anything I'd have to growl at him for."

The chances of that are vanishingly small. "He'll try to rile you."

She snorts again. "He's a cat."

He's a cat who's taking way too long to get here. I sniff the wind, frustrated by my feeble human nose. "Maybe I'll shift and see if I can track him."

"Kel and Rio are on that."

Something in me eases. We're being careful. Good. Reese is a friend, but this still makes me really nervous.

He's a good guy, and he thinks he knows what we've been through, but I can still think of a dozen ways this could go wrong.

Ebony's shoulder bumps against mine. "Trust your pack, remember? And trust that big lug you kiss a lot and claim isn't your mate."

"Don't push." It's an absentminded retort to a conversation that happens several times a day. My pack thinks I might forget Hayden and how I feel about him if they don't remind me every ten minutes.

She grins. "I'm a dominant wolf. If you expect me to be shy and retiring, you're shit out of luck."

Even my shy-and-retiring packmates get in on this game. My wolf doesn't mind. She agrees with them.

I look around the woods. Reese and some of his trackers might have made a couple of passes to get the lay of the land, but there's no way he's going to sneak all the way up on a new alpha. He's a cat, not an imbecile. He'll be darn hard to spot, though. He's the biggest bobcat I've ever seen, but he's the same color as tree bark.

Ebony's eyes are up in the trees. Smart wolf. He also likes dropping down on unsuspecting dominants for kicks and giggles.

Usually he's the only one laughing.

It isn't a bobcat who finally slinks out of the trees, though. Reese steps out of the shadows wearing a bright red, fitted flannel shirt that's the latest in sexy-man-in-the-woods fashion. Kennedy and Ghost are flanking him, looking dusty and determined and proud. A really annoyed Kel is following at a safe distance, which for Kel means close enough to strangle our visitor at any moment.

Ebony's eyes widen.

I swallow a snicker. Reese came in full performance mode.

His eyes meet mine, and there's so much there. Joy. Guilt. Relief. Grief.

I reach for him. He's the first cat I ever met, and he's always been the best one. "Thank you for coming." They're weak words for six years of absence.

He somehow manages to hug me tight and still feel like he could spring at any moment. Given the low growls emanating from my betas, that's probably a good idea.

He pats my shoulder and steps back, scanning them casually. "You two are overkill. You've got some damn good sentries."

"You noticed *them*." Kel's voice is full of quiet menace. "You didn't notice me. You might want to remember that the next time you cross into our territory without permission."

"I was invited," says Reese calmly. "And I have good reasons to be careful."

"You were invited weeks ago." Ebony's voice is as steely as Kel's. "Next time, call."

Reese smiles. Which makes both of our betas eye him suspiciously until they realize he's still jerking chains and they've just passed another test.

Their matching scowls probably aren't something I should find funny.

Reese shakes his head. "You hang around with some grumpy wolves these days, Liss."

Ebony snorts. "You haven't met the grumpiest one yet." She flashes me a grin. "Just wait until Hayden gets a whiff of you smelling like cat."

I roll my eyes. Troublesome wolves. Ones who've apparently clawed at a cat enough for the moment, thank goodness.

Reese brushes imaginary lint off his sleeves. Then he winks at me. "Okay, sweetheart. Take me to your leader."

My snicker makes it all the way out this time.

The banked grief in his eyes eases a little more. He puts his arm around my shoulder and leans in. "I'm so sorry. I didn't know what was going on here, but that's no excuse. I should have tried a lot harder. I should have known you wouldn't have all disappeared like that, asshole alpha or not."

Samuel only met Reese once. He made it very clear what he thought about lifestyles that didn't resemble his own. Cats have a lot of those. "We couldn't reach out. We had reasons."

"Kennedy told me." Anger whips through his body. "I knew things were off. I could have sent my guys in, dug up some answers. I should have done at least that much."

Kel snorts. "If you want a guilt trip, get in line."

Reese meets his eyes. "I don't need your permission for how I feel."

Ebony's lips quirk.

Kel studies the face of the man with his arm around

me and finally nods. "Thank you for coming. It's good to know we have reliable neighbors."

Reese snorts. "We're cats. We're unruly and unpredictable and annoying as fuck."

Kel almost grins. "That, too."

My wolf lets out a sigh of relief. So far, so good. One big hurdle left.

KENNEDY

I sling my arm around Ghost's shoulders. I can feel her relief and her weariness and her pride. We got him here. Now it's up to the big kids to deal with him. I bend my head toward hers. "I am so eating all the chocolate that's left at the den."

Kel shoots me an amused look.

Ghost snorts. "Liar. You give all yours to the pups."

Not all, exactly. Just most. "Fine. Maybe we can find a watermelon or something." They're kind of a pack joke, so Shelley buys them a lot. She's also trying to grow them, but so far they're just leaves and flowers.

Ghost grins. "We should check Hayden's backpack."

I can see Reese's ears flickering, following our silly talk. That's fine. I want him to know our alpha is a good guy. I try to keep an ear on his chatter with Lissa, too. She seems to really like him, which helps make my wolf less nervous. She knows Reese, but there are pups at the den, and she's not used to letting anyone near them who's not pack.

Reese drops back so he's walking beside Ghost. He glances over at Kel. "Does he know you're a better tracker than he is, or do I get to tell him?"

I kind of want to growl at him and lick him at the same time. Especially when Ghost gets her dazed, happy look again.

Kel just shakes his head and keeps scanning the woods.

I know what he's looking for. "He had two trackers with him. They both left."

Reese raises an eyebrow.

I raise one right back. Finding him was Ghost's job. Making sure no one snuck up on us was mine.

Ebony snickers. "Please tell me you chewed on their tails."

I sigh. "I wanted to, but it would have made too much noise."

Which made my wolf cranky, but we tracked Reese down just a few minutes later. I would have missed him, but Ghost didn't. She dropped out of a tree right in front of him and even bobcats look really surprised if you do that. He didn't hiss at her, though. He hissed at me plenty, but that might have been because I gave his tail a good nip for making us run through the dusty part of the forest for so long.

My wolf doesn't like dust.

She likes making her betas happy, though, and Ebony and Kel aren't just proud of the best tracker in our pack.

They're a little bit proud of me, too, and that feels good, even if all I did was follow Ghost and try not to eat too much dust.

I squeeze Ghost's hand. We're a baby pack who did good. Now we have to wait to see if it worked.

HAYDEN

I knew someone was coming. I didn't expect them to be wrapped around Lissa when they showed up.

I manage to get a hand on the scruff of my wolf's neck. It's bad manners to bleed visitors the instant they show up unless they obviously deserve it. My wolf has been packmate to plenty of cats, but something deep in the ancient parts of his DNA needs to growl at them first. Which the guy watching me clearly knows, judging by the grin on his face and the not-so-silent hiss from his inner feline.

I don't waste my energy growling back. This kitty clearly isn't going to run.

Lissa watches me, and there's way too much worry in her eyes. None of it is because of the cat who's got her tucked against his side, though.

I get a better grip on my wolf. Any friend of Lissa's is welcome here, no matter how much he riles my more primitive instincts. The pack moving in close behind me is reinforcing the same message. This man is no threat to anyone I'm trying to protect, and I have plenty of experience dealing with annoying.

Lissa smiles at me, gladness in her eyes, and steps away from her guest. "Hayden, this is Reese Tofino, alpha of the Lonely Peak cats. Reese, this is Hayden Scott."

"It's good to meet you." I try to get a better read on him as I hold out my hand. Cats rarely choose alphas, and Lissa wasn't willing to spill many of the beans on this one. Something about our animals needing to sort things out before our humans got involved.

He looks me up and down, not hiding his measuring stick any better than I am. "I've heard you're not an asshat like the last alpha."

"He was evil." I keep my voice quiet and calm, but I let him see the truth in my eyes. He doesn't flinch, which earns him points from me and my wolf. "I make mistakes, but none of them involve intentionally causing harm to my pack."

He nods his head fractionally. "That's a decent start."

My wolf tries to growl. I whack his nose. He needs to behave, impertinent cat or not. Lissa will not appreciate any displays of Neanderthal canine.

He pouts, but he settles.

The cat alpha smirks.

I shoot him a dirty look. "You're not helping."

He laughs, which means he's got balls of steel—and a good understanding of just how touchy wolves can be when a mate bond is forming.

I exhale slowly. An annoying guy with a sense of humor and decent radar, I can work with.

Someone snorts from behind me. "Are you two done yet?" Myrna steps around me and pulls Reese in for a hug. "Because I haven't seen this man for years, so if you don't mind, maybe we can all greet him properly and then the two of you can get back to your alpha pissing contest."

Reese tugs on the ends of her hair. "Wolves have pissing contests. Cats just win."

I smother a laugh. The cats of Whistler Pack drive my mother crazy every chance they get. She also actively recruits every single one of them that can tolerate wolf-shifter hierarchy. Something about them being the best antidote ever to alphas with big heads and a pack structure getting too stiff for anyone to breathe.

I should be fine. My head gets deflated around here on a regular basis.

Myrna glances at me. "Early lunch?"

Reese scowls. "You have to ask permission to feed a guest?"

She elbows him. "No. Quit causing trouble. I've never been in a pack as good for submissives as we are now."

I don't miss the fractional widening of the cat alpha's eyes.

Or the pride that moves through my wolf.

Lissa steps forward. Robbie is tucked into her side, looking up at the new arrival with curious eyes. "Lunch would be good. I think Shelley and Eliza were putting together sandwiches."

I can hear the happiness in her voice, the simple pleasure at being able to welcome a guest. It shakes me hard. Every damn time I think I know what my pack has been through, something like this happens to make me realize I'm full of shit.

"Is this your son, Liss?" Reese squats down, his eyes over-bright, and smiles. "Robbie, right? I heard you bit your alpha the first time you met him. That's just what a smart cub would do. Maybe you're part cat."

Robbie shakes his head.

"Hmm." Reese makes a face. "Part bear, then? I hear you have a good friend who's a bear."

I shoot Kennedy a look, but she's staring at the back of Reese's head with her eyes narrowed. She clearly didn't tell him that. Which means he's a smart cat who did his research.

Reese looks up from his crouch and meets my eyes calmly. "I've been reading your newspaper, just like everyone else. Thank you for doing that. There are a lot of us who have missed our friends here, and it's been really nice to see their faces."

There are quiet hisses and whimpers and indrawn breaths all over my pack. I try my damnedest to ignore them. The secrets in this pack need to unwrap in their own time and place, no matter how much my wolf thinks teeth and claws could speed things up. "Reilly and Myrna put that out. I just try not to be the headline."

The cat alpha shoots Myrna a grin as he stands. Then he unerringly finds Reilly, who's standing quietly in the background holding Kelsey's hand. "You take good photos. They tell a real story."

Reilly blushes and looks at the ground, mumbling something that comes out mostly bear. Kelsey pats his arm, which makes Reese grin and send her a conspiratorial wink.

My wolf wrinkles his nose, correctly recognizing that I probably won't let him chew on a cat who's being kind to pups and submissives, especially when he's clearly not doing it to curry favor with me. "Stay for lunch. You can tell us why you're here, and Reilly can take some photos for the next edition."

Wry amusement glints in eyes that are more cat than human. "I came for the usual reasons. To see my friends and steal some of Shelley's cookies."

I hide a snort. He's a wise-ass and he's also not telling me anything close to the full truth, but this is not my first cat rodeo. I keep that knowledge to myself, however, and start moving in the general direction of where we eat, scooping up a couple of pups as I go.

Reese follows, his shrewd eyes taking in the well-developed seating around the fire pit and the detritus of pack life spread all over the ground. He looks over at the tiny woman walking beside him. "I heard you burnt down your den."

His tone is light, casual, amused.

My wolf sighs. Definitely no chewing.

Myrna grins and leads Reese over to a comfy log. "All of it except the kitchen. We're getting a new den this fall. HomeWild-built."

Reese makes sure she sits down beside him. "We're

looking at one of those. They're not cheap, but the designs are fantastic."

Myrna smiles as proudly as if she gave birth to Rio herself. "Make sure you order one of Danielle's polished-concrete tables."

His eyes follow hers to our resident table-maker. "I've seen photos of your samples. It's enough to make a guy want to bribe you to come live with some troublesome cats."

Danielle squirms, embarrassed, but her wolf is delighted. "I haven't made a big one yet. I don't know how it will work out."

Rio takes a seat against another log. "It will work. If it doesn't, we'll go pick some more river rocks and try again. Genius doesn't have to work the first time."

Reese nods, like he isn't at all surprised to find HomeWild's lead designer joining the conversation. Tricky cat. He did a lot more than read Reilly's articles. Which I have to respect him for, but it puts me at a disadvantage. I know his territory runs along our western border, but that's nearly all I know. Which suddenly feels like a rather large oversight.

One I can fix later. Right now, I need to follow my pack's lead—and keep a close eye on a cat.

13

KENNEDY

Someday, when I grow up a lot more, I'll be able to control my wolf as well as Hayden can. Right now she just wants to bite Reese's tail again, because Shelley left to go get sandwiches with wistful hope in her eyes, and Cori gave Eliza a corner of her t-shirt to wipe away her tears, and Rio is wrapping his arms around Kelsey because she can feel the painful wishes of her pack, even though she doesn't know what they're about.

Myrna reaches over and touches Reese's cheek. "Please. Tell us about our friends."

His smile is sad and a little confused. "You've been chatting with them on ShifterNet."

I swallow. My wolf just figured out a thing, and it's clawing at her hard. "It's not the same. Just like you had to come here and check us out so that your cat could believe what we were telling you." There's more fire in my words than I meant to put in them. I tried so hard to convince him that we were a good pack. That we were ready. That they could all come visit.

"I believed you," he says softly. "That's why I'm here."

Ghost's hand slides into mine. I hold tight, and the knot in my throat eases a little.

Myrna touches Reese's cheek again. "Our wolves haven't had any news for six years. Tell us about everyone."

The corners of his eyes crinkle. "I will, but I'm not very good at wolf songs. Maddie tells me I sound like an alley cat when I howl."

Guilt stabs my ribs. Maddie's a Lonely Peak wolf. She's mated to a cat who tells really bad jokes. I got to go visit their pack a couple of times because my wolf is a badass who can leave her territory without her alpha's permission and not rip herself in two.

Ghost's fingers squeeze mine again, and I realize she's not just helping me to be strong. She's doing what good betas do and reminding me to pay attention and do my job. I look over at Reilly. He's sitting on a rock with a sat phone in his hand, but he's not even trying to take pictures. He's just watching quietly, with yearning in his eyes, waiting to hear Reese's stories.

I didn't even know he remembered the cats.

My wolf rolls to her feet. I did this wrong. "There are sentries who know the cats. I'll go cover the perimeter so they can come listen."

Hayden's eyes soften.

I nod at him. I found a job for me. A hard one, because my wolf wants to hear Reese's stories too, but a right one.

"We'll go." Kel nods his chin at Ebony. "The two of us can cover the inner perimeter as long as we have some extra eyes and ears here on the pups."

I gulp. Neither of our betas really know the cats, and protecting the pups is real work. I can do that. And I can hold Ghost's hand, because she's still kind of shaking. "Make sure Hoot and Kenny come in." I'm not sure whether I'm asking that for Ghost or for them or for me, but Kel nods like it makes sense, and I don't have enough words left to try to explain. I just know that something important is happening today.

Something with my baby pack right at the center.

RIO

Cats are such shit-disturbers.

Sadly, this one has stirred up a bunch of seriously hopeful shit, so I can't just chew on him. I look at my alpha as we try to get makeshift den protection in place. Ebony and Kel have gone to run the perimeter, but my wolf isn't letting me join them. He's convinced that he's needed here.

I'm not sure who's going to be needing me just yet, but I'm kind of suspicious one of them might be a cat, and a baby alpha might be on the list, too.

Hayden shoots me a quick glance as he walks by, herding pups into the center of the gathering pack. I shake my head at his unasked question. Sentinels have no problem taking charge when they need to, but this isn't one of those times.

Myrna smirks at the two of us, which doesn't hide the wistful, tangled ball of grief in her chest any better than the ongoing discussion over what to feed our visitor for lunch. A discussion I should probably pay attention to, because my wolf loves to eat, but he can't. He's too damn busy cataloguing all the underwater emotion in his pack.

I steal half a sandwich as a plate goes by. The truly bossy parts of our pack are making sure the rest of us eat while we get ready to do the deep heart work that's just landed. I keep my eyes on Reese. He's floating around, chatting quietly with various submissives, meeting their pups. Asking questions that make them smile and sharing bits of gossip that make them yearn. I look up as Hayden takes a seat beside me. "He's good with wolves."

"Yeah." He takes a big bite of a sandwich that has way too many pickles. He probably put them there as Rio repellent. "Almost like he's had practice."

"He has." Shelley squeezes her way between us, which my wolf thinks is awesome. He loves seeing her throw her weight around with the big dudes in her pack. "There are three Lonely Peak wolves that I know of, and some of us used to visit quite often."

My sentinel radar goes off.

She leans against my shoulder and keeps talking, almost to herself. "It's hard for Reese to see us like this."

It's shredding him. He knows a lot more than Hayden and I do about how many wolves are missing—and how many scars the ones he can see are wearing. I wrap an arm around her shoulders. "How does it feel for you?"

She inhales, exhales slowly. "It's hard."

She's vibrating, and it isn't just from grief. I wait.

"For so long, we couldn't let anyone look. We didn't dare." She swallows, takes another moment. Casts her eyes over at her alpha. "I know there's not much here to look at if you care about material things, and we'll be really proud of that new den when it arrives. But it feels really good to be proud of who we are right this minute."

Hayden's wolf melts into a puddle of yellow-gold goo.

She smiles down at the ground.

My sentinel tips his head against hers, honoring one of his pack's most scarred warriors. "The new den is just some walls and couches to hold what's already here." I glance over at our visitor—the one carefully walking a tightrope over a lake of grief and choosing to see resilience instead. "He gets that. He sees who we are."

Hayden sighs. "He's not an entirely stupid cat."

Shelley chuckles. "He's on his good behavior."

He's got reasons, just like we do. "You've got friends in his pack, and he's got cats who want to come visit. He's a little shaken, but he's seeing what he needs to see."

She raises an eyebrow. "That sentinel woo of yours has some uses."

My wolf laughs. He likes her, very much.

Hayden snorts and rolls to his feet. He leans down

and kisses the top of her head, and then he strolls off, some kind of pack radar calling to his wolf.

I lean my head against the woman who came over here to make sure her alpha had his sea legs. "You just made his week. You know that, right?"

She snorts. "That's Lissa's job."

The big black wolf of death lolls on the grass and grins at her. The cat is still holding a few tricks up his sleeve, but it doesn't matter. This pack can handle him.

HAYDEN

Lissa joins me as I herd Braden back in the direction of his moms. She's holding two slightly green apples in her hands. "They're pretty tart, but they're local."

I wrap my hand around hers and take a big bite out of one of them. It makes my taste buds pucker, but it hints of something sweet and crisp around the corner. Fall, definitely on its way.

Ravi sits down on a log with his guitar and starts to play softly, keeping an eye on his daughter. Jade is in Reese's lap, breaking off tiny pieces of cookie and feeding them to her new kitty. For a pack that still isn't fond of dominance, we're rolling ridiculously smoothly with a visit from a guy who takes regular baths in it. He's keeping it tamped down, but cat dominance doesn't have an off switch like the wolf version. "He's an interesting guy."

Lissa takes a bite out of my apple and chews contemplatively, watching Reese murmur something to Ravi. "His dad died the year before Samuel took over here."

My heart aches for a man I hardly know. "Was his father alpha?"

Lissa shakes her head. "No. The cats were less organized then. Mostly family groups."

Not unusual. "What happened?"

She smiles. "After the funeral, he invited them all to some island down in Mexico for two months. When they came back, he was alpha and they had a plan. They started up a bunch of small businesses and a school, and a really amazing program for local human kids who want to be naturalists and forest guardians."

My wolf raises a curious ear. The forest guardian program started at Whistler. My mother's idea on how to turn young humans into allies of shifters and wilderness areas both. I spent two summers being the first real shifter most of them had ever met. "You're telling me not to underestimate him."

She laughs quietly. "That, too."

I sigh. She never lets me get away with being pain-in-the-ass teeth and claws. "And that he's a good guy."

"He is." She pauses. "He pulled his pack together when everyone was grieving, including him. He did it with sand and sunshine and dreams, and he's here because he's a lot like you. He tries really hard to do the right thing, even when it rips him to pieces." She grins and kisses my cheek. "So, don't chew on the kitty. Even if he absolutely deserves it."

I pout, because it always amuses her, and because I want to distract her enormous, tender heart that's bleeding some today, even if it's for a really good cause. "You never let me have any fun."

She laughs. "That's not what you said last night."

My wolf pounces as her cheeks turn pink, delighted with her. And sighs as a small head batters into us a second later. Robbie, come to join in the game with Mellie hot on his heels.

The damn cat has the audacity to laugh.

I scowl. I might have to chew on him at least a little.

Lissa pets me, which helps. Robbie rubs his cheek against my chest, which helps more. I sigh. Shelley's right. We have a long way to go—and we can be really proud of who we are today.

I look up to find a cat watching me with something resembling approval in his eyes.

My wolf snorts.

I ignore him. He turned into all bark and no bite about two minutes after the annoying kitty arrived. I watch as Reese reaches over and picks up some knitting that's sitting on a log. He eyes Myrna consideringly. "You making blankets?"

Her eyes light up. She's already worked a couple of deals in the ShifterNet online trading forum, and it's unleashed a menace. "Dozens. You need some?"

"Yes." The cat alpha's reply is emphatic. "All of ours have holes, and you know cats have no patience for knitting."

Myrna snorts. "I know *you* don't. It can't be helped if you're setting a bad example for the rest of your pack."

Reese replies with an entirely delinquent grin that makes her cackle.

My wolf watches with interest. We've reached the nuts and bolts of this visit, and the guy is clearly planning to ignore me. Rebuilding easy relations with the rest of my pack while treating me like vaguely boring wallpaper.

I roll to my feet as Myrna starts discussing possible trade items and hide a grin. If he thinks doing business with my submissives will piss me off, he has a long wait coming. I grab one of the platters Shelley has just arrived with and nod at her to sit down.

I can be on sandwich duty. My pack's got this.

REESE

He's handing out freaking sandwiches.

Cats try not to be impressed by anyone, but Adrianna Scott won us over a long time ago. I expected her son to be a spoiled little shit, though. He's not. He's also not the powerhouse I was expecting. Samuel was the most dominant wolf I've ever met, and Kennedy said the new guy won in a fair fight—or as fair as it gets when he tries to take the high road and an ugly street brawler tries to cheat.

I would have offered him respect just for getting rid of that blight, but I didn't expect to like him. He makes it damn hard not to, though. Every shifter in this pack obviously adores him. The pups treat him like friendly furniture and the submissives go out of their way to pat his wolf on the head. Power doesn't earn you either of those.

They love him.

And he clearly loves the fuck out of Lissa, which isn't going to hurt his standing with me or my cats either.

I sigh. It still isn't going to be easy. My cat isn't done trying to shred my insides, and I thought I was prepared for this visit. There are so many wolves missing, so many holes where friends once stood. I'm hearing snippets, small murmurs. Some are still around, although my cat's not sure what kind of shape they're in.

I'm sorely tempted to send my trackers to check, but sadly, tromping all over this alpha's territory would violate my sense of how to treat a decent neighbor. I intend to have a very long conversation with him, though. After I'm done with the far more important ones.

The small pup in my lap turns furry and heads out on the dead run, chasing another wolf her size. Eliza drops down beside me, laughing. "I'm amazed she sat still for that long. Did you get any of that cookie or did she eat it all?"

I let her laughter soothe my cat. "I'm good. So are the cookies."

Her head rests briefly on my shoulder. "It's really good to see you here."

I lean in. We were juveniles together, part of a group of friends who ran easily across packs and found food and a place to sleep when we needed one. "Where is everyone, E?"

She winces. "Some are around."

Not nearly enough, but if their alpha can wait for that story, then I'll damn well duct tape my cat to a tree and make him wait, too. Which is going to be one of the hardest things I've ever done. Nobody plots revenge like a bobcat—and one of the chief architects of the evil that happened here is still living.

I stroke Eliza's hair gently, offering wordless comfort to her wolf and my cat. Which doesn't last long. Her head lifts up off my shoulder, her eyes suddenly worried.

I turn, my cat getting a sniff of Kenny's wolf before I see him. Which is good—I'm not sure I would have recognized him otherwise. He was the oldest in our juvenile cohort, but he doesn't look it now. His eyes are those of a man who aged decades in the last six years. I heard he stayed pack beta under Samuel. It's one of the reasons I never got worried enough. Looking in his eyes, I understand just how badly I fucked up.

I roll to my feet, my cat desperate to put paws on his broken wolf. I wrap my arms around him as soon as I'm close enough. I don't wait for permission. I don't think I would get it, and his wolf needs the touch of a friend who remembers the good in him more than he needs to breathe.

He doesn't move. He just stands there quietly with my arms wrapped around the shell of him.

My cat moves a trip to polar-bear country way up his

list. I keep that promise quiet, though. Vengeance isn't what the whipcord guy who can't hug me back needs.

He needs forgiveness.

I look around, because no way can I give it to him, and his pack maybe has good reasons not to—and see four shifters circled around us. Reilly, who I mostly remember as a round, squishy toddler. Kennedy, watching us with eyes that are going to give me nightmares now that I know more about what turned a rambunctious kid into a lethal weapon. And two more teenage girls, who are eyeing her and waiting for instructions.

My cat smiles. Kennedy has a girl pack, complete with bonus bear—and apparently they've adopted Kenny. I shoot Hayden a quick glance, because I only know of one wolf who tolerates that kind of cat antics in her pack.

His lips quirk.

My cat snorts. Fine. Apparently I know two.

I give Kenny one more squeeze and let him go. I need to warn my cats. Ravi's wolf is healing. This one isn't, yet, and wolves don't heal their most wounded in the middle of a pile of fur the way we do. Which means I can't show up here with thirty cats and party supplies like we planned. For lots of reasons.

With this many missing wolves, it would be a fucking wake.

Which means I need excuses, ways to start sending small groups back and forth, because otherwise my cats will mutiny.

Fortunately, I came equipped with several.

14

KENNEDY

Uh, oh. I know that look. That is totally a scheming-cat look.

I eye Reese. He just flattened Kenny's wolf. He needs to not cause any more trouble for a bit.

He grins, because he's an annoying cat who doesn't listen to silent warnings. "My pack has some thoughts on how we might start working together. You guys remember Sienna and Sierra, right?"

They're Maddie's twins. Cat shifters with wolf eyes. We used to make cookies and mischief together.

Hoot's eyes shine. Her scrappy wolf loved visiting Lonely Peak.

"Do they remember me?"

I frown at the bear who just blurted out that question. Reilly was only four when we stopped visiting with other packs. Sienna and Sierra used to love reading to him, but I've never heard him talk about them. Ever.

Reese nods, his eyes gentle. "Yes. They read every single article you write and zoom in on every photograph you take and they're so proud of you. They don't think you remember them, though."

Reilly doesn't say anything. He just curls his knees a little tighter into his chest as tears drip down his cheeks. His mom comes up behind him and wraps her arms around him, making the noises that used to soothe him when he was a small bear.

Sierra and Sienna used to make those noises, too.

Hoot leans into Ghost's shoulder, her eyes wet.

My wolf wants to shred things. Her baby pack is so sad right now. All of them. I just want to let out an awful wail for what we lost and won't ever get back.

Hoot reaches for my hand.

I take it, but I don't let my tears fall. I can't. I didn't lose nearly the most, and my wolf is way too angry to let her feel all the way sad. I keep ahold of Hoot's fingers, though, and I watch Reilly's tears, and I let them cry a little for me, too. And I let my brain work, because Hayden says that wolves need jobs when they're wounded, and even Reilly has a wolf in him, and maybe the scheming in Reese's eyes could be a very good thing.

I sniff and look at him. "What do Sienna and Sierra want?"

I catch a flicker of relief in his eyes before he grins. "They want Reilly. And some wolves who are good in the woods."

Hoot sits up so fast she nearly bangs her head on Ghost's chin.

I put a really different kind of warning to Reese in my eyes. He needs to be careful. So, so careful. Our woods have lots of secrets, and almost all of them are Hoot's to keep.

He nods slowly, a cat who doesn't ignore messages when they're really important. "Let me tell you what they're proposing, and then you can tell me what might be a good fit for your pack."

He's looking straight at me. Trusting me to take care of Hoot's secrets and a bear's soft heart and anything else that might matter.

My wolf looks over at Hayden, alarmed.

He catches the pickle falling out of Braden's sandwich and smiles at me, like a baby alpha handling tricky negotiations for her pack is totally normal. That can't possibly be right, but Hoot's eyes are shiny and Reilly is a bear statue and somebody needs to do something really soon.

I swallow hard. My wolf remembers Sienna and Sierra. Maybe this is just about teenagers, and not as important and official as it sounds. I look at Reese and nod. I can help him be careful about the woods.

He smiles. "A couple of years back, they started a video channel. FollowTheCats.com. You might have heard of it."

Reilly lets out a soft, awed sigh. "They do that? They're famous."

I'm kind of lost. "We haven't had much internet. We

have it now, but it's summer, so only some of us use it. Like Reilly. He does a lot of research."

Reilly's cheeks turn pink.

Reese nods, like it's totally normal for a ten-year-old bear to be smart like that. "They post video blogs, mostly following a couple of local wild bobcat families. It started as a side gig to our forest guardian program, because after the human kids went home, they still wanted to know about the wild cats they had seen."

"They make awesome videos." Reilly's hands are waving like they do when he's really excited. "They tell a whole story, about the wild cubs and how they learn, and how cats know when a new season is coming, and what it's like to be a bobcat teenager, and sometimes they add funny parts about being a shifter, too."

Reese glances over at Myrna and Hayden. "Those are carefully screened. We're meticulous about keeping pack life private, and also about respecting the wild family groups they follow. The girls won a big naturalist award last year. It's very well done."

Hayden huffs out a laugh. "I know. Whistler Pack has a group subscription. We were some of your biggest fans."

That troublemaking look lands back in Reese's eyes. "I figured that was just the pack's teenage girls."

Rio snorts. "Don't say that where Adrianna Scott can hear you. She loves that channel almost as much as she loves Reilly's photo essays."

Reese blinks, and his cheeks turn kind of pink just like Reilly's. "The girls are going to die when I tell them."

"Tell them not to do that." Hayden's voice is casual, but something in his wolf isn't. "I'm sure she'd love to meet them the next time she comes to visit."

My wolf sits up fast. That's alpha permission for something no one has said out loud yet. Reese knows it, too. I grin at him. "She's really nice. And only a little bit scary."

He makes a wry face. "They'll ask her to do a video appearance. They're completely jealous that Reilly got a big scoop when she came to visit you guys."

Reilly's eyes shine. "Maybe we can do something together."

Reese smiles slowly. "Actually, that's exactly what they have in mind."

HAYDEN

I know what cats smell like right before they cause trouble. This one is stinking of it. Sadly, I think it's the good kind of trouble, and Kennedy's baby pack is practically quivering. Even Kenny is paying attention.

Reese is playing to his audience, but I don't miss the smirk in his eyes as he very intentionally doesn't look at me. He's not asking for permission anymore. I'm impressed he did at all. I hope he realizes I wasn't giving it to him. Kennedy might have some growing up to do yet, but helping Reilly be a cub reporter for a couple of teenage cats is entirely in her wheelhouse.

And I don't know enough about what Hoot is protecting to have this conversation.

My wolf tries to whine about that. I tell him to be fucking glad that this many people care about his pack, instead.

Reese glances casually at his larger audience. "The girls have a big following for their cat stuff. They've also done ravens, and occasionally a bear when I can get one to cooperate. But their viewers have been clamoring for wolves since forever."

Something he clearly had the smarts to veto. A wild wolf could pretty thoroughly mess with a young shifter bobcat.

Reese turns his attention back to Kennedy's baby pack. "The girls would like an hour of video a week, which takes about ten hours of raw footage to put together."

Ghost clears her throat. "Just wild wolves, right?"

Reese nods. "Absolutely. We aren't going to turn shifters into reality TV, although some of our cats do like to narrate in front of the camera. Whether you did or not would be up to you. Sienna and Sierra are happy to do voiceovers."

My wolf only needs one look at Reilly's eyes to know how that's going to turn out. So he keeps his focus on the cat alpha, who has just offered up real work for some of the shifters in my pack who are most in need of something to do. As overtures of pack friendship go, it's a really excellent one—and also oddly psychic. I try to remember if there were any hints of bobcat in the diner.

Every cat I know is willing to eavesdrop for the greater good.

Reilly clears his throat. "I don't know how to use a video camera. I could learn, but I bet they're really expensive."

I wince. Good point, kid. One we'll solve, but a ten-year-old bear shouldn't have gotten there first.

"Won't be a problem." Reese leans back against the log. "The proposal comes with an offer to split revenues. I can have them email Lissa the details, but your share will easily cover a couple of video cameras, a laptop, and probably the monthly mortgage payment on a HomeWild sleeping module, too."

Reilly squeaks. My wolf doesn't make any sound quite that undignified, but it's a close thing. That's hella bigger than an overture of friendship.

Reese definitely smirks this time. He finds Lissa in the crowd, staring at him with big eyes. "I hate spreadsheets, but that's what they tell me. They're also offering additional revenue splits if you've got a couple of wolves who would be willing to hang out in the online forums and chat. It's mostly enthusiastic kids with questions, and we have adult moderators to keep everything safe."

Lissa tries to speak and nothing comes out. She clears her throat and tries again. "You can't be serious about the sleeping module."

Three bedrooms and a small common area that snap on to a shared walkway. I know what they cost. Lissa has a dozen of them on her most secret wish list.

Reese snorts. "I'm totally serious. Half my pack's

income is earned by teenagers." He grins at me. "Be warned, it makes their heads big. They're the primary reason we're about to buy a bunch of stuff from your sister."

I hope he told Jules that story. Clients who make her howl with laughter get much better prices.

I lean back and look at him. It's a generous and very sneaky offer. Submissives are far better at getting close to the wild wolves. He's not just encouraging friendly relations. He's fortifying the women and pups of my pack. Arming them. Doing what he can to make sure that what happened to them never happens again.

I can play the fall guy for that. "You said revenue share." Thanks to my gaming royalties, that's the one financial concept I mostly understand.

His eyes glint. "Yes. Our pack will be making nice money off this as well."

Smart, tricky alpha. Generosity without a whiff of charity. I sigh. If you can't beat a cat, it usually pays to join them. "What kind of a team would typically handle an hour of video production a week?"

He manages to keep a straight face. "It varies, but at least a couple of people who know how to use a video camera and a couple more who are good trackers. More if you want to handle editing and on-screen reporting."

I sit back and grin as Kennedy literally jolts. Sometimes there's nothing more awesome than watching lightning strike a wolf.

KENNEDY

Hayden said I would know. I want to leap into the air, because I totally do, but baby alphas are supposed to listen and not do all the talking. So I sit on my wolf, which is crazy difficult, and elbow Hoot. Hard.

She sits up straight, her eyes wide. "Reilly can learn how to do anything, and I bet he can teach me how to use a video camera. I'm a pretty good tracker, and I know where the wild wolves live. There's a small pack a couple of hours from here." She grins at Reese and hugs her ribs. "They just had pups in the spring. Twins."

He makes a wry face at Lissa. "Make that two sleeping modules."

Reilly swallows so hard his throat clicks. "We could earn money for the pack? For real?"

Reese nods. "Yup. You'd be helping both of our packs. Wolf videos would pull in new subscribers, which is good for revenues, but it also means we'd have more people interested in keeping our forests awesome, which is a big part of why we do this. I saw your SchoolNet lesson on black holes the other day. The girls do live video chats sometimes. I bet they'd love your help with those."

I sigh. My wolf is feeling really bad she bit his tail. It's time to be nice to a kitty, teenager style. "Seriously? You watch school lessons? In the summer?"

Reese smirks at me. "We're cats. We like to be smart."

I throw a pinecone at his head.

He catches it and rolls his eyes. My baby pack snickers, even Kenny.

Reese looks at Hoot and Reilly. "It sounds like you'll be the ones leading things over here. I'll tell Sierra and Sienna to contact you." He glances at Hayden. "Their version of that will probably be to run over here as fast as they can convince someone to drive them."

Hayden's lips quirk. "I figured."

I hug my ribs just like Hoot did. I haven't seen them for ages and Hoot and Ghost haven't seen them for six years and neither have a bunch of the sentries and this is going to be so good. Hoot knows exactly where all the ghosts in the woods are, and she can make sure we do this without disturbing their peace.

I grin at Reilly. "You're going to be famous."

He looks delighted and horrified and awed and excited, all mixed up in one adorable bear.

Reese laughs. "You can stay behind the camera if you like. But I'm pretty sure you'll hear the girls screaming from here if I tell them they have a new bear reporter."

Reilly looks over at Myrna, a little frantic. "I can still do the newspaper." His eyes shoot to Ebony and Kel. "And my pack chores. And my lessons."

Ebony grins at him. "Duh."

He turns around to look at Danielle, who's sitting right behind him.

She just gives him the kind of smile that the very best moms give their pups when they're really proud of them.

My wolf wriggles in delight. A job for Reilly, and it's real and important and it sees exactly who he is, and the whole world is going to love him because he's sweet and smart and awesome. The job for Hoot is quieter, but it's special, too, and it will give her lots of time at the den and it can fit with what she does for Bailey.

Danielle looks at Reese shyly. "If you have video cameras that need repairs, I could try to help."

He snorts. "We're cats who break things and suck at fixing them. We tried sending our broken gear to the ravens to get fixed. They sent it back missing all the shiny parts."

Reilly giggles. "My mom can fix anything, and she doesn't collect shiny parts."

Reese winks at Reilly. "That would be great. We have three broken video cameras, and probably a couple more I don't know about. If your mom fixes those, they'd be more than enough to get you started." His gaze travels casually back to Danielle. "If you're willing, I'll send over a truckload of other broken things so that we don't drown you in repair work when you come for a visit."

When. I cuddle my knees. We're going to have visits.

Reese carefully ignores the sniffles and tears as that sinks into our pack and grins at Lissa instead. "Since all my wishes are apparently being granted today, we could also use some spreadsheet help."

She eyes him, curious and a little hesitant. "How much help?"

"So much. Save me, please." Reese bats his eyelashes at her, which makes Hayden growl and the rest of us laugh. "We run four small businesses, and all the cats who've tried to wrangle our numbers have promptly quit.

We use a human bookkeeper in town at the moment, but I think she's getting ready to kill me. Something about the indecency of paying with fish and berries instead of real money."

Lissa laughs. "I made some spreadsheets that allow for barter payments, if she'd like a look at them."

Reese pretends to swoon, which is really brave, since Hayden is sitting close enough to chew on him. "Please tell me you've trained a minion we could borrow."

She makes a face and shakes her head.

My wolf wants to wriggle backward and hide, just in case they try to pick her. She hates numbers.

I tell her to focus. Maybe this is another baby pack job. It doesn't feel like it, though. Reilly is good at numbers, but he has a big new job already, and Hoot and Ghost are both wrinkling their noses just like I am. I glance at Kenny, but he used to get Evan to help Jason with his math homework.

Evan.

My wolf snaps to attention. "I know someone."

Lissa stares at me and so does Reese. Hayden just has this funny smile on his face.

"Evan's really good at math." I wince and face my alpha, because it's not nearly that simple, and it's hard to put what my wolf knows into words. "I know he's been a jerk and he hasn't earned back his den privileges yet, but I saw him kicking a tree and wishing he could be anywhere but here. I think maybe his wolf needs that to get better."

Reese's eyebrows go up. "You want me to give my spreadsheets to one of your asshole dominants?"

I gulp. "I think maybe you should take him with you, instead. But I don't know what's right for you. I just know what's maybe right for Evan." Even that part sounds really arrogant, and he's not in my baby pack.

"She might be right."

Kenny's gravelly voice totally surprises my wolf. We all turn to look at him.

He grimaces. "He's a decent kid who ended up running with a bunch of bad influences. He's got a layer of jerk on him, but nothing a bunch of cats couldn't handle."

Reese smirks.

Kenny makes a face. "He deserves a chance. He moved into town with the rest of the guys, but he doesn't want to be there. And he is good with numbers. I don't think he's ever seen a spreadsheet, but he's smart when he applies himself. He'd learn."

I can't believe he's agreeing with me. "I think a cat pack might work out okay for him. He likes to be different."

Reese studies me thoughtfully. "I remember him when he was younger. He was a good kid."

"He was our friend," says Layla quietly, taking Miriam's hand. "Back when a lot of the pack still had trouble with our relationship."

There's real happiness in Reese's eyes. "I'm glad to see that's changed."

She smiles back at him. "It has. But Evan was one of the first."

Reese tips his head side to side a couple of times. Then he looks at Hayden. "I'll take him if he's willing to come. On the condition that I get to go to the house in town and yank on some tails while I collect him."

Hayden smiles. "Sure."

Reese's eyebrows shoot up.

I grin. It's hard to surprise a cat. Hayden's a really good alpha.

Hayden smiles at me instead of at Reese. "That's a really good idea. I hope Evan is smart enough to take the offer."

Reese snorts. "I know how to be persuasive."

Hayden leans back, amused. "Really? I haven't seen that yet."

My wolf isn't watching the two of them, even though they're really funny. She's watching Kenny. He isn't saying a word, and he's not watching the alpha comedy act either.

He's staring off at nothing.

And he's smiling.

15

RIO

Kelsey snuggles into my lap. Her wolf is at least as happy as mine is, even though she doesn't have a clue what spreadsheets and video cameras are. She can feel the flowers of her pack opening to the sun. I keep my eyes on Kennedy and a certain cat, because I don't think the sun is done shining just yet.

Reese turns to look at Shelley. "I've got a second offer. From our gardeners."

My wolf snickers. There we go.

I shake my head at him. He doesn't even like green stuff.

He ignores me, and for good reason. He might not eat lettuce, but he adores the wolves who tend it and grow it and use it to transform their trauma into potent, fertile, pack-feeding soil. Shelley is practically levitating, her eyes glued to the cat who's apparently decided we've passed all his tests.

Reese smiles at her. "We have a large garden and a makeshift greenhouse. That lets us grow a few things that are tricky in these parts. Tomatoes, squash, watermelons."

Every set of ears in the pack perks up.

Shelley wriggles happily. "I planted some watermelons. Rio's going to help me build something to keep them warm in the fall."

Reese glances at me. "I have a teenager who's rigged together some plans for a fancier greenhouse."

The big, black wolf of death knows a setup when he sees one. "Plastic or glass?"

Reese shrugs. "Whatever we can afford, but if we build two of them, the shipping of materials we'd need from down south would be a lot cheaper."

Hayden pitches an entirely unnecessary pinecone at my head. I snort and throw it back at him. "The HomeWild sleeping modules have a long wall that could easily be modified to add a greenhouse. We could look at turning one into a modular school so the kids could help with the growing."

Silent, happy fireworks go off all over my pack. Kelsey sings a wordless melody, one that's nothing but pure wish. Reilly just looks at me, every kind of hope shining in his eyes.

My wolf shakes his head. They're pulling out the big guns, and they don't need them. He's so damn easy. I look down at the small singer in my lap and put words to her song. "So, we take the money Reilly and Hoot are going to earn, and we use it to build out a school and a greenhouse. Watermelons all year round. That sounds easy enough."

Especially once Jules gets wind. There are a lot of northern packs with short growing seasons.

Reese isn't sure why watermelons are making my whole pack happy, but he knows how to land on his feet. "Two greenhouses."

I can play this game. "Design services will cost you. What do you have to offer in trade?"

Myrna cackles.

Reese rolls his eyes, but I have a solid read on his cat. He's so freaking happy that he's forgotten he's sitting in the middle of a bunch of wolves, and I just tossed him a pitch right in the middle of his strike zone. "Plenty of fresh fruits and vegetables during the summer. We trade with a local farm for eggs and butter and milk, so we can offer some of those, too. We've got a similar deal going with the ravens."

Shelley's wolf is going to explode from happiness any minute. I grin at her. "If I get cookies out of this arrangement, we have a deal."

She laughs, and it's the purest version of happiness I've ever heard from her.

Kelsey sings along in my lap, a pup who knows exactly how to celebrate joy.

Reese looks at the two of them and turns into a feline puddle. "Elsa is head of our gardening team. She's human. She met one of my cats in the tool aisle of the hardware store a couple of years back and they were a done deal by the time they got to the hammers. She's going to be really happy to meet the two of you."

"We're three," says Shelley quietly, smiling at Ghost.

The cat looks chagrined that he missed a beat.

My wolf shakes his head. Silly cat. Offering the moon and the stars and feeling guilty that's all he's got.

Ghost smiles at him, which does way more to help with the guilt than anything a sentinel could do. "I chat with Elsa in the gardening forum. She has some really good ideas about vertical growing and cross-cultivation."

I blink. The cat isn't the only one missing beats. Those sound like things the greenhouse designer should know about, and he's clueless. "Those don't sound like ways to grow cheese."

Kelsey giggles in my lap. Ghost rolls her eyes. Kennedy's eyes narrow. One baby alpha, hearing a beat the rest of us haven't heard yet. She looks at Reese. "How do we get the green stuff and cheese from you?"

I wince. My truck is not going to make it through this unscathed.

Reese shrugs casually. His cat isn't nearly that relaxed. An alpha paying very careful attention—and watching a teenage girl for the cues he needs. Which is not hurting his standing with the pack's more recent immigrants at all. "For the veggies, we can meet you in town, or deliver here if you'll let a couple of teenagers and a truck onto your territory. We generally head out to the ravens once a week May through October, and we could add you to that run. Every two weeks in the winter if you want milk and eggs."

Kennedy grins at me. "We could do some of the driving."

I shake my head. "You're fourteen. You can't legally drive my truck for two years yet."

She doesn't even pause. "Hoot's sixteen."

I smother a grin at what I can hear coming.

Her eyes sizzle with sudden glee. "Learner drivers need an adult in the vehicle with them, right? Kenny could do that."

If looks could kill, both of us would have just died.

The big, black wolf of death snickers. After two decades of following Kel around, he's immune to glares of all kinds. "That could work." I can't think of any better or more annoying therapy for Kenny than spending hours every week stuck in a truck full of teenagers. And it will give him a chance to visit people who can do for him what we can't. Reese's brief hug earlier offered him something priceless—the simple, uncomplicated assumption that Kenny's a good guy.

Which means I'm going to hand over the keys to my truck and not even whimper much.

Shelley nods. "That's settled, then. We can sort out a rotation of visits along with the deliveries back and forth."

Reese bats his eyelashes at her. "Do drivers get cookies?"

She laughs. "If you're a good cat."

I grin. I'm pretty sure he's going to leave here drowning in them.

LISSA

This is going to break my spreadsheets. I have no idea what the exchange rate for zucchini and cookies should be, and that's before we add in Rio's design services and reasonable delivery charges for eggs and cheese and Danielle's repairs and whatever else Myrna is quietly scheming.

My wolf doesn't care. She knows the answer doesn't actually matter all that much. Reese has come and yanked on our tails and then handed us exactly what I hoped he would. Connection. A chance to contribute and earn and receive in the wider world. I just didn't expect it to be quite this big or have so many forms of currency.

My fingers are itching for my laptop. I'll make it work.

Hayden smiles at me. "Think your spreadsheets can handle this?"

I laugh. "No."

Reese grins. "Figure it out, hotshot. And then show Evan."

That's going to be interesting. And good, I think. Evan has always chafed under authority, and Reese is really good at being bossy in invisible ways. So is Hayden, but Evan can't take the steps that would bring him home to find that out. Maybe a new path is just what he needs. "The financial geeks have been talking in the ShifterNet trading forum. I have some ideas."

"Good." Reese reaches out to touch Eliza's knitting

again. "The ravens would probably like to get in on this. Dealing locally is a good thing. They'll want knitted blankets. They've got a couple of hatchlings due in the fall."

Eliza sighs happily. She loves knitting tiny things.

Reese looks over at her and smiles. "We've got a cub on the way, due in midwinter to a mated pair who've been waiting a long time. If you can make a few special baby items, I know a lot of cats who would be looking to trade."

Eliza shoots me a careful glance. She's not the only one who loves knitting tiny things. "We can do that."

Reese sits very still, but I can see his cat radar going off. He might not know how many knitters we have in the woods, but he can sense that something important just landed. "I don't want to overload you, but we also have a bunch of littles who are making do with hand-me-down blankies."

Myrna glares at him. "There's no charge for cub blankets."

He raises an eyebrow. "Fine. Watermelons are also free."

I snicker. Tricky cat. One who also understands that the details don't truly matter. There's value going both ways, and we haven't even gotten most of the Lonely Peak crew or the shadow pack involved yet. But we have some first steps, and those will give the rest some space to happen, and even though this is a big deal, I can't feel anyone who's nervous or anxious or scared.

They're all too busy figuring out the trade value of Shelley's cookies.

Hayden's wolf wraps around me before his arms do. He kisses the back of my neck as I lean into his warmth. "You were right. It's good that I didn't bite his tail."

Reese probably would have found that funny. "I didn't know he would bring this much." Partly because I didn't know just how well all their businesses have grown and flourished. It makes me sad to realize all that we've missed—and it gives me hope. "Did you see Reilly's eyes when the school idea came up?"

He chuckles against the back of my head. "Life forms in the next galaxy saw those eyes."

Our pack has gotten so weirdly, adorably geeky. I wrap my arms over his. It's time for another secret to come into the light. "Bailey was our teacher. Before."

A quick, astonished inhale. "You're kidding me."

My heart aches for all that she's missed, too. "She was really different back then. Always feisty, but she had huge patience with the pups."

His fingers lace themselves with mine. "That's not the part that surprises me. She still has that patience. The young wolves I've met who live out with her are the most capable, well-adjusted shifters in this pack."

That's a compliment the Bailey of six years ago would cherish.

He rests his cheek against my ear. "It must have been really hard for her. To know her pack needed a warrior instead of a teacher, and to let go of so much of herself to deliver it."

My eyes close. Even without most of the soul-crushing details, he sees. "Yes."

A long silence as he nuzzles my wolf. Comforting her. Seeing her, too. "The new school will be an excellent bribe."

I laugh. "You're such an alpha."

He grins against my neck. "You're the one who's going to figure out how to trade zucchini and video-camera repairs for a school. I'm just the guy who holds stuff while his pack does all the hard work."

At some very deep level, his wolf actually believes that. It's his greatest vulnerability—and perhaps also his greatest gift. "You just want to get rid of all our vegetables."

He nips my ear, which makes me squeak. "Wolves do not eat vegetables. We're carnivores."

Says the man who makes sure Ghost has enough salad to eat every single meal. I cuddle into his acceptance, his easy flexibility with who every wolf in his pack needs to be. And look out at what today has wrought. There are small conversations breaking out all over as knitters and sewers and growers and trackers and wolves who know how to use a computer all start to think and plan and scheme.

A pack ready to join the wider world.

GHOST

This is crazycakes.

I've been talking with some of the gardeners on

ShifterNet. Reilly helped me find them and they're really sweet and helpful and it's been nice to have smart things to tell Shelley. But that didn't feel like this. This isn't just about vegetables. My wolf is hearing something far more important.

We weren't forgotten.

The earth and the moon are still here and so are friends and a whole big world that cares that we exist. Which matters, and I should have known that. I know all about hiding. Sometimes you start to believe you're actually invisible, but we're not. They've been waiting for us all this time, sad that we were missing.

I take a deep breath and check in on my baby pack, because this has been a really big day. Kennedy's happy. I think maybe she hasn't figured out yet that she made sure all of us got special new jobs except for her. That's okay. We're smart wolves and an even smarter bear, and we'll make sure that's not how it turns out in the end.

I grin. We better find something she likes better than hunting zucchini, though.

I want to go talk to Shelley some more, because she's really excited about seeds and fresh farm eggs, but Kel says I'm supposed to listen hard to my wolf, and she thinks there's something I'm still missing. It's not Hoot or Reilly, because they have their heads together with Danielle and Ravi and Miriam, and I don't know what they're cooking up, but they all look like they landed in a vat of Myrna's berry jam. Kenny's scowling, but he's also talking to Eliza with actual words instead of just grunts, and that's pretty awesome.

I sigh. There's something. It's like tracking. When I'm following a really tough trail, I don't really see it—it's more like hearing its echoes.

My wolf frowns. Big pack gatherings have too many smells and sounds. It's hard to hear the wind.

I scratch behind her ears. We'll get better at this.

A shadow sits down beside me. I know it belongs to Kel without looking, because it arrived without making any noise. He does that, even around the den where it just makes people startle. I think part of him still believes he needs to be invisible.

"You're thinking hard."

I shrug. Kel never starts with what he really wants to say. "We all are."

He doesn't say anything.

I sigh. "My wolf can smell something, but I don't know what it is."

"Your wolf has damn good instincts."

I blink. "You can smell it, too?"

He snorts. "All I smell is cat."

My wolf grins. Cats are really stinky. Which is good, or we never would have found this one in the forest.

Kel stretches his legs out and crosses them, one over the other. "Alphas and betas have really different jobs. Hayden and Kennedy and Reese did well at theirs today. Ours hasn't really landed yet."

It makes my wolf feel all strange and wobbly inside when he talks like that. Like I'm wearing clothes that are a size too big but I might grow into them someday. "So they figure out what needs to happen, and we help with the details?"

He chuckles. "Sometimes they have moments of brilliant insight, but mostly, good alphas just listen to their pack and know when to push."

I grin. "Like when Kennedy elbowed Hoot in the ribs to make her talk."

"Yes." He glances at me. "Would Hoot have spoken up without the elbow?"

I make a face. She would have wanted to, but she's got responsibilities. "Maybe. The wild pups are really cute."

Kel huffs out a laugh.

I take a breath. "If alphas listen and push, what do betas do?"

He snorts. "We clean up the messes they make."

I look around and shrug. "I don't see any."

"Exactly."

Huh. "So what do we do?"

"Maybe nothing." He's quiet for a bit, and then he sighs. "Or, you get ready for everything."

My wolf likes that. She gets the feeling he didn't want to say it out loud, though.

He watches me and finally nods a little. "In the middle of a fight, you deal with what is, with what's happening in the moment, because that's how you survive. That's basically been your last six years."

That makes me sad, but he's right.

"In between the fights, sometimes you take the time to look at what could be and make contingency plans in case some of those things happen." He pitches a small pebble into the river and sighs. "But mostly you go talk about growing watermelons and remember that you're fifteen years old. Your pack has plenty of adults who are supposed to be the ones dealing with eventualities."

I just look at him.

His lips quirk. "You're damn good at that silent-stare business."

I smile a little. It's useful, especially when people talk a lot or not quite enough.

He shakes out the knee that bugs him sometimes. "When my wolf is feeling twitchy, sometimes it means that I need to spend some time considering the possibilities. So that I can be ready for them, whatever they are. Most people think that's fairly paranoid, and they're right."

My wolf nudges me. I look at him. "Kennedy. Whatever it is, I think it will be about her."

"That's why you came down from the trees."

I nod quietly.

"You know her. You know how she might react. So think. Plan. Find me or Ebony if you want backup, especially of the annoyingly paranoid kind."

I just might. "I can't be ready for everything."

He chokes off a laugh. "I've been telling my wolf that for forty years. He's crap at listening."

I grin. I like his wolf.

He nudges my shoulder. "Go. Tell Shelley to plant more watermelons."

I snicker. "The greenhouse isn't going to be that big."

His lips quirk. "Bets?"

Nope, no bets, because Reilly and Hoot are going to make so much money and everyone will vote to spend it on watermelons and happiness, even if it means a greenhouse as big as the sky.

I smile. That's so not going to be invisible.

16

HAYDEN

I eye the guy who's about to head off into the woods with a wolf-sized travel bag over his shoulder. Which isn't all that convenient a load for a bobcat to carry. "Sure you don't want a ride?"

He snorts. "I'm not even going to make it halfway back before my cats smell these cookies and start falling out of the damn trees."

Halfway back is still wolf territory, but that line is about to get porous enough that it's not worth posturing over. Especially with a guy who just rained treasure down on my pack and somehow made it look like we're doing him favors. Which we are, but I'm well aware of just how differently this day could have turned out, and how deftly he navigated the minefields. "Thank you."

His lips quirk. "I didn't do it for you."

I roll my eyes. "Duh."

He laughs. "You grew up with too many cats. You're hard to annoy."

I have a pack full of wolves who are drunk on happiness. He'd have to try so much harder to rank as even a mild annoyance. "It sounds like you'll get more chances." Lissa and Shelley were already in ShifterNet chat, sorting out logistics with some of the Lonely Peak cats.

He grins. "As soon as I get home, I'm eating all our watermelons."

I lean against a tree. "I'll be eating Shelley's cookies. Every single day."

He snorts. "Fine. You win." He turns to go—and then he turns back, and I can see the reason he's the alpha of a bunch of cats riding in his eyes. "This offer isn't for you, either. If you ever need strong backs or soft hearts, know that I've got them."

"You'll need both for Evan," I say quietly. "Thank you for taking him." It hurts my wolf to let him go, but I had a quick chat with Kenny. If he can get his head out of his ass, Evan will thrive with the cats. They tend to appreciate initiative and snark in equal measure.

"We've got a good crop of young cats. Ones who think for themselves and manage not to fuck things up too badly. It sounds like he hasn't had much exposure to decent shifters his own age. Or an alpha who sees him as anything other than dominant cannon fodder."

I wince. That kind of history doesn't fix overnight. "If he's causing problems, you know where to find me."

Reese smirks. "I don't need you. Sienna and Sierra are cats, but their mom is a wolf and a badass. She also runs our business that has the most complex bookkeeping needs. She'll have him straightened out in no time."

I might feel sorry for Evan if he hadn't so thoroughly earned what's coming for him. "In that case, maybe I'll call her."

Alpha eyes. "She's mine. You can't have her."

I laugh. "I don't poach happy wolves."

He shoots me another look, mostly warning, with underlying glints of amusement. Then he turns toward the woods he emerged from this morning.

I watch as he disappears into the trees and turn back toward the den. Most of my pack won't need me for days —they're too busy trying to figure out how many knitted blanket squares make a reasonable trade for cheese and eggs. But there are a few my wolf needs to check on.

Starting with a baby alpha who did her pack proud today.

KENNEDY

I scowl at my wolf. Reese is gone and my baby pack is all chatty and content. It's been a good day. She can chill.

She just shakes her head slowly.

I wrap my arms around her neck. Maybe she's just stressed by having a visitor so close to the pups. Silly wolf. Reese is no threat. Kelsey kissed his cheek, and she's never wrong about anyone.

My wolf doesn't settle. If I were furry right now, she'd

be pacing the perimeter, watching for the storm she can smell.

I frown. The storm has already happened, and it was good. Lots of new jobs for the pack, lots of happy wolves, and I might even get a chance to drive Rio's truck again. Kenny might run the truck into a tree on purpose to see if he can get himself fired, but that's a small problem. I know how to handle that one. I need to go talk to Bailey about Hoot's new job, and that's a bigger problem, but my wolf already has some ideas about that, too. Bailey really likes cheese.

My feet pace in circles around the small clearing, trying to unclog whatever my wolf knows and I can't see. It's probably a detail. Sometimes I ignore those because my wolf likes big problems, not little, niggly ones. Maybe I'll ask Ghost. She's really good at niggles.

I turn and face the den and close my eyes. Lissa says that Hayden sees his pack on the back of his eyelids, but I don't. Not the big one or my little one. I can feel my baby pack, though. They're like invisible gravitational beams that attach somewhere inside my ribs.

I breathe in and try to do one of the counting exercises Dorie taught me, the ones that are supposed to quiet my brain but mostly make me feel like a squirrel instead. If my baby pack is inside the big pack, maybe I have gravity beams that run to everyone.

My wolf stops her pacing, intrigued.

That's interesting. I show her the gravity beams, let her feel them.

She licks my nose, like I'm a cute pup but maybe one who isn't very smart.

I roll my eyes and keep looking around in the dark inside me. I should at least have a gravitational beam that runs from me to Hayden. And maybe one to Lissa, too, because that's how alpha pairs work. That's what Myrna says, anyhow. She's maybe just being a troublemaker, but my wolf really likes Lissa, so she's okay with that.

I shake my head. Brain squirrels. Focus.

I don't feel anything. I hope that doesn't mean anything bad. I don't want to be the baby alpha of a rogue small pack. I want us in the middle of everything, growing lettuce and learning how to build a greenhouse and driving and making video stories about wild pups.

My wolf snaps to attention.

I frown at her, but it isn't a brain squirrel this time. It's the very edge of an idea.

I snort. It better not be about growing lettuce.

She laughs at me. Squirrels taste so much better than salad.

I roll my eyes. Squirrels are annoying and speedy and way too likely to run up a tree to be worth the effort. Besides, Ghost made friends with a squirrel family once, so she gets a sad face if anyone hunts them, because it might be the great-great-grand-cousin of the squirrels she fed nuts to that winter.

I grin. Bailey thought that was really dumb, but she still had Fallon trade with Maitland for extra nuts.

Fallon. Bailey. Ghost.

Squirrels and nuts and real jobs and being in the center of everything.

My eyes go wide as I stare right straight at the suddenly raging storm inside my head. It's huge and it's crazy and there are so many gravitational beams and some of them don't attach to anything and that's so much of the problem, but I know how to fix it.

My wolf whines. She wants to bite the gravity beams, chase them to where they need to go.

I shake my head. Teeth and claws aren't how we do this. I spin around, because I need Hayden and I can somehow smell him, and there he is, standing on the edge of my small clearing and watching me like he knows what it's like to have a crazy wolf storm inside your brain.

I gulp. Maybe he does. "I need you to come with me."

17

HAYDEN

I owe Kel and Rio an apology. I used to go on rampages like this, dragging them all over Whistler Pack territory without giving them any information. I'm only now figuring out how just how annoying that was.

My wolf lopes after Kennedy and tells me to chill. He can feel her urgency and he knows where she's headed and this is way more fun than being nice to a cat.

I snort as we angle off toward the part of our territory that's loosely Bailey's turf. I've never been out here alone. I come when I'm invited, and I'm well aware that I've never been to the most important parts. The pack runs through sometimes, following the call of the moon, and there are more voices singing with us on those nights. But even then, there's a veil of caution.

Kennedy is acting like it doesn't exist.

My wolf's alpha instincts stir.

I tell him to enjoy the run and wait to see what she's got brewing. I could see it churning in her as she stood absolutely still in the woods, but she's fourteen years old. She's allowed to do dumbass things for years yet, and if all this accomplishes is another encounter with Bailey or a chance to get the attention of a stray wolf or two, that's plenty of reason to be following a baby alpha on her run through the woods.

I smell incoming angry shifter before I see her. My wolf whirls to face the threat, because Bailey's wolf is streaming dominance and a very clear list of all the ways she plans to detach my limbs from the rest of me.

She never gets the chance.

A teenager in human form steps in between us, holds up a palm, and stops a charging wolf in her tracks.

My wolf blinks, hard, because he has no idea what to do with the human suddenly in his path—or her steely demands for obedience.

I grab him by the ruff and shift, never taking my eyes off the bristling red menace staring me down. I knew Bailey was strong. I never really put that together with what years in a war zone can do to a wolf. The first time I met her, she was at a disadvantage. This time it's on her turf and we both know it.

I pull jeans and a shirt out of the travel bag Kennedy was carrying and try to look like an alpha who has his shit together as I get dressed. Which takes more balls than usual, because shifters in human form don't win fights with angry wolves, even when they've had years of lessons from Kelvin Nogues.

Kennedy growls at the red wolf. "Don't be a stupid-head. I brought him. I need to talk with both of you."

That sounds like an actual plan. I dig into the travel bag, hoping we grabbed one stocked with snacks. I pull out a container of jerky and one of watermelon slices. My wolf grins. He thinks the pink water tastes funny, but he knows it's in the bag because his pack is really fond of his human's foibles.

I keep my eyes on Bailey and slowly lower myself to sitting. "If you're going to stay furry, I'm guessing you'd rather have jerky than watermelon."

Kennedy snickers and tosses a spare shirt and shorts at the still-bristling red wolf. "No fur. I need you to be able to say actual words. And the watermelon is really good."

I extract a slice and take a nice, juicy bite.

Bailey shifts, glaring at me and at the bright green tee she pulls over her head. "This damn shirt probably glows in the dark."

I hide a grin. As far as I know, she's never actually met Kel, but she channels him just fine.

Kennedy steals my watermelon. She sits down with it, takes a bite, and looks at Bailey expectantly.

Bailey sighs. "Are we seriously letting her boss us around like this?"

If there were any teeth in that question, I'd show mine, but there aren't. "Yes."

She growls and sits down, far enough away that she has time to react if I suddenly develop a case of bad manners. Which makes my wolf sad. He knows that it isn't that she doesn't trust him in particular—she can't let herself trust anybody. Not far enough to believe she's completely safe, anyhow.

Kel used to do the same thing.

Bailey takes some of the jerky Kennedy holds out. "Next time give me some warning, or I'm putting teeth marks in his ass."

Dealing with the devil she knows. That's fine for now.

"We need to talk," says Kennedy quietly. "I know something, and it's big, and the two of you would have to agree for it to work, but I think it could change everything."

My wolf blinks. That's a hell of an agenda—and she means every word.

KENNEDY

This is crazypants. Bailey still wants to bite someone because we got too close to her camp and my head hurts because the storm inside it hasn't gotten any calmer and Hayden is just sitting there eating watermelon like I invited him on a picnic.

My wolf leans into that. He's had way more practice at this alpha stuff.

I take a deep breath. If I start talking from the middle of the storm, I'm not going to make any sense. "I had a video chat with Adrianna Scott a few days ago."

Bailey's eyes widen.

I hope Hayden understands why I'm starting there. "She said some really smart things that made my wolf feel better about who she is. She says a baby alpha can be a good part of her pack." It's hard to say those words, but this won't work if I don't.

Bailey makes a face. "Duh."

I look over at Hayden. His eyes are easy. Proud. Ready.

I swallow. I can do this. "She said I could have a baby pack, a small pack inside the big one, that could be useful."

I can see Bailey's wolf thinking really fast, trying to figure out if this is the start of a good idea or a dangerous one.

I swallow again. It's both. "I think you have a baby pack, too."

She snorts.

My wolf is so sure. "I know it's bigger than the main pack, but it's still a baby pack."

Hayden goes crazy still, and Bailey looks like I just stabbed her.

She knows how big the shadow pack is and he kind of knew, but I just made it part of the story we all know together, and that changes everything. I don't care. I'm *trying* to change everything. "You might have more wolves, but you're not the main pack. You don't want to be."

Bailey finally nods.

My throat feels like I just ran in the dusty forest for

hours. "You're not a baby alpha like me, but you're something kind of the same. A leader for your group, who can help the main pack see your shifters and what they need and what they can offer."

They're both listening to me so hard they're barely breathing.

I keep my eyes on Bailey, because she has to choose first. "I think I know how the main pack and the baby packs can work together better."

She scowls. "We're working together just fine."

I think about how gentle Lissa gets when she talks to Bailey sometimes. "You sent the sentries when the pups needed protecting, and that's a really big deal. The den is sending lots of food out to the woods. That's a really big deal, too."

Bailey just looks at me.

Hayden's fingertips brush my arm. "You see more that we could be doing."

I keep my eyes on the wolf who still has to choose. "Maybe. I have a really big idea, and I need the two of you to help me figure out if it's a good one." I pause, because this is the hardest part. "I'm going to have to tell a bunch more truth to explain it, though."

Bailey's eyes don't look angry anymore. They mostly look sad and tired and hurt and confused.

My wolf cracks. She can't do this. Not if it will just make Bailey hurt.

"If you wanted to be alpha, my wolf would let that happen."

We both turn to look at Hayden, our mouths hanging open.

He smiles, mostly at Bailey. "You're an amazing leader and you've made sacrifices for this pack he's never going to be able to match. He would gladly be the slightly immature baby alpha who hangs out and eats watermelon and tries to make you laugh at inappropriate times."

Bailey's lips twitch. "Isn't that mostly what you do now?"

My wolf can't laugh yet. She's too shocked about what Hayden just said.

He shrugs. "Pretty much. And you're still out here working like crazy with too many wolves and too many responsibilities and not enough resources. It sounds like Kennedy has some ideas about how to fix that. I say we hear her out."

She grimaces, but she's actually considering it. Which is huge. And necessary. My wolf knows who her alpha is, but she loves Bailey so much.

She finally nods at me. "I hope you know what you're doing."

I make a face that usually makes her laugh. "Um, no. I'm fourteen and my feet engage before my brain, remember?"

She snorts.

I take another deep breath. They aren't really working, but I don't know what else to try, and the jumble in my brain will start making way less sense if I take all its oxygen away. "Reilly has this book about aliens. They aren't shifters, but they have fur, just like us, and they run a space station. When spaceships come to visit the station, some of them park and some of them go into orbit around the station and some of them head out into the galaxy on trading runs and come back again in a few weeks."

They're both staring at me like I accidentally forgot to put my eyes in my head when I got up this morning.

Bailey finally looks at Hayden. "You turned her into a science fiction nerd?"

He laughs. "Nope. That's Reilly's fault."

This is the last time I'm ever talking about anything I read in a book. "I think our den is like a space station and baby packs are like ships. If things are working smoothly, everyone finds a nice parking spot close to the den or a good orbit, and they have shore leave and drink fizzy drinks and hang out together."

Hayden and Bailey look at each other and make really weird strangled noises.

I glare at both of them. "When it's not working, ships run into each other and space shuttles get accidentally lost and nobody comes to drink the fizzy drinks and the people who live on the space station are sad because they don't get to trade for cool stuff from other galaxies or see their friends."

Mirth abruptly vanishes from Hayden's eyes.

I wait for Bailey to catch up. She's the one who got Reilly hooked on spaceships and galaxies. She used to tell him Star Trek stories before bed.

She looks at me and doesn't blink for a really long time. "You're saying we need more organization. Air-traffic control and orbital coordinates and ship-to-station communication."

I wrinkle my nose. Reilly's book wasn't so big on details. "I think so. Maybe. What are orbital coordinates?"

Hayden chuckles. "A black hole we shouldn't go down right now." He glances at Bailey, amused. "Remind me to introduce you to a guy named Scotty."

She looks kind of like I do when I have to eat salad for dinner.

Hayden's gaze shifts to me and I suddenly feel like a really small baby alpha. "You're saying that we need to act like one pack, with a plan for all of our baby packs and how we work together and communicate and share resources and get all the jobs done that need to happen in a big, complicated pack."

I nod slowly. That sounds kind of right.

He tilts his head, looking at me, his eyes the yellow-gold of his wolf. "Those are still the wrong words. They're the kind of words my mother would use. You see something else. Something more specific, maybe."

I exhale. I feel like I'm talking from the middle of the storm again.

Bailey is suddenly sitting beside me, leaning into my wolf. "Find somewhere and start, kiddo. It doesn't matter if it's the beginning. Just talk and trust us to listen and to help you sort it out."

The first time she said that to me, she was still my teacher. My eyes sting a little. She never made me feel silly for not being able to find the beginning. I take a deep breath and lean into that. "My baby pack feels like gravity beams inside me."

Hayden nods. "Pack sense. Alphas have a lot of it."

I try not to feel silly. "I guess gravity beams are kind of weird."

He tugs on the ends of my hair. "I see lines of light. Rio hears drumbeats. Kelsey sees flowers. There are no right ways. What do your gravity beams tell you?"

My eyes are feeling scratchy again. "I tried looking for the ones that attach to you, because we're part of the main pack, right? At first I couldn't see them, but then I could see so many. Some are jumbled and blowing around, and some are too big or in the wrong places, and it's all this great, big mess."

He nods slowly. "Yes. Exactly that. I feel it differently, but I feel it."

I gulp and look at Bailey.

She rolls her eyes. "You two are the alphas. I'm just a wolf who got stuck with the job when nobody else was available. But anyone with half a brain knows we're a mess."

Knowing rises up in me again, hot and fierce and true. "I think I know how to fix it."

BAILEY

It's an insane idea. I listen as Kennedy explains the nuts and bolts of what she sees in her jumble of gravity beams and how to rearrange them. It's complicated and naive and bold and full of about a million things that could break or go wrong.

I can't look into her eager eyes and say any of that, though.

Because she's somehow still capable of innocent hope.

And because she's right.

I glance at the guy calmly feeding her the last of his watermelon and sigh. He's going to let her do this. It's been written all over his wolf since her second sentence. Which means I either need to play the big, bad wolf and do it fast, or I need to do something my wolf is going to absolutely hate.

Hayden meets my eyes, and there's nothing naive in the gaze that pins me where I sit. I resist for a moment. He tried this shit the last time we met.

Then I realize the message his wolf is trying to send. It isn't one of pressure or of pack or of dominant insistence. He's asking me to help him do right by the fourteen-year-old who brought him out to my woods—the one I love so fiercely and have spent six years putting in harm's way because there was no one else to send.

The one who has somehow found her inner sunshine and lollipops and is fully expecting me to tell her they need to die.

I shake my head at the man with yellow-gold wolf in his eyes. Insightful jerk.

His lips twitch.

I switch my gaze to Kennedy. The furry red demon inside me is definitely going to hate this.

Kennedy watches me carefully. She knows I'm the one most likely to take her shiny idea and break it into a million pieces—and she brought it to me anyhow.

I sigh and take the first step into the ooze. "We need a bigger meeting."

She keeps staring at me, her wolf a little slow on the uptake.

Hayden's isn't. His grin lights him up like the middle of a freaking solar system.

I scowl at him. The rest of my day is going to suck, and I'm quite happy for that to be his fault. I take one last bite of jerky and pull a stupid green t-shirt off over my head. It's going to be a long, hard afternoon, but I know the wolves that Kennedy needs for this harebrained scheme of hers, and I can probably get most of them to show up.

Because they love her, too.

18

RIO

The good shit always happens when I'm gone on a grocery run.

I look around at the chaos that is our den and snort. It looks like ground zero for a mobile crisis response team. Kennedy is busy scribbling on an old-school whiteboard that two cats delivered this morning, and she's got Ebony and Lissa looking over her shoulders. I have no idea what they're working on, but it's making Lissa glow.

She isn't the architect, however. This show is in fourteen-year-old hands.

Hayden is the kind of calm that happens when an alpha is letting a typhoon hit his pack and standing ready to rescue anyone who gets accidentally tossed into the water. Which means a sentinel and two betas are standing ready to do the same thing. We got very little information this morning, but our alpha did issue some edicts.

Ask no questions, and be ready for anything.

Which isn't all that helpful, but he knows that. It beats the instructions he handed out to the rest of the pack, though. We have incoming. No names and no quantities, which means Myrna and Shelley are making a stack of pancakes taller than I am, the groceries I just arrived with are being processed by an assembly line of helpers, and even the smallest pups are working hard to get our den ready for an invasion.

I badly want to shift so I can feel the earth under my paws and hear what's coming, but Kelsey is tugging on my fingers and we already have several faces in the den who are normally up in trees on our inner perimeter. I need to be patient. It's going to be worth it. Even a sentinel who has to work with his annoying human form knows this is going to be one of those mornings that his pack will sing about for a very long time.

Reilly snaps a photo of the food assembly line and grins. Then he spins around and scans the den, a reporter smart enough to document what he doesn't yet understand.

Or maybe he does. Kennedy's baby pack is oddly calm.

My wolf shakes his head. They don't know any more than the rest of us. They just fiercely trust their leader.

Fair enough.

I look around for Robbie, who can sometimes get lost in this level of bedlam, and find him sitting in Kenny's lap. My eyes widen. That's a huge level of trust from Lissa, especially when she's not right on top of them. Myrna is, though, and flipping pancakes won't stop her from reacting if Robbie signals distress. Which he isn't. He's happily staring at the pages of a picture book along with Jade and Braden.

"Kenny's solid." Kel drops a hand on my shoulder as he passes by with an armload of wood for the fire. "The chaos is centering him. We should have upended his world a long time ago."

I have some responses to that, but I'd be talking to Kel's retreating backside, so I don't bother. I just grin down at Kelsey. "What do you need my help with, cutie?" I got tasked with being her assistant.

She smiles wordlessly and holds up a sizable handful of flowers.

"Those need water, I bet."

She shakes her head.

I realize why a few seconds later. Sentry calls announce friendly visitors, but my wolf barely hears them. He's too busy drinking in all the new paws he can feel, and the maelstrom of emotion coming with them. The hesitance, the uncertainty, the fear—even from their leader. Wolves who aren't at all sure of their welcome, who aren't at all sure this is safe.

Who aren't at all sure this is home.

I look down at the flowers in Kelsey's hand and smile. I can't count them precisely, but I don't need to. Our small pack psychic has her answer ready.

She'll have one for each of them.

KENNEDY

They're here.

I drop the bedsheet down over the whiteboard. It's not quite done, but it can change as we go. It needs to be able to do that. I talked to Bailey about who to bring, but I don't know who will actually come, and my wolf couldn't calm down enough to see gravity beams this morning.

Hayden walks over and takes Lissa's hand, and even my scatterbrain can see the bond shining between them. They smile at each other and then they look at me.

I wait for them to turn around to greet the people who are about to arrive.

Hayden grins at me instead. "This is your show."

My wolf tries to panic. She didn't expect this. This is a job for her alpha. She's teeth and claws and she isn't very good at explaining hard things and a lot of the shifters who are coming need someone smart and calm and in control to make this work. "I told you all the big parts."

His arm wraps around me and my wolf. "They're not here because of me. They're here because of you."

I grab my wolf before she bites him. She's just scared.

He strokes my hair like I'm a fractious pup. "You've done the hard part already. Do the rest and trust your pack to catch you."

My throat feels funny as I try to breathe. "I don't even know how to start."

Lissa reaches around him and gives me a squeeze. "Try saying hello and offering them some pancakes."

That makes my wolf laugh a little. She can do that.

I take a deep breath just as Bailey walks out of the trees. Her eyes scan the den in one fierce swoop before they settle on me.

I can't really worry about her. It's all the shifters behind her who have my attention. There are so many of them—way more than I was expecting. Dorie. Elijah. Stinky, who's already grinning at Reilly and Hoot. Katrina. Blaze. Heron. Moon Girl, who's in her fur and trembling with how hard it is to be here, but she's here. Terrence. Ben. Glow. Fallon. Teesha.

Some of them are gawking because they haven't been anywhere near the den in forever. Some have no idea who the new people in our midst are, and some can smell pancakes and look really hungry.

But mostly, they're looking at me.

I turn to look at my alpha, but my wolf already knows. He can't do this. They don't know him. They know me, and they know my baby pack, who are somehow suddenly all standing right next to me, using their gravity beams to hold me up and push me forward and kick the ass of the storm inside me so that I can hear something besides my heartbeat in my ears.

I take another deep breath. I'm a baby alpha. I serve my pack. I can do this.

I smile, so big my face hurts with it, and start saying names. All of them, starting with Dorie and ending with

Wrinkles, and then starting again with Kelsey and ending with Kel.

Bailey and Hayden both smile at me when I finish, like I've done something really important and right. They should smile at Ghost. She's the one who taught me that names matter, that being seen matters, even if you're used to being invisible. Maybe especially then.

"Well, come on in." Myrna steps forward, delight in her eyes and brisk orders in her words—the same kind that get pups out of the river and dirty dishes headed to the kitchen. She gives Dorie a fierce hug. "We've got breakfast for those of you who are hungry, and our alpha has promised to wash the dishes. He needs practice, so you should all eat some pancakes."

That makes everyone smile, even Moon Girl. Mellie walks over and lifts her nose, greeting the trembling wolf whose fur matches hers. That gets everyone else unstuck, somehow. The shifters of the den match themselves to shifters from the woods, finding them a place to sit, a plate of food, a pup to hold or some knitting or whatever will help them settle.

My wolf just stands and watches. She still can't see the gravity beams, but she knows a bunch of them are already finding places to land and she hasn't said a single word yet.

I grin quietly. My pack is kind of awesome.

There's a click beside me. Reilly, taking my picture. I make a face at him. I'm not the news today.

He makes a face right back, which makes my wolf want to lick him. Silly bear.

Bailey looks at me and raises an eyebrow. "We're here. Start talking."

Kel snorts. He's sitting by Dorie, holding two plates of pancakes while Jade gets settled in the older cat's lap. "Be nice or you won't get any more pancakes."

Lissa throws a pinecone at his head. He catches it and tosses it meditatively. His wolf is really chill. I wasn't sure he would be, because some of the wolves who just showed up aren't even kind of submissive, but he looks almost happy.

Hayden meets my eyes and says the same thing Bailey did, only silently and a lot more gently.

I blow out a breath and walk over to my whiteboard. Bailey used to have one for teaching classes outside, and I can't believe I'm using it, but it was the only way I could think of to show all the gravity beams inside my head.

I turn to face everyone. There are so many eyes. My wolf butts her head against the inside of my ribs. That's the whole point. I stand up straight. "We're the wolves of Ghost Mountain." I glance at Dorie and Fallon and Teesha. "Well, most of us are wolves, but all of us are pack."

Dorie smiles at me. "That we are, girl. Your idea's a good, strong one, what I've heard of it, anyhow. You've got a brain to go along with your heart and most of us know it, so spit it out."

Sneaky cat. I grin at her. "You don't know who I put in your baby pack yet."

Her eyebrows go up. So do a whole bunch of others.

Crap—I'm starting in the middle again. I take another

deep breath. "We're all pack. One pack. It's time for us to start acting that way. That doesn't mean everyone will be at the den. Some people aren't ready to live here and some don't want to and some need to get to know Hayden better first."

A few heads nod. Not all of them, but their ears are listening.

I gather up some of my very favorite bits of the den for those ears. "Even if you don't live here, you might want to come in sometimes, because Hayden kisses Lissa and makes her cheeks turn pink, and we eat Myrna's magic ribs, and Ravi plays the guitar, and Shelley's cookies taste the best when they're still too hot to bite."

Stinky looks completely convinced. And a few more heads are nodding.

That was one of the things my wolf said really loudly yesterday. Way more people need to come visit the den, because some of them will stay and all of them will get to taste things we can't package up and send out into the woods. Pack isn't something that can be loaded into a box, not all of it, anyhow.

But some of it can, and my wolf had a lot to say about that, too. "We need to set up a way for everyone to be part of the pack—a real, visible, contributing part, even if they're not at the den." I look at Hayden and Bailey. They both nod. I haven't messed up too badly yet. "Some of you know that I'm a baby alpha. That means my wolf wants a pack of her own, but she would totally be a menace if she had one, so instead, I have a baby pack. A small one inside the big one."

Dorie nods. "Cats do that."

Bailey snorts. "Cats do all kinds of dumbass things."

Dorie just laughs. "True, but this isn't one of them." She eyes me. "They have baby packs down in Whistler. Lots of them."

I make a face. I wasn't going to say that part. "Yes. Some of them are like families or friend groups. Other baby packs have special jobs within the main pack."

A lot of ears twitch when I say that part.

I straighten again. Wolves like jobs. I can talk about that. "The Lonely Peak alpha came to visit two days ago, and we worked out a bunch of new pack jobs so we can trade with them. We're going to make knitted blankets and fix stuff that's broken, because cats suck at those jobs, and they have cheese and vegetables, and we're going to build a school and a greenhouse and make special videos about wild wolves."

I wince. That came out all jumbled.

Wrinkles nods slowly. "That's a lot of work. You'll need help."

I smile at her. My wolf loves Wrinkles. "Exactly. But we won't just be trading with the cats. You need food and school supplies and a sat phone to read Reilly's newspaper, right? And we need some of Brown's smoked fish and the teas you make."

She frowns. "I sent some of those."

I nod. I'm the one who collected them. "But it's all disorganized." Which Wrinkles hates. "You don't know what teas the den ran out of and Shelley doesn't know what kind of cookies Brown likes best."

Wrinkles grins. "Oatmeal with cranberries."

I have no idea why anyone likes oatmeal. "The thing is, Shelley wants to know that about every wolf, and all the pups and juveniles and teenagers need to have a connection to the school program, and we need to send salad to shifters who want to eat it so that I don't have to."

A whole bunch of people laugh at that.

My wolf grins. She will happily deliver lettuce to anyone who wants some.

I shake my head at her. She needs to focus. This is so not about lettuce. I move over to my covered whiteboard. "I tried to draw a picture of one big pack with a bunch of little packs inside it so that you could see. It ended up really confusing, though." I try to pull the sheet off in a fancy flourish, but it gets tangled. It takes a while to get it off the corner of the whiteboard, and by the time I turn around, every single person is staring with their mouth open.

My heart drops. Crap. My drawing looks too much like a storm. "I'm sorry. This isn't going to help." I try to throw the sheet back over, but it slides off again. "Maybe Hayden and Bailey can explain it better."

"Don't you dare cover that up." Bailey's eyes are studying my whiteboard like it's some kind of treasure map. "Let us sort through it for a minute."

My wolf sits down, hard. I look at my whiteboard to make sure someone didn't fix it and make it smart when I wasn't looking, but it's still a mess of squiggles and lines and circles that look like a birthday party exploded. It doesn't make any sense at all.

Except that can't be true, because my pack isn't just staring. They're moving and breathing and whispering and tilting their heads.

And they're already reaching for gravity beams.

HAYDEN

She has my mother's instincts. Not all of them, but I thought I understood Kennedy's plan yesterday. Looking at the messy genius on the whiteboard, I realize I didn't understand the half of it. She has Adrianna Scott's feel for pack structure and how it can be bent and molded and reconfigured to serve every wolf in its domain.

My wolf can feel the radiating rightness, and he's still working on sorting out just the lines that connect straight to him.

Which means he's missing the forest for the trees. I tear my eyes away from the purple circle with my face in it and take in the whole board. There are so many names. Photos of some wolves, sketches of others. Nicknames for many, but they clearly have meaning to the people staring and pointing and murmuring and sitting with silent, streaming tears.

My wolf finally gets it.

His whole pack is on there.

Every. Single. Wolf.

That alone would be a contribution beyond measure, but Kennedy has gone so far beyond. Every wolf is assigned to at least one baby pack, and if my dazed brain is making sense of the lines, most belong to more than one. Some of her lines, especially the ones attached to den leadership, are really more about communication than they are about pack structure, but it doesn't matter.

Gravity beams will work just fine as a pack vocabulary.

What does matter is that every single wolf is on the board—and every damn last one of them is attached to a line that leads home. Some of those lines are faint or dotted or there's a question mark hovering over it, but what she's tried to do, as rough as it is, is genius.

And the wolf who did it is struggling to keep her head up.

I roll to my feet. Her alpha is going to fix that right now. Or he is until he catches Kel's hand signal.

I stop, not sure why he's put me in a holding pattern, until I see Reilly, walking forward with a look in his eyes that says this is all about to get sorted and I'm on cape-holding duty again. I sit back down and grin at Lissa. She makes sure I get lots of practice.

She ignores me, smartly watching the far more important action at the whiteboard.

Reilly reaches out and touches his name. "I'm in your baby pack. So are Hoot and Ghost." He frowns a little. "They're not in Bailey's pack anymore."

Kennedy gulps. Rightly so. Bailey was not happy about that part. My wolf had to flex his muscles some and make a couple of promises he's not going to regret a bit.

"Bailey's pack is too big. It needs to be smaller so that she can do her most important jobs and the rest of us can take care of some of the others."

"Like me," says Dorie, an older woman with gray hair and mischievous eyes, nodding. "That's smart. I've got most of the youngsters and the knitters."

"And me." Reilly smiles shyly, touching the line that connects him to Dorie.

Kennedy's head bobs. "That's our baby pack's job. We're going to be the communicators. We live at the den, but we know the wolves in the woods."

It sounds so damn simple when she says it. Truth that resonates so easily that it feels obvious. Except we didn't see it. We weren't brave enough. We didn't see what could be built if we were willing to rip everything asunder first.

"To make that easier, each baby pack is going to have a base camp." Kennedy grins at Bailey. "Orbital coordinates."

Bailey snorts.

I give it three hours before every wolf in my pack knows what orbital coordinates are. Reilly will be in geeky bear heaven.

Kennedy looks at her baby pack, who are all listening with sharp attention. "We're going to visit each of them and deliver what they need and carry messages and help coordinate so that Ravi can go out and play music and Shelley can make birthday cakes and knitters can make blanket squares to trade with the cats and all that stuff."

Dorie nods. "Regular pack business."

My wolf wants to lick her, even though he's pretty sure she's a cat. Regular pack business is a wild leap for a bunch of wolves who are too wounded to get within miles of the den. Which Kennedy's wolf somehow neatly weighed and measured and translated into a mess of dotted lines and just enough gravity to start tugging each of them in the right direction.

Intricate, carefully calibrated hope.

Reilly's eyes are back on the whiteboard. "There's a baby pack for the new business, too."

Kennedy smiles at him. "I figure some of the wolves in the woods can help you with tracking the wild pups and shooting the video footage." She looks at the shifters who came in from the woods. "We'll be earning money doing that. Lots of it. It's a partnership with the cats and it's going to pay for a school and a greenhouse. Lissa has it all worked out."

Lissa hasn't got it anywhere close to that, but it doesn't matter. Kennedy just said words of pure pack magic and she knows it.

It's not the diagram that's her real genius. It's the understanding, embedded in every line on the whiteboard, of the need of every wolf, even the most wounded, to provide for pack. She didn't just set up friend groups and social support systems. She wrangled it so that every baby pack is going to tangibly contribute to the finances and trade goods that support all of us.

This isn't the gentle, incremental change I've been

working on, the kind that was intended to give a traumatized pack a chance to stay on its feet and keep its balance. This is a revolution. Kennedy just broke our pack, and there's so little panic that Rio is sitting on a rock eating gummy bears with Robbie.

Because she found the right reasons. The story that somehow makes this no big deal. The narrative that yanks off all the veils of secrecy in the name of cookie deliveries and building a school and making sure Reilly's newspaper is easier to circulate. But the part of me that is my mother's son sees underneath the story.

Kennedy just smashed us.

The shadow pack doesn't exist anymore, every wolf is connected to the den, we have several small businesses that will no doubt be fully incubated by lunch, and it's going to take pack leadership at least a week to catch up to what she just wrought. I only know one other wolf who might have pulled that off, and I don't know that she could have done it in an hour with nothing but a few dry-erase markers and sheer faith.

Kennedy just drew the future and gave us all our marching orders.

She watches as we all stare some more, tracing lines, working out the details, trying to decipher some of her quirkier scrawls. She flinches as the silence stretches too long for her wolf. "I can try to explain it better."

"Don't be silly. We can all read." Dorie stands up. "Myrna, let's make a plan for the knitting. Then I need to talk to you, Reilly, and after that to Ravi, and then to

Fallon, because I think we need to swap two of our wolves." She glances at Kennedy. "Should we update your diagram as we sort out the details, or do you want to do that?"

Ebony walks over with a fistful of markers. "I've got that."

Two shifters who I think are a mated pair stand up next. "We're on the video team, so we need to chat with Reilly. And Shelley, because our baby pack has a birthday coming up. And Lissa." The smaller of the pair smiles. "We have some trade goods you don't know about yet."

Bailey snorts. "That's because you don't share very well, Fallon."

The spritely woman with wild hair grins. "We'll share for books and cheese."

Lissa is already moving, her laptop in her hands. She gets intercepted long before she gets to Fallon. My wolf watches, bemused, as his pack descends into chaos for the second time this morning. The productive, planning kind that involves makeshift lists and spreadsheets and markers and wolves calling out over the ruckus and pups running to tug on hands.

The only one not moving is a baby alpha, standing entirely still in front of her whiteboard, gazing on what she's done.

I will her to see it. To feel it. To trust what her pack sense and her heart and the gravity beams inside her already know. There's a fierce red wolf, one who gave up much today, standing on the other side of the din, silently willing the same thing.

I don't know if Kennedy hears either of us, or if what lives inside her finally speaks loudly enough for her to hear. I do know that when she finally smiles, I literally feel the *thunk* of the gravity beams landing.

19

LISSA

There are at least a dozen wolves I want to hug. I don't have time. I'm too busy being the chief financial officer of a pack that just exploded.

In a good way, but that isn't making it any less messy. If I had ever dared to dream of this day, I would have assumed it would be drowning in tears. Instead, it's making its very best attempt to break my spreadsheets.

I nod at what Kel just said. "Yes. We'll have a sat phone for each baby pack." Which we're apparently going to pay for with Danielle's repairs. Three hawks just dropped off every broken cell phone in Whistler Pack. We can keep one for every three we fix. Danielle is already hard at work—with seventy-three broken phones in her lap.

Kel exchanges glances with Ghost and Dorie and nods. The three of them have designated themselves as the logistics team. With Ghost in charge. Most of Kennedy's baby pack is leading from the front. Reilly is busy sorting the video crew and walking awed shifters through Rio's rough sketch of what a school attached to a greenhouse might look like. Hoot is talking to the people who will have most of the ghost wolves in their baby packs, selling Kennedy's plan at the much-lower volume that will be necessary for it to work for our most wounded and scarred.

Which is only right. Hoot has been their guardian for years.

My wolf closes her eyes for a moment. This is so big, and there are so many moving parts—and at the core, it's so simple.

We are pack.

When I open my eyes again, Bailey and Hayden and Kennedy are all looking at me, their alpha radar pinging. The jobs they've assigned to themselves are less obvious than most. Kennedy is chatting with Ebony a lot, and every time she does, more gravity beams get sorted on the whiteboard.

Yes, we're a pack with gravity beams now. Nobody could resist.

Hayden is quietly making sure he talks to every person who came in from the woods, often with someone from the den as a guide. I saw him scratching Moon Girl's ears a few minutes ago. Kelsey was with him, easing the way, but it still brought tears to more than one set of watching eyes. A very wise alpha, calibrating welcome to what each wolf in his pack can handle.

My wolf preens. Smart wolf. Sexy alpha.

I snort at her. She's not even kind of objective anymore.

"He's as good at this as you told me he would be." Bailey sits down on the grass beside me and puts her chin on my shoulder.

I turn and rest my cheek against hers. "You brought them."

She grunts. "I didn't know how many of them would come."

Every wolf here, den residents included, would follow Bailey Dunn through fire. And now she's giving them up. "How's your wolf doing?"

She shrugs a little and scans the den, her chin back on my shoulder. "She knows this isn't her job anymore. Kennedy was smart enough to leave her with a few scraps, so she'll deal."

Bailey's wolf has always been a pragmatist, and those "scraps" include some of our most fragile and damaged wolves. "I guess you're going to be out in the woods a while yet."

My best friend snorts. "I'm already coming back next week to help Rio with the school design and Reilly with a video lesson on wild wolves."

My heart delights. They're inviting her teacher to come out and play. "Robbie wants a run with you. I'll bring him out in a day or two. We'll come visit your new base camp."

She scowls. "I might move it."

She can try. "Eliza's bringing a crew around on Saturday to build platforms."

Bailey blinks. "Platforms? What did I miss?"

I laugh quietly. I've been asking that question every two minutes for the last several hours. "Somebody was talking to one of the cats and Reese messaged me. They have two dozen fancy canvas tents they use in the summer for their forest guardian program. They set up on wooden platforms and come with sleeping cots and fire-safe lanterns. He says we can have them for the winter."

Bailey glances down at my spreadsheet. "And you're making him accept what in return?"

I grin. "Smoked fish. It wasn't a hard sell." At all. He had cats drooling over his shoulder.

Bailey chuckles wryly. "Damn cat, always sticking his nose in."

One of our biggest fears for six years was that he would stick it in too far and get a pup killed. It's so very good to feel that ebbing away. "We've got lots of fish."

She nods. "Between Brown and Reilly and a couple of my wolves, we'll get a smoker running and keep it filled."

I wonder if she can hear just how easily she's pivoting to these new conversations. "Wrinkles is already talking to Eliza." Chainsaw skills are suddenly in hot demand. "They're figuring it all out. I'm just keeping track."

That earns me a disbelieving snort. "Eliza's a good choice. Pinning us all down to a base camp is going to take some delicate maneuvering, and her wolf is submissive enough not to trigger anyone."

Which is also a skill suddenly in high demand. I know Hayden's kicking himself for not figuring this all out weeks ago, but neither did a bunch of us who know the lay of the land far better than he does. Reese brought work for the submissives. Kennedy somehow turned that into the mortar of our rebuilding.

And my best friend somehow found the courage to let it happen.

Bailey lifts her chin and raises her voice. "I want that blue. I need a new sweater."

Myrna turns around from the big computer screen Rio usually works at. She's got Ronan and Aurelia in video chat, with an explosion of yarn behind them. They're negotiating a trade that sounds like it involves multiple plane trips, the naming of future children, and an intercontinental bear alliance. "The aqua or the navy?"

Bailey scowls. "Navy, like proper wolves wear in the woods."

Ronan's laughter booms out of the screen. "We charge extra for boring colors."

Myrna eyes him. "Not on my watch, you won't."

Aurelia snickers. "He's just grumpy because someone found his last jar of huckleberry jam this morning and helped themselves to a taste. Sadly for him, she's about three feet tall and giggles when he growls."

Myrna's eyes light up with pirate glee. "I guess that

means the two dozen jars I just sent back with the hawks will have higher trade value."

I groan. Those aren't even in my spreadsheet yet.

Bailey laughs softly, her grip on my arm suddenly fierce. "Gods, Liss."

I can feel her wolf shaking with what's just hit her. I lean into my best friend while she works out what it is, because no one on the planet deserves it more than she does. And no one will find it harder to decipher. Every one of us at the den has had exactly such a moment sometime in the last few weeks—or several of them—but it hits hardest the first time.

The entirely strange sensation of feeling all the way happy.

HAYDEN

I watch Rio as he takes a marker from Ebony's hand and adds a line connecting himself to Bailey and all her dotted lines. They're the wolves I know the least about, and the ones I presume need his sentinel most. Including a name said in only the quietest of whispers.

Rennie.

I don't know who she is just yet—but my wolf has already made her promises. I eye Rio. "Bailey isn't going to want your help."

He snorts.

Right. Sentinels don't ask for permission. "Anything

else major that needs adjusting?" He's been oddly absent from the whiteboard editing, and sentinels are fluent in the language of gravity beams.

He shakes his head slowly. "No. Kennedy nailed most of it, and the baby pack leaders are cleaning up the details just fine. Nothing's ringing wrong. A few stray whimpers, but no major fault lines."

I eye the board that so very obviously came out of Adrianna Scott's playbook. Capable wolves in leadership, baby packs with a purpose, and a really clear path of evolution as most of them disappear or re-form or relocate themselves to the den. "It really is that good, isn't it?"

"Yes." A wry smile. "I had no idea, if that's your next question. I had Kennedy down as loyal teeth and claws with a damn strong wolf, a playful rebel streak, and a heart the size of Banner Rock."

Which would be more than enough, but it isn't all of who she is. "I checked in with a few people. She didn't miss a single wolf. Not one." Not even the ones off to the side and apparently not currently anywhere near our territory. There are lines running to them, too.

He glances at me. "How's your wolf?"

I snort. "You're over here because you can smell him."

"He is kind of stinky."

I laugh. "Fortunately, that name belongs to someone else." A really cute kid who ate more pancakes than all the rest of the pups put together and who shook my hand with solemn pride when we talked about his baby pack.

"His group will be at the den by winter, and a couple

others will be close behind." Rio smiles. "The bossy wolves on scheduling are also making sure you have plenty of regular visitors to charm."

His math is the same as mine, then. Kennedy and her baby pack will hook people up to gravity beams. The den will haul them in. With significant assists in some cases, but my wolf already has plans. She gave me exactly the job I do best. The magic I'm still trying to wrap my head around is that she did the same for dozens of us. "Are Kel and Ebony breathing yet?" Security isn't exactly going to be a cakewalk.

Rio chuckles. "Kel took tactical possession of the territory map. Bailey's helping. They're locating base camps so that a perimeter can be held by baby packs working together. In some ways, it's easier than maintaining a single tight perimeter around the den."

Easier, maybe. Also more porous, but Kel isn't going to let a steady flow of traffic in and out of the den make us less safe. Not when it's going to make us better in every other way. "Do we need more betas?" Whistler Pack has a very flat leadership structure, but the betas are the level that makes it all hold together.

Rio makes a noncommittal sound. "The three who should get the title next will all bite you if you try to make them take it."

My wolf grins. He has such an unruly pack. "Only two will bite. The third will look at the ground and try to make herself invisible."

He smiles. "She might surprise you."

She might. She's managing some pretty scowly dominants from the woods with no trouble at all. "So basically we put our feet up and let Kennedy's crew handle most of the work because everyone thinks teenagers are cute and harmless?"

Rio nods cheerfully. "Yup."

It's a good thing the adults in this pack don't have big egos. "Are there any terrible mistakes I'm making?"

"As you sit here eating cookies and doing nothing?"

Exactly. I've touched every single wolf who will let me anywhere near them, but aside from that, I seem to have run out of useful work to do. With the possible exception of annoying my sentinel. I grin and pop in the last bite of a really good cookie.

His wolf seriously contemplates growling at me.

I keep a mostly straight face. Rio has the wisdom of the ages inside his skin—and a sweet tooth to rival Braden's. "Wrinkles and Shelley just made them. If you go to the kitchen and look sad enough, they'll probably take pity on you."

His lips quirk. "Kennedy's only mistake was not leaving the two of us enough to do."

We both know that isn't true—there's at least one job coming very soon with both our names on it. But I have no problem fortifying myself with cookies until it's time. Especially if it will give me another chance to hang out near the quiet brown wolf who looks like Mellie, smells like bravery, and sat in the doorway of the kitchen pantry and took a whole minute to start breathing again.

KENNEDY

I scrub my fists over my eyes like a small pup who's fighting a nap. It's not even lunch yet, but my wolf is exhausted. She can't stop now, though. There are so many things going right, but all it takes is one spaceship without orbital coordinates and we'll have a big mess.

My wolf shoots a pointed look at the one shifter in her baby pack who is definitely not paying attention to air traffic control.

I hold on tight to her scruff. We need to wait to deal with that, and right now he's in a good parking spot. He has a pile of board books as high as his nose, a jumble of pups in his lap, and Stinky and some of the sentries looking over his shoulders.

I hope we don't break Kel. Perimeter security is a little sketch at the moment.

"Do you think we can swing a night run through Teesha's camp, or will that freak out too many of her shifters?"

I blink at Ghost, who has the same kind of light in her eyes that Braden gets when he's eaten way too many berries. "Maybe ask Hoot?"

She snorts. "I would, except she just left with Moon Girl and Ravi and half the new batch of cookies."

Visiting the wolves who aren't here and trying to make some of the dotted lines more solid. Which is a really good thing—I just didn't expect it to happen quite so fast. "I kind of thought people would eat pancakes and talk and start the hard stuff tomorrow or next week."

She leans against my shoulder. "I don't think that's how gravity beams work."

I groan. "That's not going away, is it?"

Her giggle is light and adorable, just like Reilly's. "Nope. You will be forever known as the wolf who turned us into a bunch of science nerds."

I hide my head in her hoodie. "Just kill me now."

She laughs again. Then she elbows me. "Can you take a group out in a few days? Sienna and Sierra are coming for a visit and they want to see the wild wolves."

I get my brain in gear. "Did you ask an adult wolf?" Baby alphas should not be left in charge for any longer than half a morning. Then they need naps.

She grins. "I did. Kel said to ask you. He said your wolf obviously needs more to do."

Troublesome beta. "We'll need to know where all the base camps are and what areas Hoot and Moon Girl are designating as off-limits." That's the idea Kel and Ghost and Bailey worked out so that we can keep things like video shoots and pack runs from being an accidental disaster.

She nods. "I'll have a map ready, and snacks, and Reilly sent a hawk to pick up the broken video cameras so that Danielle can fix them and we can get a lesson on how to use them. Also, Brown is maybe coming because Wrinkles says he knew how to use the old-fashioned video cameras and even a really cranky old shifter should learn some new tricks."

It's going to take me a whole week to catch up to this day. I bump the shoulder of the person who is somehow holding it all in her hands. "You're pretty awesome. You know that, right?"

She smiles down at the ground. "Sienna and Sierra are so excited. They're talking about one channel for the wolf pups, and another one that's more generally wolf, and maybe one for owls, too. Wrinkles knows a nest that we can film from far enough away."

Baby owls are stinking cute, but that's so not the important part of what Ghost just said. I look at her carefully, doing my baby-alpha job and listening as hard as I can. "That sounds like a pretty big deal."

Her eyes are so fierce. So proud. "Sienna and Sierra are buying four sleeping modules for their pack, K. *Four*."

I have the best baby pack ever. "We can't let cats show us up."

Her grin splits her face. "Exactly." She grimaces. "You might have to sit on Reilly, though. He's talking about a bear channel."

Yikes. Wild wolves are pretty timid around shifters. Wild grizzlies aren't timid around anything. "Maybe we can find some cute black bears." I glance over at Stinky. "Or some skunks."

Ghost shakes with laughter as she pats my head like a pup who shouldn't be let out of sight. "Maybe don't put that idea on your whiteboard just yet."

Right. Check.

No skunks.

ADRIANNA

I peer at the emailed picture, zooming in on it so that I can see the details, just like I do with Rio's designs. It isn't Reilly who sent the photo this time. It was Lissa, along with a quiet note of heartfelt thanks for helping their baby alpha find her calling.

The slightly blurry whiteboard squiggles and lines speak so very eloquently of that story, of a young woman who let her wolf *know* and then spoke that truth out loud to a pack who was able to hear it. I look at the marker lines of trust and resonance and faith and let myself cry a few tears, because it isn't every day you get sent a photograph of resurrection.

It's a diagram that says so much of who Kennedy is, and who she believes they can all be, and she's springboarded all of it off the simple idea of finding her baby pack something to do. I touch my fingers to the big, beautiful pack Kennedy ripped apart and stitched back together on instinct and teenage chutzpah—and smile at the gorgeous geometry of a baby alpha who put her baby pack right at the very center.

And then I take a deep breath and consider what to do about the story hidden underneath the diagram. The one that so easily could have been mine.

The answer doesn't come from me, or from my wolf. It comes from the gentle man who has always seen the innermost recesses of my heart.

I wipe my cheeks and thank him. Then I turn away from my screen and lift my flannel shirt off the back of my chair. I got a terse note from Ames about half an hour ago, filing her version of a flight plan for bright and early tomorrow morning. It will evidently take that long to stuff half of Whistler Pack's yarn into her cargo compartment.

I'll drop by and let her know that she'll need to stuff a wolf in there, too.

20

KENNEDY

I hand the stick and its droopy toasted marshmallow over to Hoot. We only built a small fire, but it hasn't burnt down to coals yet, and she's mostly managing to set her marshmallows on fire.

She hands it around the circle to Kenny.

He tries to pass it to Reilly, but bears can be really stubborn when they want to be. The second time Kenny tries, Reilly even growls.

My wolf snickers. Her baby pack is badass. I take out one of the sandwiches Myrna packed for us. I tried to make them myself, but she muttered things about demon teenagers loose in her kitchen, so I didn't try very hard. I think she maybe didn't want me to scare Moon Girl away. She stayed almost the whole day, and that's a really big deal.

Reilly reaches for a sandwich, too. He doesn't actually like marshmallows all that much, and Myrna put extra honey on our bread along with the ham and cheese. He sighs happily as he catches a whiff of the honey. "This was a really good day."

Ghost settles back onto his shoulder, nearly asleep.

I feel a little bad about that. I knew I was giving my baby pack a big job, but until I watched today happen, I didn't really understand how big. "We maybe need some more help with air-traffic control. I didn't mean for all of you to have to work so hard."

Hoot snorts. "You're a genie who came out of her bottle and granted everyone three wishes today, so quit worrying and let your wolf grow a big head for an hour or two." She grins at me. "We'll squish it back down to size for you in the morning."

I stare at her as my wolf abruptly settles.

Ghost laughs quietly from Reilly's shoulder. "Nice one."

Hoot dusts her fingers on her t-shirt. "I have moves."

Kenny snorts. "You have a marshmallow that's turned to coal."

Hoot holds up her stick and makes a face at the smoking black lump on the end. "I did this one really slowly, just like you said, Riles."

I don't listen to whatever Reilly says in reply. The rest of my baby pack might be fine, but my wolf thinks I need to pay more attention to Kenny. He didn't even want to come have a campfire with us, but Ghost glowered and said something the rest of us couldn't hear, and he took the pitcher of lemonade and the bag of marshmallows and followed us out here.

He catches me studying him and gives me a look I remember from back when he was beta.

I wrinkle my nose because both of our wolves need me to. He's not the boss of me.

He shakes his head, but I see his lips twitch inside his beard.

I reach over for another sandwich. My wolf yowls in protest when it gets close enough to my nose. I take a closer look and grimace. "This one is half lettuce." It has ham, though, so it's not for Ghost. Hers have tomatoes and this crazy thing called an avocado that I'd never seen before a few weeks ago. They're green and slimy and they make Ghost and Kelsey give Rio big, sloppy kisses.

Which is so weird. Slime should not make people happy.

Ghost looks at me with half-asleep eyes. "Those are for Kenny. He likes lettuce."

I stare at him. "Since when?"

Reilly giggles. "It's nice and crunchy and it makes my tongue notice the honey and ham more. You should try it."

I mime death by gagging. "Shortly after I eat earthworms."

Hoot grins. "Those are pretty good if you toast them first."

I start to laugh. Then the sound that just came out of Kenny's wolf sinks in. The four of us turn to look at him, which isn't really necessary. Pain has a smell.

He looks down at his hands. Then he looks up at Hoot, and his eyes are full of something wretched. "Please tell me you haven't actually had to eat earthworms."

Oh, crap. I want to stop Hoot from answering, but that isn't fair to her. I inch closer to Kenny instead. I don't actually care if he eats lettuce, but he needs to stop eating guilt, and that can't happen until we find some of its gravity beams and get them off him.

She shrugs a little. "I only ate them a couple of times. Fallon knows how to cook them."

Fallon is a raven. She taught us how to eat all kinds of weird things.

I touch Kenny's shoulder. "Some of the ghost wolves have trouble hunting. It's too violent. So they forage and eat what the woods offers." It didn't sound so bad when we were doing it, but it's really hard to think about while I'm holding a honey-ham sandwich.

I guess it's even harder to be the guy who ate hamburgers in town while his pack fried up earthworms.

I look around at my baby pack. It's time to deal with the piece I left for last. I wanted us to rest a little more first, but Kenny's wolf needs us now. They all nod at me, their eyes sad and ready.

I swallow. This is going to be hard, but I listened a lot. My wolf is tired and confused and shaky, but she's also proud, because three of the shifters in her baby pack got something they really wanted today. A lot of somethings. Hoot gets to live at the den and love Bailey and help the ghost wolves come home. Ghost gets to be a quiet badass, one everyone sees and respects and turns to because they want to hear the wise things she notices. Reilly gets to tell stories and lead the work that will give our pack a school, and nobody will ever be able to make him feel weak again, because there will be a whole building that says he isn't.

What Kenny wants is both a lot simpler and a lot more complicated. Especially because I don't think he knows he wants it, yet.

I leave my hand on his back. Hayden does that a lot. "You didn't say much today."

He shrugs. "You assigned us work out in the woods. I need to stay far away from that. I'll help out around the den and keep out of the way of the visitors."

I wrap my fingers around his gravity beam. "No. You won't."

His head jerks to face me, his eyes spitting mad. "Moon Girl shook when she saw me today. Do you really want me out there, delivering pain everywhere I go? I might deserve that, but they don't."

His gravity beam is writhing, trying to escape like a wild thing, but I don't let it go. I hold on as three other sets of hands take hold, too. I left Kenny for last—but he's the answer my wolf knew first. "That's *exactly* what they deserve. Hoot is in charge out there. You aren't. You'll be listening and serving and apologizing with your paws, because that's totally what the wolves out there deserve."

His eyes are almost glassy with confusion.

I let my wolf be just as bossypants as she wants. "If Hoot tells you to leave, you leave. But the rest of the time, you run deliveries and take messages and write down birthday cake orders and bring back smoked fish and help Eliza make tent platforms and whatever else your pack needs you to do."

His mouth moves, but nothing comes out except some croaking.

I wrench on his gravity beam. "It will work. Reilly and Kelsey like you now because they've had time to see you being a decent wolf. Lissa let Robbie sit in your lap this morning while you read him stories."

Hoot snickers. "Myrna was really close with her frying pan, though."

I roll my eyes. Bad jokes are a big part of why the ghost wolves love Hoot. "Duh. We're not stupid. We're just willing to give chances."

Kenny's head shakes almost violently.

I'm holding really tight, but my wolf is worried. This is the right answer, but Kenny's not listening. I don't know if he *can* listen.

Then I hear the low, rumbling growling from the woods. Hayden and Bailey step out of the trees looking like avenging warriors in the night. Bailey looks like that a lot, but today she mostly looked sweet and a little wrecked, and Hayden usually looks like a silly, playful puppy.

They don't look like that now. Even my wolf is a little wide-eyed. I asked for their help, but I didn't expect it to be quite this rumbly.

Ghost sits up and smiles. Her eyes don't look sleepy anymore.

Bailey walks forward, her eyes drilling into Kenny. "Quit being a dumbass. You need to do this, and you'd know why if you stopped to think for two seconds instead of being an idiot. You're going to be a symbol, just like that damned bandana."

Kenny makes his croaking sounds again.

She smiles a little, like maybe she understands them. "A symbol of redemption. Of dominants who serve and listen. Of wolves who matter, even when they're broken."

Kenny spasms.

My baby pack slides in closer. I reach for their hands. I had it wrong. So wrong. It isn't our job to convince him. It's our job to hold him while the big wolves of the big pack hit him with lightning.

Hayden takes two steps and crouches down so that he's looking straight into Kenny's eyes.

My wolf stares in awe at the great big gravity beam he's carrying.

"It will be the hardest job you've ever done." Hayden's hand settles on Kenny's knee, the big alpha of the big pack delivering lightning as gently as he possibly can. "But your pack needs you to do it."

I glance at Bailey, because I thought maybe she might bring a gravity beam too, but she's staring at Hayden like he just grew horns. The good kind.

Nobody moves.

My wolf frets. We're all waiting for Kenny to do something, but maybe he can't. Gravity beams are really bossy. I try to move in a little closer, but my wolf won't let me budge. The right alpha has spoken. The baby one needs to stay quiet and not mess things up.

I shoot Ghost a look, but she isn't looking at me or Kenny. She's looking at Hoot. At the person who knows, better than anyone, how to apply gravity beams to battered wolves—and who has really good reasons not to help this one. Hoot finally sighs. Then she scoots into Kenny's side, bumps against him with her shoulder, and holds up her stick with a still-smoking lump of coal on the end. "Marshmallow?"

His laugh is weird and gravelly and fragile.

I think maybe that's what the best gravity beams sound like when they land.

21

HAYDEN

I sit down beside Lissa and look around. Carefully. There are new people here for breakfast. And a few who have already wandered in and left again, coming in with cautious faces and heading back out bearing snacks and sat phones and crayon drawings and whatever else has been deemed necessary baggage by the eager wolves of the den.

Lissa snuggles against my dazed wolf. "Are you on den duty?"

Kel gave up on sentry visitor alerts late last night. They were waking the pups. He's designated teeth and claws to pay extra attention in the den instead. There are more of those, too, including a couple of quiet wolves standing quietly over by the trees. "Did Glow and Elijah get breakfast?"

She laughs. "I'm not in charge of feeding people,

thank goodness. But I can't imagine Ravi and Robbie and Shelley are letting anyone go hungry."

I shake my head. I stopped by the kitchen this morning to see if Shelley wanted more help and discovered her nearly brimming over with glee as she oversaw several helpers and huge bowls of muffin batter. "Who's the woman with red hair in tiny braids?" She came in with Fallon, who is a raven. I have a shiny rock in my pocket I hope she likes. My wolf likes ravens.

Lissa's eyes brighten. "Cheri's here?"

I calm my wolf. He grew up in a pack of eight hundred shifters and managed to keep them all straight. He'll have all of his wolves sorted soon enough. "She's Brown's daughter, right?"

Lissa laughs. "Depends on what day and who you ask. She inherited his temper."

My wolf grins. He likes feisty packmates. "Should we be letting her near the baked goods?"

"Ah, such a cute alpha. He thinks he can protect the muffins." Ebony drops to the grass in front of us, snickering. "You should let Fallon and Cheri have all the muffins they want. They know where we have a stream that regularly offers up pretty gemstones."

My wolf has been gem-hunting with plenty of ravens. "Trade goods?"

She nods. "The local ravens changed leadership while we were incommunicado, but Reese hooked me up this morning, and Myrna knows the new beta over there. They're already talking beryl and topaz and garnets.

Apparently our territory has them in colors and quantities the ravens covet."

I eye her skeptically. I know how ravens do business. "We don't want shiny rocks back in trade."

She chuckles. "We might, actually, and Jules might want some for the concrete counters and tabletops Danielle and Eliza will be making. Bears would go nuts for polished jewels in their tables."

I lean into Lissa and kiss the top of her head. "And to think I've occasionally worried about how this pack would make money." Worries she listens to in the quiet of night and kisses into quiescence. We still don't have the kinds of revenue streams that will easily pay for big-ticket items, but watching my pack revel in the joy of small luxuries has given those concerns a good kick in the pants.

Lissa smiles, like she can hear my thoughts. My wolf thinks that's entirely possible. "The bears put in another order for fresh fish this morning. Reilly finally has enough ShifterNet store credit for that handmade bookshelf he wanted to order. I thought the Siberian bear on the other end of the video call might die from all the cute."

Reilly used his very first credits for a purchase even Lissa doesn't know about. A suncatcher for the new den, modeled on Kelsey's flowers. Whistler Pack's most famous artist might still be sniffling. "I won't ask how you're keeping track of all of this. I'll just ask if you need help."

Lissa hugs her computer like I might try to steal her spreadsheets.

Ebony laughs. "They're all yours, lady."

I eye her. My betas are probably way ahead of me, but it's entirely weird that my pack seems to have this all sorted without me. A good kind of weird, but still. Revolutions should not be this easy. Kenny's been my hardest job so far, and I'm not convinced I was needed there, either. "Do we need more teeth and claws?" Those have been our biggest shortfall ever since I arrived, mostly because I have a penchant for tossing the stupid ones out of the den.

She shakes her head. "No. Bailey is sending us people. Dorie, too."

Dorie waltzed in with most of her baby pack this morning, which promptly resulted in a game of hide-and-seek that offered up some pretty good clues about where our sentries gained their tree-climbing skills. Her crew might live at their new base camp just beyond the old perimeter for a while yet, but I'm damn sure the new school will get underway in the fall with her charges sitting at tables inside it. Or sitting somewhere. I'm not sure the new school actually has tables. Something about students who learn better when they can move their hands and feet.

"We need to free Bailey up from security concerns." Teachers as good as I expect she is shouldn't be organizing perimeter security.

Ebony smirks at me again. "Way ahead of you, Alpha."

I roll my eyes. "Is there anything useful I can do this morning?" Second-guessing my betas is going to get me growled at soon, and Lissa is already typing things into a spreadsheet that makes my eyes hurt just looking at it.

"Well, you could consider an invitation you just got."

I squint at my beta. Her voice is way too casual. "Which would be what, exactly?"

She shrugs. "Moon Girl is out of cookies."

I stare. Moon Girl has a baby pack full of ghosts, but there aren't that many of them. "She left with dozens of cookies."

Ebony smiles. "She asked for more." A pause. "And she asked for you."

KENNEDY

I climb into the passenger side of the truck and pull the door closed behind me. We're about to head out onto public roads. The kind where fourteen-year-old wolves who are maybe still a little unclear on the difference between the brakes and the clutch shouldn't be driving.

Rio pats the steering wheel. "It's over, sweetheart. She's safely chained to the passenger seat. She can't hurt you anymore."

I grin. He did great. He only squeaked a couple of times, and we did get kind of close to that one tree. "She's an awesome truck. Are you giving Hoot a lesson later?"

He shoots me a look that says maybe I shouldn't ask that question quite yet. I pull out the grocery list instead, the really long one Shelley wrote and shoved into my hands after breakfast. "I bet fifty pounds of butter is going to cost a lot."

Rio snorts. "Shelley's cookies are like printing money. It will be worth it."

I'm so glad my brain doesn't have to figure that stuff out. "I hope we still get some. I heard Myrna trading with Whistler Pack this morning. We might need more planes."

Rio's laugh fills the truck. "Don't let Ames hear you say that."

I only met Ames once, but it was enough to know that I never want to make her mad. She hangs out with polar bears for fun. "She ordered a blanket. One of the expensive ones Myrna put up on ShifterNet with special squares from the pups." Which means squares with holes in them, but if you're Mellie or Kelsey, apparently that's cute. "She traded it for two delivery runs."

Rio just shakes his head. I don't really know what that means. My wolf has no idea what deliveries of rocks and yarn and fish should cost. "Ghost says it was a fair deal."

He smiles. "Given how much Ames likes Kelsey, I'm guessing everyone feels that way."

That part makes sense to my wolf. Things have more value if they attach to good smells. That's why I'm wearing my hoodie this morning, even though it's kind of warm in the truck. It smells like campfire smoke and lightning strikes and a wolf choosing to belong.

I glance carefully at Rio. "I didn't see Kenny this morning."

He navigates a big pothole in the road. "He went out with Reilly."

My eyes snap wide. "Alone? Just the two of them?"

His lips quirk. "Do you think we're brand-new at this job?"

Oops. "No, sorry. It's just that Reilly is really sweet and Kenny might not be after last night, and I don't want anything bad to happen."

He chuckles softly. "Said every alpha ever."

I scowl. "I'm just a baby alpha."

"That's just a matter of degree. You know that. Especially after yesterday."

A lot of people talked to me about what I did yesterday. He wasn't one of them. My wolf suddenly finds that worrisome. "Did I make a mistake?"

His eyebrows go up. "No. Did someone say you did?"

I get the weird feeling that if I say a name, they're going to get a visit from the big, black wolf of death. Which is silly. I have lots of teeth and claws I can use to protect myself. "No. I just thought it."

He watches the road ahead of us for a long time. "Being a baby alpha is a bit like being a sentinel. Most days your pack could live without you just fine, so you play with the pups and wash dishes and go on grocery runs." He pauses. "And then there are the days when you step up and use all the power inside you and act as the big lever your pack needs you to be."

My breath whooshes out. "Yeah."

He reaches over and squeezes my shoulder. "You want so badly to be ordinary teeth and claws."

My tears prickle, hot and itchy. "We need teeth and claws."

"Yes. But you're something different, and your pack needs that, too. We need you to be that powerful lever sometimes." He grins. "We also need you to help load fifty pounds of butter into the truck the next day, so don't get a big head."

That steadies my wolf some, just like when Hoot said it. "So I can go back to being ordinary now?"

He snorts.

Crap. "Mostly ordinary?"

His smile is wry and makes me feel good, even though it isn't the answer I want. "I think your pack is going to need your particular talent for a while yet. Your alpha in particular."

I blink, suddenly lost.

Rio chuckles. "The two of you are quite the pair."

My wolf sits up, vaguely horrified.

He reaches over and pets her hair. "He's still in charge, sweetie. Don't panic in there. You have different alpha strengths, and he can use yours to make his better."

My wolf is breathing again, but I'm still lost. "I have a baby pack. That's it. All I did was show the rest of the pack how they could have one, too."

"Exactly." He stops the truck, and we both watch, amused, as a deer and her two babies meander across the road in front of us. I guess she can't smell our wolves inside the truck. "And in doing that, you showed us how to shape ourselves to be a truly functional pack. You moved all the connections around in one fell swoop so that everyone has a place to belong and a way to contribute and a direct link to home."

I tilt my head. "I guess. I didn't think about it that much. I just put what my wolf knew up on the board."

"I could have done something like that, given enough time and enough knowledge of each shifter in our pack. But pack design isn't my true strength. I'm better at helping wolves get well enough to come home. Adrianna Scott does that kind of restructuring brilliantly. Hayden can do it some, but it's not his true strength, either."

My wolf growls.

Rio's wolf just snickers. He's so not scared of her. "That's not an insult, warrior girl. It's just simple truth. You know him well enough. What's his alpha superpower?"

I think about what Hayden did yesterday. How he touched every single wolf from the woods, even the ones who started off really scared of him, and how he always seemed to know when someone needed a sandwich or a cookie, and how many times he smiled at someone right after they did something brave. "He makes the other end of the gravity beam feel really good."

Rio laughs again, the big kind that makes the truck rock.

I grin. "I got a call from Scotty this morning. He's sending me a t-shirt. I'm an official geek now."

It takes a long time for Rio's chuckles to roll all the way to a stop. Then he stops the truck, leans over, and nuzzles my wolf. "That's exactly right. That's Hayden's superpower. He was already using it, but yesterday you moved a hundred gravity beams around and put them in the right places and gave him so much more room to work."

My wolf finally gets it. I didn't challenge my alpha, or go around him, or threaten him. I *helped* him.

I stare into eyes that are fearsome and honest and so proud of me.

And finally let myself feel a little bit that way, too.

MYRNA

I flop down on the grass beside Shelley and Ebony and sigh dramatically. "Ronan is an evil bear."

Ebony laughs. "What terrible thing has he done now —sent you all the glow-in-the-dark orange yarn in the universe?"

Probably that, too. "No. He found out we were building a school and he already worked out a secret deal with Reilly for two sets of schoolbooks, fifteen student laptops that hook up to ShifterNet, and a robot kit."

Shelley flops over on her stomach giggling, which is a sound I thought I might never hear again, so I allow it. I shoot Ebony a thoroughly aggrieved look, though. "He traded laptops for fish, and Reilly is so proud he nearly stabbed me with a marshmallow stick, so I can't very well make him renege on the deal."

Ebony manages to breathe, in between choked sounds that seem an awful lot like she might be laughing at me, too. "Maybe it's not as lopsided as you think. Our fish are worth a lot in trade. I've seen some of the deals Lissa is making with the northern bears."

I glare at her. "The robot kit is life-sized."

Shelley sounds like she's having a seizure. "You could always get even."

I nod vigorously at an innocent passing cloud. "Oh, I plan to. That man is getting so much huckleberry jam, he won't know what hit him." And the unending gratitude of an elder who spent six years fearing that she was presiding over the death of her pack, but jam is easier to send by hawk.

"Good one." Ebony grins at me, pure mirth in her eyes. "You show him who's boss."

I don't think anyone will show Ronan that in this lifetime. He's too big and too wild and he cares far too much. "He also quietly haggled with Kelsey. He traded three of her best flowers for a special journal made of handmade paper that smells like honey." I sniff a little. "She's giving it to Reilly for his birthday."

Shelley elbows me fiercely. "Don't you dare argue that Kelsey's flowers aren't worth it."

I sniffle a little more. "She hasn't been willing to trade her flowers to anyone else. Or her songs."

Ebony blinks. "What did I miss?"

It's a question getting asked a lot these days. I pride myself on knowing every damn thing that happens in this pack, and I'm nowhere close to keeping up. "She recorded a song this morning. One of her special ones that she makes up as she goes along. About cookies. Reilly put it up on ShifterNet."

I snuck a very quiet copy onto Hoot's sat phone before she headed out to the woods, but I'm not saying anything about that. Or about the link I sent to the email account my youngest son occasionally checks. There are some wolves who will stay the quietest of whispers, no matter what dynamite our baby alpha lit yesterday.

"It was a really pretty song." Shelley's eyes are all soft and goopy. She was there when Reilly and Hoot decided that Kelsey's impromptu singing session was good material for their first video shoot. It took Danielle all of fifteen minutes to have one of Lonely Peak's broken cameras up and running this morning. Which is apparently something only old women with cast iron frying pans consider at all suspicious.

I'm not saying a word about that, either. I did send Reese an extra jar of berry jam, though—the kind with spicy chilies he loves so much. I might not be keeping up with all of today's gossip, but I can at least stay on top of our bribery. "We need to throw Reilly a big bash." It will be the first den birthday to happen since hope arrived in our woods, and he's our best bear cub besides.

Shelley counts on her fingers. "Three weeks."

I nod. "Should we do it here at the den, or out at one of the base camps?"

She hums a minute, thinking. Kennedy might have figured out the fancy stuff yesterday, but Shelley Martins added an awful lot of devious details. "At the den. Three weeks is enough time for people to come in for a visit or two and let their wolves acclimate."

There's been a whole lot of acclimating going on already. It's wondrous.

Ebony nods. "I bet the closer satellite packs all come. Probably Wrinkles and Brown, too."

I snort. That cranky old bear took about ten seconds to fall in love with Reilly when he first arrived, a shy and careful baby who had seen way too much in his short life. Even back then, Brown mostly lived in the woods, but he didn't miss those first birthdays and he won't miss this one. "We could do up a big grill. Fish for the bears and other heathens, and steak and ribs for the civilized amongst us."

Ebony grins. "I like grilled fish."

My wolf likes her so damn much. Especially this version of her. Submissive Ebony was painful to watch. "Heathen."

She snickers. "I'll pass the word. I'm headed out tomorrow to sort out smoker construction and some dispute about the rogue cats upriver scaring the fish."

That will likely become Reese's problem. I add cats to my mental invite list. A small contingent. Kennedy balanced dozens of shifters on the head of a pin yesterday. None of us wants to be the blooming idiot who accidentally pushes someone off. "What kind of presents should we get him?"

"Books," they both say in unison.

It's the standard answer, the one that's been attached to Reilly since he could talk. But he's not that bear anymore, or not just that bear, and I want him to know that his pack sees him—that in the midst of the big and wonderful storm swirling through us, we didn't miss some of Kennedy's quietest, most precious gifts. "I'll talk to his baby pack."

Shelley sighs happily. "I love that sentence."

The three of us grin at each other like dopey teenagers. Which is good. Someone has to take on that role.

The real teenagers are too busy running the pack.

22

KENNEDY

I stumble out of the river, blind as a bat because Reilly's bear is a menace even when he's not trying to drown anyone, and I couldn't shift because I was dumb enough to jump in still wearing my shorts.

"Here, catch." Lissa sounds amused, and the towel that thunks into my face a moment later is actually helpful. Unlike the dozen other shifters who are just laughing at me.

I scowl at all of them once I get the water out of my eyes. Carefully. A couple of them are new and got here after I chased Reilly into the river, and I don't want to accidentally scare anyone. My wolf thinks it's okay, though. They're all grinning and even the newcomers smell like watermelon, so I'm pretty sure we're just pack entertainment for the afternoon.

Which is fine by me.

Hoot was the first act. Her driving lesson made Rio swear in languages Kel didn't know he spoke, but it was also awesome. She needed a pillow behind her back so she could reach the pedals and she had to borrow Myrna's stomping boots with the big fat heels, but she was so happy, and she hardly hit any trees at all. She also didn't get very far, so we all got to watch and giggle and cheer for her when she made the engine growl like a wolf.

She's sitting with the watermelon eaters now, regaling them with tales of Rio's snarls and the one time he covered his eyes. Which I think he maybe did to give her a better story. He's a very sneaky sentinel.

"You were leaving yourself wide open to an attack down low."

I turn and blink at Kel, who's sitting in a campfire chair holding one of Myrna's fancy drinks with an umbrella in it. "What?"

He grins at me. "When you get water in your eyes, you forget everything you know about fighting."

My wolf wants to bite the umbrella in his drink. I tell her to use her brain. There's no way Kel is spouting off about my fighting in the middle of a lazy afternoon for no good reason. I glance around out of the corners of my eyes. Sometimes the lesson he's teaching isn't very obvious. I don't see anything, but a lot of wolves are paying attention in a lazy kind of way. Which might be the point. Kel knows a lot about how to make fighting not so scary. I scrunch some water out of my t-shirt and offer him a pugnacious grin. "I wasn't fighting. I was wrestling with a bear."

He snorts. "Same difference."

Reilly steps up quietly beside me. Watching. Listening. A bear trying to figure out which way the wind is blowing, because he knows all about Kel and his sideways lessons.

I lean against him and cross my arms. He tries the same thing, which nearly knocks us both into the river.

Kel's lips twitch. "Let's try a demonstration. Kennedy, you face the river and work through a basic kata. Shelley, why don't you come over and hit her with that attack sequence we've been working on?"

Shelley jumps up like she just sat on a cactus.

Myrna whoops. "Go get her, girl! Right hook straight to the nose."

Ebony snorts. "Let's maybe avoid bloodshed."

Myrna pouts. "That's no fun."

Goofballs. My wolf hides her grin. Shelley actually looks like she might try this, and that's so stinking cool. I can totally take a punch to the nose for that.

Kel ignores everyone's antics and looks at Reilly. "You're going to hang out in the river and periodically make sure Kennedy gets water in her eyes."

I sigh. More distraction lessons. At least it's not pinecones. My wolf is really tired of those.

Mellie starts clapping wildly and making hawk sounds at Reilly.

Kel's lips twitch again. "Permission granted to make some of us wet."

Layla, who's got Mellie in her lap, rolls her eyes. "Oh, sure. Thanks a lot."

"Here. I'll take her."

Everyone stares at the guy holding out his hands.

Kenny smiles faintly. "I don't mind getting wet."

Mellie, who is adorable and fickle, jumps over to his lap and shifts to her wolf so she can lick his nose. Kenny mutters things, but he doesn't mean them. Not really. Toddler gravity beams are kind of fierce.

My wolf wants to whoop like Myrna, but she doesn't. Instead, I face the river and start one of the flowing forms that Ebony has been teaching me. Not one of the basic ones, because if I followed all the instructions Kel would probably worry, and besides, Shelley will get more openings this way. Or at least more things that look like openings, and I'm pretty sure my job is to keep them that way.

I tell my wolf to pay attention, because gentle blocks aren't all that simple, and if I actually get punched in the nose, Kel will probably laugh, but Shelley will be upset.

She walks over, looking a little worried. I grin at her. "Two against one is so not fair, Kel." Reminding her about Reilly's water assist, which is going to be really annoying.

She laughs and winks at the fuzzy brown bear sitting happily in the river. Then she turns and squares off with me in a fighting stance that's totally decent, except it's way too far away. I start to say something, because I've been helping drill the beginners, but then I remember this isn't my lesson. It's Kel's. I'm just a cute, bedraggled prop.

He doesn't say anything, which makes my wolf curious.

Shelley glances over at him, and I ready myself for a simple punch or kick sequence. She's been working on both, and for a wolf who spends most of her time baking cookies, she's got some really good footwork. She just keeps watching me, though, so I move into the second stanza of the form. It's got some awkward parts, especially when you're wearing wet shorts.

I shake my head a little. I so need to think before I chase Reilly into the river next time.

A huge whoosh of water hits my chest and heads straight up my nose. Shelley shrieks like a hooligan and runs at me, her arms doing a crazy windmill thing that I have no idea how to block gently.

I drop into a low stance, thinking I should maybe topple us both into the river.

Reilly's second wave hits.

Darn bear. I catch one of Shelley's fists and try to find the other one before it hits either of us in the nose, which is hard to do when I can't see.

Half a breath later, her neat, carefully executed kick takes me out at the knees.

I land flat on my back in the river and just lie there, blinking up at the sun, as Myrna whoops and Reilly shifts back to cheering human and fifteen people pile into the river to congratulate Shelley.

I grin up at the sky as my wolf yips happily into the din. Today is apparently one of those days I get to be completely ordinary.

HAYDEN

I shake my head as I finally figure out what Kel was up to. Kennedy's wolf has just relaxed in a way I've never felt, a dominant letting completely go of her need to protect and defend and keep her strength on a short leash. All neatly handled by a guy in shorts and a straw hat who never even put down his fancy drink.

Kel salutes me with his glass. "Shelley's too tough for her. You might be more her speed."

I scowl at him like a well-trained alpha. "I'm busy eating watermelon." And cuddling Lissa, but he's even less likely to find that a good excuse. He spent half my teenage years finding a good reason for me to stop cuddling someone.

He cracks a grin that says he hasn't forgotten those moves. "I have it on good authority that you need a refresher course on water fighting."

Lissa giggles into my chest.

My wolf grins. He'll happily lose a water fight to her any day she wants. Especially if there are cuddles afterward. However, I'm pretty sure Kel is up to something other than amusing himself at the expense of the alpha wolves in his pack, and given that he's been paying attention to den dynamics for the last hour and I haven't, I should probably indulge him.

Or not. My wolf studies him and decides this is lazy Kel at work. Just a small tweak that happened to present itself while he was chilling by the river.

Given the size of the grin on Shelley's face, I can't

disagree with him. And neither will Kennedy. Her wolf does math like mine does. She'll happily let any shifter in this pack use her to build up their own confidence.

Lissa rubs her cheek against mine. She can feel my wolf's contentment. He's having a really good day. This morning, I headed out to Moon Girl's turf. I dropped off cookies and spices and sandwiches and brought back some dried green stuff that smelled nasty and made Myrna's eyes light up. Moon Girl stayed in her fur while I was at her base camp, but she didn't tremble—and there were at least four wolves watching us from the trees.

Sussing out Kennedy's new gravity beams.

I smile and close my eyes. I've been doing that a lot so I can look at the web of light on the back of my eyelids—the new and improved model that has every Ghost Mountain shifter connected to pack, even if some of the rays of light are really dim. I've been trying to figure out all day how to thank the wolf who built it. It didn't occur to me to have a submissive beat her up and a bear drown her.

It should have. Belonging matters to every wolf, but it matters to Kennedy in deep, hidden ways I don't fully understand yet.

I look back over at Kel, thinking that maybe an alpha and a lazy, frothy-drink-slurping beta should join in this game, when I see his wolf snap to attention. I don't have to ask why. Kennedy is crouching rigid on the edge of the river, trembling with whatever just hit her. I beat Kel to my feet, but neither of us are faster than Reilly. He's next to Kennedy in an instant, his eyes full of horror.

It slams into me. She looks exactly like he did, right before the first time I saw him shift—desperately trying to hold his bear inside and losing.

Fuck.

I can feel my pack moving, wrapping around Reilly and Kennedy with instincts older than shifters. I want to move them back, clear them out of harm's way, but even as I think it, I know it's wrong. Even this close to blowing up, Kennedy's not leaking a single drop of dominance. She's containing herself.

Which means there's only one direction this is going to blow.

I shoot Kel a look, but his eyes are those of a warrior riding into a battle he didn't expect. Whatever he was trying to do, it wasn't this.

Which is a misfire he can beat himself up about later. Right now, we have a baby alpha on a ledge, and we need to get her the fuck down before she makes the dumbass decision that the one wolf in this pack who's expendable is her.

KENNEDY

I grab at my wolf's scruff, at her ears, at any part of her that might listen.

It's useless. I'm not even sure she knows I'm here. Every part of her is trembling with the awful, horrible realization that somehow slid out while she was lying on her back in the river being happy.

I want to wail, because I know the mistake I made. For one small, sunshiny moment, I forgot that she's too much.

I yank on her fur. If she will just listen, I promise I won't ever make that mistake again.

She shudders. It's too late. She's seen it and felt it and the instincts that make her what she is won't let her walk away from power like that, even if it will blow up all my chances to be happy. She's spent too much of her life being teeth and claws who weren't quite strong enough.

Now she is.

She can't, she won't pretend it's not true. Someone, somewhere might need her to be this strong one day.

My human heart chokes on her tears. *This* pack needs her. *These* wolves. I want to stay.

Her answer is fierce and stoic and all wolf. This pack has leaders, strong and worthy ones. She will not challenge.

My puny human growl makes no difference at all, but I hurl it at her anyhow. I would never challenge Hayden. Ever.

Her heart reaches for mine. She knows that. We will go.

I want to shriek and windmill and kick and see if I can somehow land her flat on her back in the river, but I know it won't make any difference. The answer will still be the same when she gets back up. When I do.

She's so much stronger. So crazy much stronger than even a few days ago.

I want to pretend that I don't know why, but I do.

I did this to myself.

I attached the gravity beams. I hooked my baby pack to me and every wolf to my baby pack, because we're the air traffic controllers, the ones who know all the safe parking spots and orbital coordinates. Which made so much sense in Reilly's book, but I didn't realize one really important thing about gravity beams.

They don't just make the wolf on the other end stronger.

I wrap my arms around my belly and my heart and try not to puke. I know what I have to do. I've always known. I just didn't expect to be the stupidhead who made it happen this soon.

I made myself stronger—and now I have to go.

23

RIO

Fuck.

I speed through the trees that edge the den, leaving fur on several of them because my wolf can feel the intensity of the crisis that just landed. He can also feel two very important sets of paws charging in from farther away, but he has no idea if they'll arrive in time.

He has no idea if he will.

I crest the small rise that was getting in the way of my sight lines, my sentinel almost frantic with the need to get between Kennedy and what she's about to do to herself—and yank him to an abrupt, hair-pulling, yelping halt when I see that he isn't going to be the one doing the containment.

Kel and Hayden are wide-eyed, frozen in place as their wolves figure out the same thing. As we all watch four shifters arrange themselves in a quiet, fierce square and implacably demand control.

Kelsey backs into me, her small red wolf trembling. I shift and scoop her up, because I already know everything my paws can tell me. I cuddle her into my chest as my sentinel stares at four shifters he somehow entirely underestimated.

Ghost is facing Kennedy, a lithe, solemn teenager with fire in her eyes and the gravity beams of the whole damn pack in her hands. When she speaks, her words ring with that collective might. "Don't you dare."

Her words land on Kennedy like bombs.

They don't shake her baby pack, though. The four of them stand firm, their eyes full of fierce conviction and unified intent.

I gape at what I can suddenly so very clearly see.

A bear full of bravery and kindness, and just maybe the power to edit Kennedy's story. A scrappy wolf who shares her heart with a human who knows how to use tenderness like a scalpel. A scarred shifter who just can't let go of the beta wisdom he was born with and who somehow still has the capacity to care. And a teenager who listens to the wind and knows her own worth and forged them into a unit.

My sentinel bows his head.

He fucked up.

I saw her baby pack. I didn't even begin to see their power.

GHOST

I can't panic. I can't. Even though I really, really want to, because Kel said to have contingency plans, but I didn't expect to actually use them. Not like this. Not when it matters this much. I want to look at him to see if maybe he's got a better idea, but I don't dare. Kennedy's wolf is dominant and she needs me to hold her eyes and to not be afraid.

I gulp. I'm not scared of Kennedy. I'm scared of what she might decide to do if I don't get this exactly right.

If *we* don't. I'm not alone. Hoot and Reilly got here in just as big a hurry as I did, because we talked about how she might need us fast. But none of us got here quicker than Kenny. He was way over on the other side of the den, and he made it here at almost the same time as the rest of us.

He's behind her, just far enough to the side that I can see his eyes. They tell my wolf something really important. He might have grumped a lot when we talked about this, but he's not grumping now. His feet are planted and he means it, which is a really big deal. We need him. His wolf knows things about this kind of fight that none of the rest of us do.

I hope it's enough.

I take a deep breath and look straight at my very best friend and hope the wind told me the truth. "You can't leave."

She jerks like my wolf just raked claws across her belly.

I will if I have to. "You belong here. Your wolf is maybe thinking some dumb stuff, but you need to say it out loud so that your pack can hear it and fix it." She taught us that.

She shakes her head wildly.

Reilly's bear growls.

Kennedy's eyes snap to his.

I'm so proud of him, so stinking proud, because when we talked about this before, his eyes were all sad. He thought maybe we didn't matter enough for her to stay, that he wasn't worthy enough, that he was just a weak bear like the lieutenants used to tell him. But he isn't letting her see any of that. He's growling like an awesome bear who knows that he matters and that he won't let her go without a fight.

Hoot's pinecone hits, and Kennedy whirls, temper blazing in her eyes.

My wolf cringes, but Hoot knows when to be gentle and when to be annoying and when to be scrappy, even when someone is full of panic and fury.

She grins at Kennedy. "In case you aren't speaking bear very well today, what Reilly means is that you should stop being a stupidhead and use your words."

This was our plan. We can't fix everything, but we can help our big pack see Kennedy all the way inside where we see her, just like she did for each of us.

I thought it was a good plan. A smart plan. A sneaky one.

I think maybe it was. It's just not nearly big enough.

Kennedy spins to the final corner, to Kenny, and for

one awful moment, her wolf actually considers trampling him to escape.

He doesn't growl. He doesn't even try to look tough. He just looks her straight in the eyes and speaks quietly. "Sometimes the hardest thing of all is to tell the truth."

I hear her gut-punched exhale, and the wheezing breath that comes after.

Her eyes drop to the ground. Her words are so hushed, I barely hear them. "I have to go. My wolf is too strong to stay."

KEL

I'm a fucking moron.

I know everything there is to know about being a warrior who believes that their particular kind of power is more likely to break their pack than sustain it. I can't even imagine the horror of feeling that way at fourteen. Of feeling that way for a whole lifetime, because this part of Kennedy's story didn't start six years ago. It started with a tiny wolf chewing on the basket she got abandoned in. A baby thrown away because she was too strong to stay.

Rio caught that story and scented its power, and Hayden's alpha instincts worked out even more, and I'm supposed to be the guy with his finger on the pulse of everything—and we're all standing here watching a fifteen-year-old put her contingency plan into action because the leadership of her pack knew all that and still managed to drop the fucking ball.

Which we need to fix. *Now.* We don't have much time. Dominants don't drop their eyes like that, ever.

My heart lost most of its blood years ago, but it sheds a few aching drops for a baby alpha and her anguish. Then I apply a field dressing and stand the fuck up, because I have an ass to kick. Really damn carefully.

Hayden glares at me, but I ignore him. This part isn't his job. He needs to catch her when we're done. I nod at Ebony, who's positioned herself on Kenny's other side. The man might not ever accept a beta title again, but today he's earned it. And we need him.

Then I meet the eyes of the young woman on the other side of the square who is leading us all. I've seen a few acts of submissive shifter bravery in my time. Stepping in front of the second most powerful wolf in North America as she was about to go nuclear is as big as it gets.

And Ghost is still far more worried about her best friend than she ever was about herself.

I send Reilly and Hoot quiet hand signals to flank Ghost, in case Kennedy dials up her stupid. To their eternal credit, both of them look at Ghost before they comply. Which is a power struggle most betas would squash flat, but today they've entirely earned the right to trust their instincts first.

The look I get from the three of them as they move into position is identical.

We'd better not fuck this up.

My lips quirk, even though the wolf grenade in our

midst is still ticking. Then I focus, because that isn't going to last, and we have shit to do before she takes the most obvious course out of her current pain. I glance over at Ebony. Kenny is distinctly unhappy to be standing between us, but I don't give a damn. What Kennedy needs right now is the tough love of shifters who have been to hell and never quite come all the way back.

The three facing her are Kennedy's rock. We need to be her hard place.

I clear my throat so that her wolf has a fighting chance. I don't knife people in the back, even when it might be more merciful. "That's the biggest load of crap I've ever heard."

Her head snaps up as she spins around, her eyes entirely wolf.

I'm not surprised—but I'm damn impressed she's still in human form. Barely, though. Her brain is damn close to furry. Which means we need to use small words and carry a big stick. "You think you need to leave because you're too strong for this pack to handle? That's some arrogant bullshit. The kind you need to prove. You want that title, you need to flatten my ass."

The three mouths falling open behind her would be fun if this weren't so utterly serious.

Kennedy swallows. "You can probably beat me in a fight. But this is about wolf dominance. Your wolf is submissive. Mine knows it."

I snort. "Go ahead. Knock him on his ass."

The two wolves beside me clearly didn't see that coming.

Good. I don't pull out this party trick until it's really damn necessary.

The whimper that comes out of Kennedy wrings more blood out of my bloodless heart, but I don't let her pain stop me. I can't. We need her wolf's full attention, and that means we need to let her human hurt like fuck for just a little while longer. I fold my arms across my chest and smirk. "That's a big claim. I say we need some evidence."

She looks entirely horrified. As she should. I'm daring her to challenge her pack's hierarchy and traumatize her packmates, all in one stupid move. But Rio hasn't stopped me yet, and he would if this was going to break anyone. I put the troop leader I once was into my voice. "Prove it, Kennedy. Show my wolf who's boss or stop with the dumbass teenage theatrics about needing to leave and let me get back to my drink."

Most of the pack glares at me for my spew of disrespectful nonsense. I'll ask their forgiveness later. Ungluing a wolf with Kennedy's level of control isn't all that easy.

The growl that comes out of her is almost as deep as Rio's, but her words are those of a teenage girl about to crack. "Please don't make me. Please just let me leave."

Fuck.

24

ADRIANNA

Kelvin Nogues has a heart as big as the sky, but sometimes he's a flaming idiot. Kennedy could no more blast him with dominance than she could one of the pups. Her human would never let her—and far too many warriors have helped her cement her exquisite control over her wolf.

However, he's not wrong about the message he's trying to deliver, and on that, perhaps a visitor can help.

I shoot my son a look, because there are things you never do without an alpha's permission, and this is going to involve a good dozen of them.

He rolls his eyes a little, which is a fair feat, given how worried they are.

I wish I could tell him not to be afraid, but I can feel Kennedy's wolf teetering on a precipice still. So I do the best that I can. I step forward to help Kel blow up her ledge. "I'd be happy to take her place."

Heads swivel all over the den. It pleases me greatly that very few of them look relieved. I'm not here as savior. I'm here because I saw a whiteboard diagram of a baby alpha building a pack that can hold her—and one that can live without her.

I'm here because I love her, too.

Kennedy isn't ready to hear any of that yet, though. She needs some good wolf, bad wolf to happen first, and Kelvin and I happen to be an excellent team for that. "You're a truly annoying wolf, Kel, and I haven't had the pleasure of blasting you in quite some time."

The look he gives me would quell a lesser wolf.

I smirk. He might have some well-hidden superpowers, but I developed immunity to those looks of his long ago.

I watch as he scans a trembling wolf and her baby pack and does the lightning-fast calculations of a man who never leaves anyone behind, ever. My wolf waits. She's trusted his math for a very long time. If he thinks this isn't the way, I won't push it.

Finally, he sighs. Then he pivots to face me and jerks his chin at the two wolves beside him. "You might want to move out of the way."

Kenny snorts and backs away, his hands up. To my surprise and delight, he heads straight to join his baby pack, who are all watching me with mutiny in their eyes. They aren't standing down, not a one of them. Ebony isn't either. She glares at me for a long moment before she takes a single step to the side. "Don't break him. I happen to like his annoying wolf."

Perhaps she knows, or perhaps she doesn't. Either way, it does my heart good to know he's got such a friend at his side.

I measure the distance between them. My wolf is riled enough that another step away would be better, but I know when I've pushed a beta as far as I can push her, and Ebony's eyes are well across that line.

That's fine. She can be part of the message if she wants.

I don't give Kel any warning. I just hit him with the fully unleashed dominance of the most powerful shifter wolf in three hundred years.

Ebony doubles over instantly.

Kel's snapped hand signal stops incoming Hayden dead in his tracks, which is a good thing. Grabbing a dominant wolf while she's trying not to puke is a recipe for getting his ears ripped off. And Ebony isn't the wolf who matters right now.

I shake my head at Kel, who's standing just as he was. "Still can't touch you, can I?" My heart aches for what it cost him to develop that skill, but he won't thank me for showing it.

He raises his eyebrows a carefully controlled quarter-inch. "Nope."

I look over at Kennedy. She's staring at Kel, absolutely dumbfounded. Good. Time to drive the point all the way home. "Your wolf isn't stronger than mine."

She shakes her head wildly.

I smile a little. That day may yet come, but this ledge isn't the time or place to have that discussion. "I aimed everything I have at him."

Ebony grunts. "I'll say."

I let my lips quirk. "Next time, move out of the damn way."

She snorts. "You do this often?"

I keep my eyes on Kennedy. "No. Only when it's necessary."

Her eyes are back on Kel, her stunned wolf trying to work out what just happened, and why, and what it means for the story running wild in her head.

I give her an assist. Her human has managed to re-establish a foothold, but her eyes are still pure wolf. "Some shifters have a natural resistance to dominance. The right kind of training can build that into immunity."

Kennedy's entire body goes taut. She stares at me for several heartbeats, frantically processing. Then she whirls to Kel. "Can you teach all of our submissives to do that?"

And she thinks she's dangerous. My heart squeezes.

Kel shakes his head. "No."

I speak the rest for him. That much hurt I can lift out of his hands. I inflicted it on him once when I asked the very same question. "It isn't the kind of training you would wish on anyone you love."

Kennedy's dusky skin turns a color it's not meant to have in life.

I nod gently, willing her eyes to stay on mine. Kel won't cope with pity. Most days he won't even accept gratitude. And we still have a baby alpha to navigate back to safety. "You spent most of your formative years in a pack where dominant hierarchy was everything. Where the strength of your wolf was everything. That's not the pack you're in now, sweetheart."

She shakes her head.

I'm not even sure she knows what she's denying anymore.

Kel tilts his chin. "You've been fine for weeks. What changed?"

Mute denial as a wolf suddenly careens back toward the edge of her ledge.

"She got stronger," says Ghost quietly, stepping up to Kennedy's shoulder and laying a rock-steady hand on the arm of her shaking friend. "Some when we made the baby pack, but I think a lot more when she did the stuff with the gravity beams."

Lissa frowns from her spot at Hayden's side. "Those made us all stronger."

"It's made her wolf stronger than Hayden's." Rio's calm words send a ripple of shock through the pack—and less than a breath later, a gorgeous, brilliant firming.

My wolf bows her head. Always, it's the submissives who rise.

I step back. My small part is done.

Lissa switches her frown over to Rio. "Why is that such a big deal?"

He chuckles softly. "Good answer."

Hoot scowls. "She thinks it means that her wolf could challenge him for dominance and maybe win and then the pack would be all unstable." She elbows Kennedy. "Even if she would never, ever do anything that stupid."

Reilly snorts and crosses his arms like Kel. "That's really dumb. Does that mean I have to leave when I get big enough to sit on Hayden and he can't get me off?"

Oh, the immaculate instincts of a baby alpha who picked such as these to catch her. Perfection, every last one of them.

Kennedy makes a face. "You're a bear. That's different."

He makes a face right back. "How?"

Logical, wondrous bear.

Kenny grunts. "I'm thinking it's maybe useful for an alpha to know that he could be replaced." He shrugs as the entire larger pack glares at him in unison. "I'm not saying it should happen. I'm saying that there can be consequences when an alpha can't be taken down and knows it."

It's a brave argument to make in the middle of a pack who lived through those consequences. It's also one that haunts me often. There are good reasons Whistler Pack has enough betas to topple me. Thoughts like that aren't a burden any fourteen-year-old should have to carry, but it beats the hell out of thinking she has to leave.

Kennedy's wolf shudders.

Kel glances at me.

I just smile quietly. Kennedy's baby pack is giving a master class in how to love a baby alpha. They don't need help. They're going to get it, though. I can see the heart of the pack readying.

Lissa looks up at Hayden. He kisses her forehead and nods, trusting his green-eyed wolf to handle this.

I smother a grin. We're still on entirely dangerous ground, but a better alpha pair I have not seen in a very long time, no matter what they're calling themselves.

Lissa pats Hayden's arm. "He already knows he can be taken down."

Kennedy's body snaps taut, a wolf looking for the danger to her alpha. Loyal teeth and claws, even as she teeters on her precipice—and entirely blind to what that means.

Lissa isn't, however. She smiles at Kennedy, and there's absolutely no fear in her at all. Just the gentle words of one used to explaining things slowly and carefully. "Kel could challenge Hayden and maybe win, and that doesn't seem to bother his wolf."

Kel snorts. "It didn't bother him when he was ten years old, and I could have squashed him three times a day back then."

The ten-year-old's mother might have had something to say about that. These days, she's mostly amused.

Lissa surveys the pack slowly and smiles a little when her eyes settle on a big, black wolf. "I bet Rio's a pretty decent threat, too."

Kennedy wrinkles her nose. "Sentinels are different. My wolf doesn't care about his dominance."

That makes her smarter than a lot of alphas I know.

Lissa gently, carefully reels in her baby-alpha fish. "Kel and Rio are Hayden's baby pack. He picked them when he was younger than you are." She pauses to let that fully sink in. "I don't think his wolf has ever cared about wolves who might be stronger than he is. He only cares if they serve their pack."

I can almost see the invisible cape swirling behind Lissa—and the deep, violent struggle in the teenager she's facing. Kennedy's human wants so very badly to believe, but her wolf simply won't let her.

Myrna steps forward and lays her hands on the fishing rod. "I hear dominance doesn't work very well in mated pairs, either." She looks over at me, a dare in her eyes. "Your mate was submissive."

Smartass elder. James would have adored her. "He was."

She smirks at me. "Was he the boss of your wolf?"

I grin. "Were you the boss of your mate's wolf?"

She cackles merrily. "I was."

That answer was never in any doubt at all. "Then you know exactly how it works."

Her eyes stay on me. She's not done. "You have a polar bear in your pack. A big, mean one."

I snort. Ronan will laugh for a week at that description. "He's very polite for a polar bear."

Myrna shoots me a dirty look, one that says I'm blowing my lines and she expects better of me.

I manage not to laugh. "He could sit on me and make himself alpha of Whistler Pack anytime he wanted."

A faint nod of approval. "So dominance isn't all that important, really."

HAYDEN

I should take a turn, soon. Maybe.

My wolf isn't at all sure we need a turn. His pack is hitting base hit after base hit, and his mom is no slouch either. Especially with Myrna throwing her big, fat fastballs right over the plate.

My mother glances over at me and smiles. "With enough love, enough trust, dominance is just a party trick. I'd guess that Hayden has a pack where at least five of his wolves aren't ever going to bow to his dominance." She winks at her favorite bear cub. "Perhaps six when Reilly gets a little bigger."

Ghost and Hoot catch Reilly before he falls over.

Kennedy leans into a wobbly bear. I don't even know if she's aware that she's doing it. Serving pack, even as she fights with a story that's trying to toss her out of the only family she's ever known. "Five?"

I nudge my wolf in case he actually wants to stand up for himself.

He just grins and keeps watching the show.

My mother smiles again. "Kel. Lissa. I'd take even odds on Rio. You. Kelsey."

Kelsey walks over and pats my knee.

My wolf snorts as I pick her up and nuzzle her soft hair. My mother knows me frighteningly well. I'd die before I blasted Kelsey with dominance juice. That's true for all of my wolves, but especially this one. Dominance got used as a weapon to try to eviscerate her soul.

Never again.

I look up to find Kennedy watching me, her human and her wolf.

Apparently I'm going to get a turn.

I let my wolf rise in my eyes. She needs to see, because I wasn't sure what his answer would be when this day arrived, but I know it now. "My wolf has no problem at all with you staying. The opposite, actually. You're going to help attach his wolves to pack and bring them home, and he'd be really fucking sad if you left."

Kennedy cracks yet again. Enough for me to see how much mess is left inside—and how little room there is to get in there and shred it.

My mom steps to her shoulder, the baby pack parting to let her in. "Let your wolf all the way out, sweetheart. She needs to feel his wolf. Is there anything but gladness in him?"

That should probably be a terrifying question, but I'm absolutely positive she already looked.

Kennedy's growl is that of the tiny dominant toddler she once was.

Soothing murmurs from the alpha of all alphas. "My wolf's got you. I won't let you or anyone else come to any harm. Go ahead. Let her feel the alpha who wants her so very much."

Kennedy backs up, but it's not to flee. It's to get a little space. To find her feet. To stand. A dominant wolf who needs to face this with her teeth and claws at the ready, because looking that deeply at me involves making herself wildly vulnerable, too.

I wait. My wolf can't answer her question until she asks it.

She quakes as she opens, as she lets me see. As she shows her alpha and her pack all of who she is, even when the core of her so obviously still believes she's too much.

I don't try to answer with words. I trust my own baby pack at my shoulders to contain me if I've somehow horribly misjudged what lives inside me, and I give all of who I am to my wolf.

The world goes a little weirdly blurry, and then Rio's sentinel woo is yanking me back, making sure I'm not a dumbass who gets his brain stuck in wolf gears forever.

I ignore him. I'm too busy trying to focus on Kennedy, hoping like hell she got the answer she needed.

She looks at me, her entire heart in her eyes—and then she crumples.

The arms that go around her don't surprise anyone except for Kennedy.

25

KENNEDY

I'm so hungry. I've eaten four hot dogs and my wolf is still starving. I take the charred gift Robbie is holding out to me. He and Mellie cooked this one, and Braden added ketchup. Lots and lots of ketchup. "Thanks, cutie."

His head tilts, an unspoken question in his eyes.

I grin. "Probably at least one more. If you're not getting too bored of cooking them."

He scampers off, firing hand signals at Mellie.

I take a big bite and look over at Hayden, who's eaten almost as many hot dogs as I have. I can't believe what he did. Going completely wolf while you're human isn't very safe. Rio hit him with some kind of sentinel hammer to make sure he didn't get stuck there, but still. He took a big risk for me.

And now my wolf knows, absolutely, because there was no doubt at all in his wolf. There will always be a place for her in his pack. He feels no threat, and even if I keep getting stronger, he's just going to roll his eyes and give me jobs to do.

Which makes me feel kind of silly, now that I know—but my wolf was so sure we had to leave, and my heart was too scared to listen.

He took that risk so I would be okay.

That's what it really means to be alpha.

"He's fine," says a voice at my shoulder.

I look at Kel as he sits down. He made Ghost stop hovering and go eat a big bowl of salad with cheese curds and tomatoes and a whole bunch of other stuff the cats dropped off this morning. "Are you sure?"

He eyes me. "Aren't you?"

I sigh. "Lissa says he's fine. I guess she would know." She also said smart things about being vulnerable and this pack knowing how to respect that as strength.

I might need a couple more hot dogs before I can think about that.

I don't need any more food to talk to the wolf beside me, though. I bump my shoulder against his and hope he can smell my gratitude over burnt hot dog. "You knew how I felt. You understood."

He grunts quietly. "Sometimes the very hardest thing to do is to let go of the one thing we believe most deeply about ourselves."

I let that sink in for a while. He's right. My whole baby pack is working on that. "Like Hoot thinking she's small or Reilly that he's weak." I consider for a minute, because the other two are trickier. "Or Ghost believing that she's best when she's invisible, or Kenny thinking he's bad."

Kel smiles faintly. "Yes. Or a fourteen-year-old who's convinced that she's dangerous."

My wolf grins. "I kind of still am. I'm just not the most dangerous. This pack is full of badasses."

He snorts and says nothing.

He turned into a badass for some hard reasons. "I don't know all of what you did when you were a soldier. But I want to say thank you."

Dead silence. Then a quiet squeeze of my shoulder as he gets up to leave.

Another wolf settles in his place. She chews on a bite of apple as she watches him go. "He rarely lets anyone thank him. That was well done."

I look over at Adrianna Scott, who has a wolf inside her that makes mine look like a stuffed toy. "Do you let people thank you?"

She smiles. "I came here because I saw your diagram and knew what it meant. You can thank me by fixing it."

I wrap my arms around my knees. "I didn't realize that I built it so I could leave."

"I know." She watches Braden dump half a bottle of ketchup on Hayden's next hot dog and chuckles. "That's why those of us with very strong wolves need to surround ourselves with people we love and respect and who will call us on our bullshit every time they see it."

I make a face. "My baby pack is getting awfully good at that."

A fond look at Ghost as she crosses behind the cooking fire. "Indeed, they are."

I shake my head. "Hoot was always a little bit feisty, and I guess Kenny knows how to be bossy, but Ghost used to be really quiet and Reilly was so shy you could hardly hear him talk sometimes."

"You gave them reasons to speak up."

My wolf wants to growl. I tell her to chill. She's eaten way too much ketchup to get riled. She just needs to be smarter next time. "I was stupidcakes, I guess."

"Not at all." Adrianna runs her hand down my back like Hayden does with the pups. "You were born thinking you were too much, my dear. It just came to a head. Never apologize for your strength, or your fears. They make you who you are."

I snort. "You don't have fears."

Her lips quirk. "Would you like to reconsider that statement for a second, or shall I tell you what I think of it?"

Oops. I clear the ketchup off my brain. "Sorry. That was a dumb thing to say."

"It was." She wraps her arm around my shoulders and kisses the top of my head. "But I imagine others will think it true of you, often enough. Fortunately, I don't think those four over there will be amongst them."

My baby pack has somehow all gravitated together again, even though they're supposed to be eating and recovering from what my wolf tried to do to them. Nobody said it quite like that, but the bosses of the den swooped in with salad and really fat roast beef sandwiches and an entire jar of Reilly's favorite honey.

I'm not sure what they fed Hoot. My wolf was still kind of jumbled.

I squint at them, because she's less jumbled now. "Why are they staying over there?"

"I imagine you'll figure out the answer to that shortly." Adrianna squeezes my shoulders again and stands up. "I'm going to get out of your hair and let Rio have a turn so that he can stop hovering."

He emerges from the shadows and rolls his eyes.

My wolf makes a face. "Are you guys in some kind of line or something?"

Adrianna's laugh sounds like Kelsey's when one of her flowers blooms. She doesn't give me an answer, though. She just walks off and sits down by Myrna and scoops up Jade to sit in her lap.

I shake my head. "She's amazing, and she doesn't even care."

Rio huffs out a laugh as he takes her place beside me. "That makes two of you."

I glare at him. "I made my baby pack whack me over the head with really big sticks today. That's not very amazing."

He grins wryly. "They made the rest of us look like amateurs."

They made me look like an idiot and I'm going to be stupidly grateful for the rest of forever.

He leans against my shoulder and holds up his plate. "Want something to eat that isn't burnt hot dogs?"

I don't even bother to look. "Nope."

He snorts. "Your stomach is even weirder than mine."

I catch some ketchup with my tongue before it drips off my bun. "Don't you have any sentinel stuff to say?"

He shrugs and picks up one of Myrna's honey ribs. "Do you need me to say any of it?"

I take a big bite of my hot dog, because even a wolf tongue isn't going to contain this much ketchup for much longer. I think as I chew, and let my wolf sort through what she knows. When I finish, I grin at him. "Nope."

He bumps my shoulder again, less gently this time. "Good. Go remind them why they're yours."

I roll to my feet. "They're so stuck with me now."

I heard him chuckling as I walk over to my baby pack, but I'm not really thinking about Rio anymore. I'm watching four sets of eyes, and I'm listening really hard. To what they told me before, and what they're still telling me, and what that means deep down inside where I got a totally wrong idea and couldn't let it go.

Reilly is the easiest. He knows I might need him to sit on me some day, and he's okay with that, but in the meantime, he's just going to make me read more books about black holes and gravity beams, and his ears will probably keep turning pink when I say nice things about him and his bear.

Kenny thinks he's the hardest, but he's not. He's a wolf who's too loyal to his pack to quit, even when they tried to make him. He's still not happy to be in my baby pack, but his wolf is smart enough to know that he's all the way in and we're not going to let him go, so he might as well just suck it up and deal.

Hoot maybe did the hardest thing today. Her wolf is scrappy. She dashes in and bites someone's tail and then she hides again. She doesn't stand still and dare a badass wolf to eat her for breakfast, even one she loves really a lot. But she did it and she didn't back down and she already told me that if I try that shit again, she'll drive over me in Rio's truck.

I look at Ghost last, at my best friend and the wolf who has always felt like my sister. She knew. Rio guessed some, and so did Adrianna, and probably Hayden and Lissa and Kel and some others, too, because apparently my wolf isn't nearly as good at hiding her feelings as she thinks she is. But Ghost wasn't guessing.

She knew, because she sees me all the way inside.

Because she knows how to listen better than anyone.

I sit down beside them and smile a little. There are things I want to say, but they feel too raw, yet. Too much like wolf growls without any words. Which they would probably understand just fine, but I want to find the words. They deserve them.

My wolf jolts as a pinecone hits my head.

Hoot grins. "Quit thinking so hard. We have fudge. And hot chocolate."

The plane Adrianna came on had all kinds of good stuff in it. My belly considers what it wants to eat first.

Reilly holds up the sat phone and takes a picture. Not of me, thank goodness.

Kenny scowls. "I don't want to be in your newspaper."

Reilly grins. "Tough. I put all the heroes in there."

My wolf scrambles, because the look in Kenny's eyes is totally meant to set bear fur on fire.

Hoot topples sideways into Reilly, giggling. "Can we use that app you showed me to give him a cape and a funny costume?"

I stare, but Reilly isn't even looking at Kenny, and Hoot obviously isn't scared of him at all, and Ghost is trying to hide a grin.

With enough love and trust, dominance is just party tricks.

Adrianna didn't just say those words to me. She said them to my whole baby pack, and now they know how to handle grumpy, bossy Kenny, and they know how to handle me, too. I sway, dazed, as something warm and cozy and beautiful lands in my belly that has nothing to do with ketchup and hot dogs.

Hayden granted the part of my wish that says I get to stay. They're granting the part that says I get to mostly be an ordinary wolf.

My wolf sighs and lays her nose down on her tail. She's finally figured out the thing that no one actually said, about why she's safe and why she isn't too much and why she gets to stay.

It isn't dominance that will contain her. It's love.

26

KENNEDY

I didn't know Hoot could bounce this much. I grab her shoulders so she doesn't accidentally bang her head on a tree branch.

A horn honks from down the road, and a truck screeches to a halt as two teenagers jump out the side door whooping like crazy. I let go of Hoot, because she's already running, and follow behind her in case she runs headlong into two cats and someone needs to catch flying body parts.

I grin as Sierra and Sienna wrap her up in a huge hug, the three of them jumping around like a six-legged kangaroo. I grab Reilly and pull him in, because his bear is nearly turning inside out with excitement, but he's still shy sometimes.

Sierra turns her head and gives him a big, fat smooch on his cheek. "Riles, you got so huge!"

His ears turn totally pink. "I was kind of little the last time you were here."

I see the sadness that flits across her eyes—and the steely determination not to let it show. I reach in and hug her hard for both those things, and because I really missed her, too. "Shelley made cookies and Ghost made fancy salad and Danielle thinks she fixed all the video cameras."

Sienna looks around just in time to catch the incoming group hug from Myrna and Ghost and Lissa. "Did you put the fancy honey nuts in the salad? Reilly was telling me about those and my cat got seriously jealous."

Reilly's ears turn a color that I didn't think bear ears could go.

My wolf grins at Ghost. There aren't many vegetarians in this pack, but the Lonely Peak cats have a bunch of them, and they've been bugging her for her secret salad recipes. Possibly because a baby alpha keeps complaining loudly online about all the fancy lettuce she needs to eat.

I wrap an arm around Reilly's head, just in case his bear needs some help settling. Kenny ran with him this morning, but then he went out to the woods with Wrinkles and Fallon to get ready for the video shoot and maybe to escape a little, too.

Sierra and Sienna don't know about the video-shoot part yet. Reilly talked with their team and set everything up to do a live stream of the wild pups. It's going to be epic. Or possibly a disaster, but I don't think anyone will care. He's been practicing his opening lines all morning, and he's so earnest and awesome when he says them.

Myrna keeps petting the twins' heads like she can't believe how big they got, and the mamas are crowding in for hugs, and Mellie has somehow managed to climb Sierra's leg. She's part monkey, or at least that's the excuse Miriam and Layla are going with this week.

Sierra scoops her up, laughing and nuzzles her nose, just like a wolf.

Mellie shifts and licks her cheek.

"About time you got here." Dorie shakes her head and manages to wrap her arms around five people all at once, because nobody is letting go very well.

Sienna reaches out, her eyes wet. "Auntie. It's been so, so long."

Dorie snorts. "A few months, maybe. Does Reese know how often you snuck out to meet us when we came to trade with the rogue cats?"

A voice clears behind us. "No, he doesn't."

The twins have really good innocent looks, even though they're big, fat liars. I went with Dorie to do some of those trades. The rogue cats swapped with us for food that nobody would miss, and blankets, and old clothes, and Bailey allowed it because they're cranky cats who never talk to anyone and Dorie had them convinced that we were just a few rogue wolves.

Which Reese doesn't know about either, I bet.

He tilts his head in towards Dorie's, an alpha who's decided not to create a ruckus, at least for now. "Auntie."

She shoots him a look. "Don't you dare be mad at

these two. They brought hope to my heart in some very dark days."

Guilt blazes in Sierra's eyes. She's just as bouncy as Sienna, but she has a softer heart, and she's been asking a lot more questions on ShifterNet. Dorie says she's going to be one of the cat aunties some day, but we have to let her grow up a little first.

Ghost reaches out and takes her hand. "Come eat salad. I put lots of the honey nuts in it, so if we don't get there soon, Braden and Rio will eat them all and leave us with just lettuce."

My wolf snorts. There are probably eight weird things in that salad besides lettuce, and Braden and Rio won't eat any of them.

Sierra giggles, her eyes clearing. She wraps her mostly free arm around Reilly. "So, are you ready to be famous?"

He looks kind of alarmed, but I know the secret didn't leak. There are cookies on the line. I elbow in on his other side to help it not get leaked now. "Ghost checked on the wild pups last night. They've been coming out to play in the afternoons on a rock outcropping near their den. They look like little baby mountain goats, except they have terrible balance and roll around like bears. I think they knock each other off the rocks on purpose."

Reilly shoots me a grateful look as Sierra and Sienna start asking a million questions about sun angles and wind direction and family hierarchy and whether the pups have names yet.

Myrna chuckles and shoots me an approving look. She helped Reilly write the copy for his video intro. It's really good.

I grin and let my wolf feel happy. It's going to be a really awesome day, and all she has to do is hold camera batteries and tease cats and not eat any cherry tomatoes.

Being a good baby alpha isn't so hard after all.

HAYDEN

I wince as Hoot starts waxing poetic about her driving lessons and the teenagers on either side of her shoot speculative looks at the guy walking beside me. "Apologies in advance."

Reese snorts. "Trust me, if this is about whose teenagers can spread the most dumb ideas to the other's pack, you're going to lose badly."

Myrna drops back to join us. "Might as well let it happen and get it over with. When I was young, the teenagers of the three packs used to run wild together."

The cat alpha manages to inject a metric ton of sardonic amusement into a single grunt. "I'll warn the ravens."

I eye my pack elder. She rarely causes trouble by accident, and that's an interesting idea she's just thrown into the mix. "Are the three pack territories close enough to do that?"

She grins. "Not for anyone over the age of twenty."

My wolf thinks she's funny.

I tell him to remember that the first time a horde of unsupervised teenagers causes trouble and he's the alpha who happens to be handiest. "I didn't realize the three packs have been connected for that long."

Myrna shrugs. "We haven't. We were a new pack back then. It didn't happen as much for the next generations. The ravens went through some leadership changes that were less friendly to wolves and our packs lost touch."

Reese nods. "They weren't thrilled about cats back then, either, but they're a really different clan with Tressie in charge. We've built strong ties with them in the last four years. They're open to extending that. I know there's been some ShifterNet trading happening with your pack already. I hear you have pretty rocks."

Myrna snickers.

The cat alpha laughs. "If I get rocks for my birthday, I'm coming to find you."

My wolf grins. Noted.

Myrna elbows me. I'm missing my cues, and she's probably already taken care of birthday rocks for Reese. I grab hold of my wolf, who's a little drunk on his pack's bubbling happiness, and focus on what she laid on the table. "Teenagers might be a good way to get inter-pack relations flowing again."

Reese's lips quirk. "Those are pretty fancy words for letting them run wild across territory boundaries."

He's not objecting. At all. Which is interesting.

Myrna casts a casual look Kennedy's way.

That's all it takes to have speculation land in Reese's eyes. "Rumor has it that you have yourself a baby alpha who could knock out your wolf if she wanted to."

I made sure that went out in yesterday's edition of GhostPack News. Power that lives in sunlight is far less dangerous, and my mom is pretty darn sure Kennedy's wolf isn't done getting stronger yet. "She doesn't want to."

He shoots me an amused look. "You don't give a shit, do you?"

Nope. "Should I?"

Myrna snorts. "Cut it out, you two. Reese, you've got, what, half a dozen cats who could challenge you and win?"

He huffs out a laugh. "None of them want the job."

She eyes him. "Are any of them teenagers?"

My wolf finally figures out where this is headed. He blinks. A lot. It's an interesting idea, and a crazy one. The kind a renegade elder might throw into the pot just to see if it blows up. "You're thinking about a baby pack that crosses pack lines."

She shrugs. "That's basically what we were."

I look over at a cat who has a lot of reasons to object. We've seen our baby alpha wrangle gravity beams. He hasn't.

He's a cat who's quick on his feet, however. He nods slowly, studying Kennedy as she talks to two of his teenage cats. "That could work, actually. The ones I've got that age who have a leadership bent already have good outlets, and none of them come anywhere close to matching her for dominance." He grins. "And she might actually be able to keep the ravens in line."

I've been in a pack with cats and ravens. They're not nearly as simple as wolves, and dominance only works on them sporadically. Kennedy would have her hands full and then some.

Which is exactly why Myrna is suggesting it. One pack elder who is no slouch with gravity beams, either. "Will they let her lead?"

Reese's lips quirk. "Depends on what her definition of leadership looks like. She'd have some unruly cats and ravens to keep her on her toes, for sure."

I snort. "She already has a bear, a disgruntled beta three times her age, the best tracker in these woods, and a wolf who makes all the trees whimper when she gets behind the wheel of a truck."

He laughs loud enough to have heads turning our way.

Myrna grins at the two of us. "You'll need to let her think it's her idea."

We both shoot her wry looks.

She pats our arms. "You're not entirely dumb alphas."

I tug on the end of her braid. "It's a good thing we have wise, well-behaved elders to advise us."

Reese laughs so hard he nearly walks into a tree.

My wolf is only a little annoyed that he misses.

RIO

I shake my head at Ebony as we herd the back end of the pack toward the den. Reese left his trackers out on the perimeter with Bailey, so we're suddenly idle teeth and claws. Which leaves eavesdropping to keep us occupied. "That is one scary wolf."

Ebony grins at Myrna, who's left the two alphas now that she's roped them in to her eye-popping plan, and is exchanging hand signals with Robbie that might be about hot dogs or aliens, depending on your angle.

I don't know who came up with the aliens-are-coming hand signals, but the pups love them and they make Kel splutter. "It's not a bad idea. Maybe." I look over at the wolf who does her beta job with extreme competence and zero theatrics. "You've talked to the ravens. Will they go for this?"

She shrugs. "Maybe. They're going to want some reassurances that our teenagers have decent manners."

Ravens are a lot smaller than wolves and bobcats, and they tend to hit their final growth spurts later. "Kendra's been letting her juveniles come play with us. They might find that reassuring." Hawks are bigger and meaner than ravens, but Kendra's judgment still says something important about our young wolves.

Ebony nods. "They jumped on trading trinkets online with us, and they know we've got a raven in our pack."

We do. Fallon is rapidly becoming one of my favorite people, probably because she thinks I'm cute and harmless and she shares her gummy bears with me. Her mate is a quiet guy with waters that run deep, and she's connected to some of the most enigmatic wolves in this pack. She also radiates a hesitance my wolf doesn't understand yet.

Which means someone should probably have a chat with her before we start playing nice with the local birds, but my feet aren't sensing any reasons to be more cautious than that. I walk quietly and mull over the larger idea, the one where we let the teenagers and their imaginative, resilient energy forge stronger ties across territory lines. It's not a new strategy—smart alphas have been using it forever. But it's a bold move for a pack that's still trying to get its own shit together.

It isn't all that easy to listen to the earth under my paws when they're stuffed into army boots, but the answer comes back clearly enough. The ether that sentinels listen to has always had an extra dose of fondness for teenage rebels, and elderly ones, too.

I snort. They're only rebels if you're too dumb to listen.

KENNEDY

I gulp as we walk over the rise that leads down to the river, because we have way bigger surprises waiting for our visitors than salad. I move Reilly sideways to where he can get better photos, because this is so going to be newsworthy.

Sierra and Sienna take deep, astonished breaths—and

totally get it right. They beam at Adrianna Scott on the way by and jump on Danielle and her stack of video cameras. Carefully. Sierra gives her a big, smacking kiss just like she gave Reilly and picks up one of the cameras and pets it. "You fixed them all? Seriously?"

Reilly has taken about a hundred pictures already, but he's also wearing a smile as big as Banner Rock. A bear proud of his mom.

Sienna picks up a second camera. "This isn't one of ours."

"It's one of ours." Adrianna smiles. "Since we have an expert available, we brought a couple of ours up for repair as well." She winks at the twins. "We have a lot of your fans in our pack, and some of them enjoy making their own videos."

Reese snorts as he sits down on a log. "Clearly they don't take any better care of their gear than the two of you."

Sienna and Sierra glare at him in unison.

I shake my head. Adrianna Scott is here and she's somehow making herself almost invisible and Reese is helping her do it and Hayden is busy putting peanut butter on Kelsey's roll like that's the most important thing he could be doing right now.

I have so much to learn.

Danielle is still kind of squeaking, but she looks really proud. "Digital cameras aren't very sturdy. There are a lot of small parts that break really easily, especially with heavy use." She smiles at our visitors. "Maybe Eliza and Cori can make you some carrying cases to pad the cameras a little better when you take them out into the woods. The ones you have probably aren't designed to be carried by a shifter."

"That's an excellent thought." Adrianna smiles as Eliza scampers over. "We'll take at least three once you figure out a design."

I snicker as five heads bend together and two more come over join them—and Reese and Adrianna grin at each other like two pups who just figured out where the secret candy is hidden.

Tricky alphas.

Hayden joins me, smelling like peanut butter and bearing a roll that looks an awful lot like the one he just made for Kelsey. I take it, because I'm nearly always a starving wolf, and watch as Adrianna neatly pushes Reilly a little deeper into the huddle. "How does she even do that? Sierra and Sienna have wanted to meet her forever. She's like their idol, and they're acting like she's just another wolf."

He smiles. "Part of it is that Reese has obviously raised them right. They saw Danielle's face and they've got kind hearts."

I squint, because that's some of the math, but not nearly all of it.

He chuckles quietly. "And part of it is that you rang their pack radar with one of those gravity beams of yours."

I make a face. I was hoping nobody noticed that part. "Only a really small one."

He bumps my shoulder. "You helped them understand what was important. That's what alphas do." He holds up a roll that matches mine. "And when that's not needed, we make sandwiches."

I eye him. "What else did you do?"

He grins at me. "Not telling."

I growl a little. "How am I supposed to grow up to be a smart baby alpha if you don't teach me all your tricks?"

He ruffles my hair like I'm a silly, adorable pup, which mollifies my wolf way more than it should. "You're growing up just fine."

I sigh. "I suppose you're not going to tell me what trick your mom did, either."

He huffs out a laugh. "I don't have to. You already know that one."

I guess maybe I do.

Next up: The pack is coming out of the shadows—but some of its shifters don't know how to live anywhere else. Get Raven, book four in the Ghost Mountain Wolf Shifters series.

Printed in France by Amazon
Brétigny-sur-Orge, FR

14904008R00182